Suddenly Spellbound

ERICA LUCKE DEAN

Suddenly Spellbound
A Red Adept Publishing Book

Red Adept Publishing, LLC
104 Bugenfield Court
Garner, NC 27529
http://RedAdeptPublishing.com/

Print ISBN-13: 978-1-940215-66-2
Print ISBN-10: 1940215668

First Print Edition: January 2016

Cover and Formatting: Streetlight Graphics

*To Louise
For pushing me to finish what I started.
Thank you.*

Chapter 1

THE RUSTY SHOPPING CART WOBBLED, sending tiny shockwaves up and down my arms as I strolled down the narrow aisle between two rows of secondhand designer labels. For reasons I never quite grasped, the store organized items by color rather than size, making every shopping expedition feel like a treasure hunt in the Andes. As I inched closer to the blues, I did my best to ignore the high-pitched screech emanating from my cart's wonky front wheel, but I couldn't help imagining random senior citizens wincing as they turned down the volume on their hearing aids. Then I envisioned dogs lining up outside, waiting for someone to open the door so they could rush past and investigate the earsplitting sound.

It never failed. I always managed to grab the defective buggy. Not that I had a wide selection of *non*defective carts to choose from, but shaking *and* squealing added up to an embarrassing double whammy, even amongst the crowd at the local Goodwill.

And yes, despite vigorous protests from my best friend Chloe—who was convinced I should simply use magic to conjure up designer clothes—I still shopped at thrift stores. It was a bit of an addiction, actually. Besides, where magic was concerned, I was still a novice, but I had ninja skills when it came to sticking to a budget.

In my continuing quest for the perfect spring wardrobe, I spied a practically new Michael Kors blouse sandwiched between two lesser names. The cerulean color jumped out at me, and I plucked it from the rack with glee. Jack loved me in blue. Then again, Jack loved me in anything... or *nothing*.

"Where have you been all my life?" I murmured, tossing the shirt into my basket. I cringed at the accompanying whine of the mangled cart as I rolled the rest of the way down the row, glancing at the rack as I went. *Blues. Purples. Grays.*

Oooh, blacks.

One particular fuzzy black sweater stood out from the rest, reminding me of Karma, the cat I'd rescued from a dumpster behind the private school where I taught kindergarten. It'd been five months since I'd transformed my overfed housecat into the man who'd raised me, and I still hadn't gotten used to having my father back from the so-called dead. I mean, of course, he wasn't *really* dead. As it turned out, he'd just transformed himself into a dog—then a cat—with no way of verbalizing the spell to change himself back into a man. I never figured out how he'd managed to work magic while still in animal form. Not that it mattered. Thanks to me—and my genetic predisposition to witchcraft—I had my dad back.

Ivie Marie McKie: Nonpracticing witch... um... sorceress.

My time *practicing* had been fleeting. And my hair thanked me for being on the wagon. Funny thing about magic—it messed with your chemistry. It'd taken me weeks to eradicate the fiery red streaks from my almost-black hair once I'd given up working spells. I didn't miss the magic. Not one bit.

Okay, maybe a *little*. I glanced down at my ample breasts. Magic certainly had its perks.

As I trailed behind my squeaky wheel, I spotted another rare find—especially in such good condition—across the aisle. Like a golden needle in a vast haystack, the pair of Rag and Bone jeans caught my eye and drew me in. I plucked them from the rack and clutched them to my chest for a long moment before daring to check the tag.

As if the universe had aligned itself perfectly, like—*like magic*—they were my size.

Swallowing a squeal of my own, I tossed the denim into the cart with the blue blouse, the fuzzy sweater, and the rest of my booty, and took stock of my assortment of treasures. Chloe would be so proud of me.

Speaking of Chloe...

As if Chloe's ears had been burning, the chorus of "Girls Just Wanna Have Fun" blared from inside my purse. I dug out my phone and pressed it to my ear. "Hey, shopaholic."

"Hey, Sabrina, I'm glad I caught you." Her pet name for me used to refer to the Audrey Hepburn movie, but that was before we found out I was a post-teenage witch. "Your wedding is creeping closer every day, and we need to discuss the dresses. Did you see the ideas I added to your Pinterest?"

"Mmhm." With the phone sandwiched between my ear and my shoulder and my hip guiding the cart, I browsed the racks as Chloe prattled on. *Oh, pretty.* A pair of skinny jeans in the exact fire-engine-red color my hair used to be called out to me, and I parked myself across the aisle to hold them up to my body. They would likely be tight but totally doable. I even had the perfect pair of secondhand Louboutins, and —

"Did you hear what I said? Ivie? Are you even listening to me?"

Shit! I'd forgotten about Chloe. "Hey, sorry. I'm shopping."

She huffed so hard it practically blew my hair back. "Let me guess, Goodwill?"

I grumbled a nonverbal reply and balled up the jeans to throw them in the cart.

Her musical laughter reverberated over the line. "You're marrying a *Blake* in a few months. You don't have to shop with the welfare crowd anymore."

"Chloe! I can't believe you said that!" I glanced over my shoulder to be sure no one had overheard me. Or worse, *her.* "This particular store happens to be on the edge of

Buckhead." Chloe was intimately acquainted with the exclusive area of Atlanta. It housed most of her favorite stores, including Coach, Prada, Michael Kors, and Kate Spade. "All the best clothes end up here. And a lot of them still have the tags on. I mean, I just found"—Digging through my loot, I pulled out a sheer white blouse—"the cutest little capped-sleeve *Balenciaga*."

"No shit? Balenciaga at a thrift store? Snap that one up for sure. In fact, grab one for me if you can, but when I get there next week, I'm taking you shopping for your dress. And you'd better not even *think* about looking at Goodwill. I'm serious, Ivie. We're hitting the boutiques."

My eyes drifted to the rack overflowing with used white satin, only two rows away, and I swallowed against the crystal-ball-sized lump in my throat. I hadn't lost my enthusiasm about the wedding—I couldn't wait to become Mrs. Jackson Blake—but unlike Chloe, it wouldn't matter to me if I married Jack wearing an off-the-rack gown or a flour sack. "No Goodwill. Got it."

"Good. But I have to go. I need to rescue my husband from these damn nymphos he calls fans. Can you believe I found one hiding in his dressing room last week? The bitch tried pulling that 'I'm part of the act' line on me. As if I'd fall for that!"

I suppressed a giggle and tried not to remind her we'd done the exact same thing when we'd first met Jon.

"It's as if they're all jacked up on your magical Viagra. And it's not like I think he'd cheat on me, but I just wish he didn't get off on all the attention." She groaned, and I could practically hear her scowl. She huffed out a breath, and her voice got all melancholy. "Be thankful Jack gave up the magic shows."

I thought about my sexy fiancé-slash-one-time-magician and the magic groupies who used to hang around Vlad's Castle, and I swallowed hard. I was infinitely glad he hadn't given up the day job. As far as I knew, he didn't have any groupies as a veterinarian. "I am. Every day."

Chloe exhaled into the phone. "I've gotta go. Talk to you soon."

The line went dead before I had a chance to ask her what was really bothering her, but my phone rang again before I'd tucked it away. This time, the ringtone was generic, and I didn't recognize the number.

"Hello?"

"Ah, Ivie Marie, mah wee bonnie lass." My father's thick Scottish brogue rang through the line.

I forced a smile into my voice. "Hi, Daddy."

"I need you to come to the university. There's this spell..." After twelve years as a domestic pet, my father had somehow convinced the university to reinstate him to his position as a chemistry professor. I wasn't sure I wanted to know how he'd pulled off *that* little feat. As much as I loved my father, his obsession with my newfound ability to work magic made Jack uncomfortable.

It unnerved me too, especially when I knew there could only be one reason for my father to call me in the middle of a Saturday afternoon. "Daddy, I can't right now. I'm in the middle of something *important*," I lied easily as I wandered, oblivious to my surroundings until I ended up in the toy aisle. I stood in front of what looked suspiciously like a... a *Magic 8 Ball*?

"Oh, come on now. What could be more important than yer dear ol' dad?"

I stifled a groan. His time as a cat hadn't helped with his stubborn streak. "Fine. I'll swing by the lab on my way home."

"Perfect! I've got a surprise for you."

Dad hung up before I could ask about his so-called surprise, but my sorceress sense tingled as I returned my attention to the shelf in front of me. I picked up the fortune-telling toy in both hands, turning the answer window face down, and closed my eyes. "I'm about to be in big trouble, aren't I?" I flipped it over to read the blurred display.

Signs point to yes.

My Ralph Lauren boots sank into the soft earth with a squish as I climbed out of my powder-blue Volkswagen Beetle. Each step forced me to escape the light suction holding my feet hostage as I made my way to the split-rail fence. I should've parked in the official Maxwell Farm lot rather than the muddy field adjacent to the barn, but I was in a hurry to see Jack. I spotted him across the pasture and did my best mud-dash the rest of the way to the fence.

"Jack!" A warm tingle went over my skin at the sight of him, as if it had been days rather than merely a few hours since I'd last seen him.

He pushed his Ray Bans into his hair, and even from a football field's distance away, I saw his eyes light up when he saw me. That look—as if I was the only reason he could breathe—made the trip worthwhile.

It was no accident that I hadn't been back to the farm since October. The words "goat semen" popped into my head uninvited, and I shuddered at the memory.

The field trip.

Ever since that day, I couldn't even eat goat *cheese* without breaking into hives. If not for my obsessive love of all things beef, I might have gone completely vegan.

Jack abandoned whatever he was doing and gave me a quick wave. He cupped his hands around his mouth and shouted, "Hey, sweetheart!"

Ignoring the pungent odor of manure wafting in my direction, I rested my elbows on the wooden rail and watched my sexy-as-hell fiancé jog toward me, his forehead glistening with a sheen of sweat and his damp T-shirt pulling across his muscled chest. I would have braved an entire *herd* of horny goats for that view.

"Hi." My lips tipped into a smile, and he pressed his against them in a sweet kiss. Like a magnet drawn to him,

I wrapped my arms around his neck to pull him in for more. "Got any clean piles of hay we could dirty?"

"You're killing me here." He groaned, and his fingers twitched as he gripped my hips. "I wish you weren't kidding."

We both knew my distaste for the farm was stronger than my libido. I stole one last kiss before releasing him. "Sorry. I got carried away for a minute."

"I'm guessing you didn't come all this way to visit your old buddy, Lucky the goat." He chuckled at my obvious shudder as he soaked in my appearance, from my face to my crisp white blouse and skinny jeans then down to my designer boots. "So to what do I owe the pleasure? And risking Ralph to see me? This *must* be important."

I beamed at him. "It's always important to see you."

Jack rocked back on his heels, a curious glint in his eyes.

I wiped the smile from my lips and cleared my throat. "But in this particular case, my dad asked me to stop by the university to help him with a spe—"

"No." Jack cut me off with a quick slash of his hand across his throat. His face flushed an unflattering shade of puce, and he crossed his arms over his sweaty chest, constructing an invisible wall between us. "We've already discussed this. Magic is dangerous. Bad things happen. People get hurt. Police show up." He counted off his reasons on his fingers, his messy chestnut hair flopping over his sunglasses as he shook his head. "Absolutely not, especially when your father's involved."

I flinched. He was right about my dad, but it still shocked me to hear him voice it. My lips froze in a pout as Jack stared me down. "You're right. I did promise. And I remember very well what happens when one dabbles in witchcraft." And I did. I remembered turning my one-time fiancé, Matt, into a woodland creature—and the horrible chaos that ensued as I struggled to change him back. But had Jack forgotten it all worked out in the end? Without that magical mishap, we might never have met. "But let's not forget all the *benefits* of magic."

He smirked at me, obviously thinking of the same naughty side effects, then relaxed his stance, reaching for me across the top rail. He wrapped his arms around my shoulders and brushed his lips against my ear. "That part wasn't so bad. But the rest of it... I'm sorry, it's just too dangerous, and you seem to lack a sense of self-preservation."

His words sank in, bursting my happy bubble, and I pulled away to look him in the eyes. "But my father's been *missing* for twelve years. I really do owe it to him to at least spend some quality time with him."

Jack's face twisted in contemplation, and I waited for him to work through the dilemma. "You spent loads of time with him when he was a cat." He grimaced at my pout. "Fine. But you need to give me your word you'll be safe. I know you love your dad, but you have to admit, he's a bit of a... *flake*." He winced on the last word, searching my eyes for a reaction.

I blinked a few times, giving my brain time to process what he'd said, then swallowed back an argument. "No... you're right. I'll watch from the sidelines like the dutiful daughter."

"Okay, thank you. I know I seem like an overbearing tyrant sometimes, but I worry about you." He tucked me under his chin again. "Just promise me you'll steer clear of the hocus pocus."

I stretched up for a quick kiss, crossing my fingers behind my back. "Promise."

Guilt gnawed at me the entire way to the university. I hated lying to Jack, but it just wasn't in me to disappoint my father. Playing monkey in the middle with the two most important men in my life was getting old fast. Part of me understood Jack's fears, but it wasn't as if Dad had asked me to do anything *illegal*. Just a little magic, right? It was in my blood—in my genetic makeup, for crying out loud. And I'd gotten good at it a few months ago. In fact, if I'd kept practicing, I probably would've gotten even better. So what if there were a few side effects? It wasn't as if Jack didn't love the insatiable part of me. But dangerous?

Well, maybe a little. But no more so than climbing into a pasture filled with horny goats or wandering into the wrong side of town after dark—two more things I'd managed to survive relatively unscathed. Hell, I could have died a thousand times over from eating raw cookie dough, for that matter. He was just being an overprotective fiancé. That's all. Nothing bad would come from doing a little magic.

Convincing myself was easy. Persuading Jack would be near impossible. His argument hinged on my being "out of control"—both physically and emotionally—and maybe he was right. Magic had an intoxicating effect on me. And a little seemed to go a long way.

After looping around the parking lot for what seemed like an eternity, searching for the science building, I parked beside my mother's worn-out Wagoneer and made my way inside. My father's booming voice echoed through the vacant halls, and I followed the sound to the last door on the left, pushing the lingering sense of foreboding to the back of my mind with a shiver.

Dad looked up from his gurgling beaker to beam at me. "Ivie! You made it. I'm so pleased. Liam, come meet my little girl." My father yanked off his Plexiglas goggles and dropped them to the table in front of him. Before I realized what he was doing, he'd grabbed a tall, dark, and handsome stranger by the sleeve of his fitted navy pullover and dragged him in my direction.

My face flamed as I watched the younger man approach, his blue eyes sparkling and his cheeks dimpling as he smiled. I'd never seen him before, but the way he gazed at me—as if he'd crossed a desert to drink me in—made me uncomfortable.

Dad's uncharacteristically eager expression didn't do anything to allay my anxiety. "Liam, this is my beautiful daughter, Ivie."

"Pleased to meet you, Miss McKie," he said with a faint Scottish accent and extended his hand. "Your father's told me so much about you."

His fingers curled around mine, and I darted my eyes from Liam to Dad then back again. I seemed to be the only one in the room *not* in on the secret. "It's a pleasure to meet you too, but it would seem I'm at a disadvantage. My father hasn't mentioned you at all."

Chapter 2

"OH, NOW DON'T BE SILLY." My father sputtered and coughed into his closed fist, his shifty eyes avoiding my guarded ones. "Of course I've mentioned Liam. At least once or twice."

"No, Dad, you didn't." I gave him my sternest glare then turned my attention to the stranger. He didn't *look* dangerous. But my dad—unlike Liam with his relaxed posture and easy smile—was wound up tighter than an eight-day clock. I didn't need to be a witch to figure out he was up to something.

"He's my apprentice." A wide smile cracked my father's delicately lined face, and a matching one spread across Liam's.

That prickle of intuition at the base of my neck came back. "Apprentice? What do you mean by apprentice?" *Since when do chemistry professors have apprentices?*

"Your father's helping me with an important spell." Liam's soft, lilting voice wrapped around me like a hug. "I've been waiting my whole life for this."

"A spell? As in magic?" *What?* My mouth dropped open, and my eyes shifted between him and my father. The pair of them grinned at me as if we were discussing interest rates, not deep, dark family secrets. "Are we letting the cat out of the bag all over town?" I choked back a giggle as the memory of my father the cat flashed back. "So to speak, I mean."

They both nodded.

"But I thought only... How can he...?" To say I was confused would have been an understatement.

"Oh, Liam comes from a long line of sorcerers, not the same line as ours, of course... but a long line just the same."

There are lines? As in plural? "And he's been doing *magic*?" My voice squeaked on the last word. I whipped my head around to study the young Scottish sorcerer to my left. "But your..." I reached a hand up toward his head but pulled it back at the last moment. "There's no red. When I did"—I used my finger to wiggle my nose from side to side like Samantha from *Bewitched*—"my, um, *you know...*" I glanced down at my chest then quickly looked away. "And my hair... And, Daddy, you have red streaks. But his hair is as dark as mine. How...?" I struggled to find the words.

My father waved me off. "Oh, pish posh. The red hair is a McKie family trait. Liam is a McDougall. Their hair doesn't change color."

"Doesn't change..." My head bobbed a few times as my eyes trailed down the front of my father's apprentice, searching for any telltale signs of magic. "So if your hair doesn't change... what *does* happen to sorcerers in your family?"

Liam sucked in his cheeks, a pink hue coloring his skin. "Other things."

"*Other* things? What kinds of *other* things?" My mind raced with the sorts of changes that might occur. Clearly, the guy didn't have a set of boobs swelling from his well-defined chest. I would have noticed that. But then again, neither did my father.

"Now, don't be rude, Ivie." My father stopped me with a pointed look. "Some things are best left alone."

"Oh... of course." A hot flush spread over my face and down my neck as the overwhelming desire to know exactly what *things* they were alluding to struck me.

I shot another glance at Liam, and Dad's large hands came together in a loud clap, bringing me back to my senses. "Okay, you two—it's time we gave this spell another go."

"Now, don't be shy. Take his hand." Dad nodded toward Liam's outstretched fingers.

The look of longing in Liam's icy-blue eyes made my stomach twist and clench against itself like a fist. His expression reminded me of a kid peering through a candy store window with no more than a few pennies burning a hole in his pocket as he drooled over the all-day sucker.

The part of the all-day sucker will now be played by Miss Ivie McKie.

Jack's words came back to haunt me. No good would come of working magic with my father. "Do I have to?" I heard the whine in my voice. What was I? Five? "Never mind." I shook off my niggling suspicions and patent distrust and tried to relax, reaching out to clasp his warm palm against mine.

My father closed his eyes and let his head fall back until his chin pointed toward the center of our little triangle. He cleared his throat and let the incantation fly. "Double, double, toil and—"

"Really, Dad?" I narrowed my eyes and shot him my best death glare.

Liam barked out a hearty laugh, but I refused to join in. *I gave up shopping for this?* They were nothing but a pair of naughty boys poking fun at me.

"Come on now. That was funny," Dad said in his heavy brogue.

I shook off Liam's hand and took a step back, eyeing each of them in turn. "What exactly are we doing here? What does this alleged spell *do*?"

"Do? What do you mean, *do*?" My father fidgeted with the paper in his hand, crinkling it up then smoothing it out again.

I studied the faint shadows around his emerald eyes and the shocks of red woven through his salt-and-pepper hair. Maybe Jack was right. The magic did seem to take its toll on him. "Yes... what is the purpose of the spell?"

Dad waved his hand through the air. "Oh, it's just a little training spell. Doesn't really *do* anything spectacular. But as I'm sure you've discovered, magic is a precise science—like baking." He took a deep breath. "Too little yeast and your bread won't rise. Too much and you end up with a big mess. Nothing good comes from taking a willy-nilly approach. You either do, or you don't. No dabbling. Practice—as they say—makes perfect. We can't exactly jump right into the advanced spells, now can we?"

I shook my head, certain my eyes had glazed over.

"Didn't think so. Now, take Liam's hand. There's nothing a good binding can't fix." Dad smiled and nodded toward his apprentice.

At a complete loss for words, I stuck out my hand, and Liam seized it in his.

My father slipped his glasses to the end of his nose and began to read the words scrawled out in front of him. "Cò an gobhar sin còmhla riut a chunnaic mi an-raoir..." I suspected he spoke in Gaelic, but it sounded like garbled nonsense to me. "Cha b'e sin gobhar, 'se sin mo chèile a bha innte..."

Overhead, the fluorescent lights flickered a few times, and a warm wind whipped around us, rustling my blouse and blowing my hair into my face. I felt a sharp tug from inside, as if my very life force had yanked free and was making a slow but steady retreat toward Liam.

His grip tightened, and I welcomed the strange sensation as the energy flowed from my fingers to his and back again. My body hummed, sparks licking along the surface of my skin as hot oil ran through my veins. Our two strong forces converged, and I tasted the distinct flavor of his power coursing through me—like butterscotch candies with a dash of hot pepper.

So this is what it feels like to have a magical convergence. Jack would be impressed. Who am I kidding? Jack would be livid.

Liam's pulse jumped, setting off at a pace to match mine. Above us, the lights flickered and buzzed. Then one by one, the rows of long, slender tubes exploded like a Fourth of July finale. I flinched, tugging my hand as splinters of glass rained down on us.

"Don't let go," Liam whispered, and his hold on me became almost painful.

The thrilling yet uncomfortable wrenching sensation gained strength as ripples of current surged through my extremities. Heat pooled between my legs. My body drifted toward the Scottish hottie at my side. The enormity of the situation weighed me down. I could have sworn something had slithered its way inside me and ransacked my thoughts and feelings. I felt as if part of my very soul had ripped away from me.

I didn't like it. Not one bit.

A low rumbling vibrated beneath my feet, and the walls shuddered. My pulse quickened then slowed as the moment passed. I noticed the faint scent of ozone in the air around us and the musical sound of glass clinking together as the containers on the table shook. The rumble grew into a growl, and I gripped Liam's hand like a life preserver as several beakers tipped over, pouring their contents across the steel tabletop. Streams of liquid spilled over the edge like tiny waterfalls. A high-pitched keening forced me to pull my hand free from Liam's so I could press one to each ear to muffle the sound. A wave of panic washed over me as fountains of bright orange flames erupted from the Bunsen burners, and the windows exploded inward.

Holy shit!

My father blew up the lab. Again.

"What the hell just happened?" Crouched down on the floor with my head tucked under my arms to fend off the attack of the shattered windows, I barely noticed the warm body pressed against me. "Training spell, my ass! That was—I-I don't even know what that was."

"Are you okay?" Liam took my hand and helped me to my feet. He hovered over me, picking shards of glass from my hair.

"I'm fi—" I tipped my face up to brush off his attention and froze, on the verge of getting lost in a sea of periwinkle. "Were your eyes always so blue?"

He chuckled. "They get a bit lighter when I do magic."

"That makes sense, I guess." I tried to concentrate on anything other than his magnetic stare—the glint of light in the glass fragments, the dribble of liquid splashing against the tile floor, the acrid scent of charred air—but every time I flicked my eyes his way, my pulse picked up speed. And it wasn't only my heart behaving erratically.

"Other things change too, but nothing you'd be able to see right away." His lips tipped up on one side, and he glanced down his body.

"Oh... *Oh!*" I caught a glimpse of the bulge behind his zipper and felt the flush spread from my face, down my neck, and over my entire chest. Damn magic messing with my libido again.

His crooked grin turned into a full-blown smirk, but he didn't say anything.

"Ivie! Are you okay, lass?" my dad croaked from under the table.

"I'm fine. Just a bit... shaken." *Understatement of the decade.* The wail of approaching sirens nagged at me as I struggled to break free from the glacier-blue thrall of the Scottish hottie.

"I tried to shield her with my body as best I could." Liam's fingers whispered over my cheek, sending a fresh shiver through my body, from top to bottom. "She might have a few minor scratches, but nothing a bit of peroxide and a Band-Aid won't fix."

"Good thinking, lad." Dad stood, brushing dust and debris from the front of his not-so-white lab coat. "Already taking your role seriously."

"His role?" A wave of confusion almost as troubling as the situation at hand rushed over me.

My father's eyes darted between my face and Liam's before a shaky smile tipped his lips. "As my apprentice, dear."

"Uh huh." Suspicion twisted my stomach.

Dad shook the dust from his red-streaked hair. "You worry too much."

Red-streaked hair?

My hand shot up to my own tangled mess. "Oh no! My hair! Is it... *red*?"

They both nodded.

"Daddy, I need to go." I shoved Liam out of my way while I searched for my purse and my keys. I knew I'd tossed them somewhere when I came in. "I'm sorry. It was nice to meet you and all that, but I have to make a quick stop at the store for a bottle of dark dye before I go home. Jack will absolutely *flip* if I show up with red hair."

"But it's such a lovely shade." Liam's voice caressed me, and I trembled at the sound. "I'm quite fond of it, actually." He twined a few strands around his fingers, tugging me closer to his warmth.

My breath caught in my throat as I gazed up at him. "You don't understand. I promised..." Pounding footsteps in the hallway interrupted my thoughts. "Dad, I can't deal with this right now. I need to go. I can't be here—" I was cut off again, this time by at least a dozen cops in SWAT team attire, carrying guns, at least one of which pointed directly at me.

Not this again!

"Angus McKie, you're under arrest." One uniformed officer read my dad his rights while a second cuffed his hands behind his back.

Dad sputtered out excuse after excuse, but I was too busy panicking to listen.

Liam gripped my arm, tugging me slowly away from the melee, but I wrenched free and whispered, "What are you doing?"

He splayed his hands around my waist, his lips brushing my ear. "I'm *attempting* to get you out of here before you get—" He stopped, his body rigid, as he stared at something behind me. "Damn it!"

My head whipped around to see what had caught his attention, and his grip loosened until I stood alone with several armed men surrounding me. I eyed a pair of silver handcuffs, and my heart leapt into my throat.

"Don't worry, Ivie. No matter what happens, I'll come back for you," he murmured from behind me. I spun around just in time to see Liam's form shimmer in and out of focus until he vanished.

As if he was never really there.

"So, whatta ya in for?" the haggard old blonde drawled in her thick Southern accent as she leaned closer to me on the bench. Her stale breath reeked of cigarettes and cheap whiskey, and I had to tamp down my natural urge to recoil.

"Umm... I'm not exactly sure." I shrugged one shoulder and inched slowly away. "Blowing up a lab, I guess." Part of me wondered if I'd hallucinated my entire day—like some sort of paranoid delusion. *Could my dad have been cooking up something over those Bunsen burners that made me imagine the whole thing? Peyote maybe?*

She nodded. "Meth lab? Fragile operation, I know it well."

"No!" I gasped. More like a magical meltdown, but I couldn't tell *her* that. "The chemistry lab at the university." The same chemistry lab my father apparently *didn't* get reinstated to, given the trespassing charges pending against us.

Her lips spread in a wide smile, exposing a row of chipped and rotting teeth. "Don't you worry, sweetie." She scooted closer and patted my shoulder with Cheetos-stained fingers. "Cici won't say anything."

I suppressed a shudder. "Cici?"

"Cici." She cocked her thumb toward her chest, reminding me of an old Tarzan movie. Her Cici. Me... in deep shit.

"Oh." I bit my lip and eyed the thick Plexiglas wall preventing me from escaping Cici's fascinating company.

"Well?" She made a rolling motion with her hand. "What's your name, darlin'?"

I drew a blank. "Oh... umm... Ivie?"

"You sure?" She chuckled. "What the hell were you cooking before the explosion?"

I barked out a laugh. What *were* we cooking? I still hadn't figured that out. But if I *wasn't* in some drug-induced nightmare, my father and his so-called training spell stank of secrecy, deception, and a healthy dose of Liam's baby blues. "I don't even know. I got there right before it blew up."

"Well, ain't it just your lucky day?" She wrapped a bare arm around my shoulder, pulling me in for an awkward hug.

I choked back a scream. She was too lifelike to be a figment of my imagination, and her clammy skin made mine crawl.

"No worries, though." She gave my back three sharp thwacks, nearly dislodging my molars, before releasing me. "You just stick with Cici, and you'll be fine."

Stick with Cici? I inched away again, my lunch threatening to make a reappearance. Greasy cheeseburger crawled up the back of my throat, and I swallowed it down. "So um... *Cici*...what are *you* in for?"

She averted her gray eyes, suddenly transfixed by the concrete walls. "Got into a scuffle with my roommate. She went and died."

I took a huge gulp of air. "A-a scuffle?" What did that even mean? I once got into a scuffle with a soccer mom at Goodwill. We both wanted the same pair of Burberry sandals. They were stunning: light-blue plaid, four-inch heels, big fat straps across the foot—Barbie shoes for big girls. I needed those shoes the way I needed air. She had the left shoe, I had the right, and the bitch refused to let go.

"Well, I guess it was a little more than that." Cici let out a dramatic sigh. "I stabbed her with the heel of her own stiletto."

My mouth fell open with a pop, and I immediately shut it for fear of all the germs I might inadvertently inhale. "You killed her with a shoe?" That sealed it. Shoes were the ultimate downfall for women the world over.

"Oh, no." She chuckled again. "*That* didn't kill her."

I blew out a breath, my racing heart slowing somewhat. "That's... *good*?"

"Oh, hell no. A damn heel wasn't enough to do more than slow her down. But once I had her laid out on the floor, I hit her over the head with the toaster until she stopped moving."

I gasped. "You killed her with the toaster?"

Cici's chest rattled as she laughed. "Naw. Didn't kill her with the toaster, neither."

My body leaned away from her, but I couldn't manage to wriggle completely out of her grasp.

"I finally had to shoot the sorry bitch."

I sprang off the bench as if launched from a catapult, ripping myself from Cici's side. A wicked case of the heebie-jeebies invaded my being. I jumped and wiggled to shake it off, clenching and unclenching my fists in an attempt to fire up a spark of magic. If it came down to her or me, I'd be ready. She'd make a nice gerbil—something small enough to step on without completely ruining my shoes.

"Ivie McKie?" The short, squat policeman called out my name in the nick of time.

Hallelujah. I hurried to the door, anxious to escape. "That's me! I'm Ivie McKie."

"You made bail."

Thank you, Jack!

Chapter 3

FTER I SIGNED A RELEASE form—in triplicate—and collected my belongings, the officer led me through the maze of hallways to where my fiancé paced like a caged lion in the lobby. I'd called Jack hours ago—as soon as they'd processed me and allowed me my one phone call—and by the looks of him, he'd been here waiting the whole time.

I stumbled through the door, and Jack's head jerked up to take in my appearance. I hadn't seen my reflection, but I undoubtedly looked a mess. Being in an explosion would do that to a girl, not to mention the hours I spent living through an episode of *Snapped!* His expression shifted from relief to annoyance in a heartbeat as his eyes reached my tangled mass of red-tinged hair. I still would've rather taken on his worst mood than spend another minute in a holding cell with the haggard, drugged-out murderess.

He parted his lips, pulling in a breath, then pressed them together in a hard line, exhaling through his nose.

I fought off an onslaught of tears and flung myself into his open arms, clinging to him as if my life depended on it. Despite my silent pleas, he didn't wrap his arms around me in return, and after several tense moments, he pried my hands from around his neck.

I untangled myself from his limbs and took a step back, willing my racing heart to slow. "I can explain."

"And I'd really like to hear that explanation." His features twisted into a deep scowl. "*Later.*"

Definitely angry.

"I know you're mad at me, and I don't blame you." I wrung the hem of my favorite turtleneck in my hands. So much for the black Ann Taylor. I'd never look at her the same way again. "But thank you for bailing me out."

He pushed an unsteady hand into his hair as the muscle in his jaw twitched. He looked as if his fragile control was about to shatter. "*I* didn't bail you out."

"You didn't?" With a mighty whoosh, my stomach dropped to my toes. "Then I don't understand. Who...?" My mind raced with the possibilities as I gaped at Jack's dark yet unreadable expression. Liam's last words to me ran through my head like an old newsreel, and the zing of anticipation almost brought me to my knees.

Jack shifted his attention to the tall figure in the corner watching us with an annoyed countenance of his own. Somehow, I'd sensed his presence in the room. The now-familiar tingle skipped over my skin like stones across still water.

Jack nodded in Liam's direction. "*He* did."

"Liam?" I took a hesitant step toward my father's apprentice.

Liam's lips quirked with the beginnings of a smile as he strode toward me, sending an unwelcome surge of euphoria through me. "I told you I'd come back for you." He took my hand in his and raised it to kiss my knuckles.

Before I could stop myself, I'd clasped his hand and lowered my voice to a whisper. "How did you...? You were there and then—I've never seen anything like that before."

"Ivie?" Jack's voice broke through the connection I shared with the Scottish hottie, and I spun around to face my fiancé's jealous rage. Anger rippled off Jack in tidal waves. He dragged me against him in an uncomfortable hug, my hand still gripped tightly in Liam's. "Who the hell is this? And why did *he* bail you out?"

"Uh... Jack, this is Liam, my father's new apprentice." I emphasized the last word then turned to Liam. "This is Jack, my—"

Jack squeezed me harder. "Her *fiancé.*"

They stared at each other like a pair of mountain goats ready to lock horns over the female in heat—*me.* A jolt of desire took me by surprise. My overactive hormones couldn't decide which man to focus on.

"Ah, yes, the fiancé. I've heard so much about you. It's nice to finally make your acquaintance." Liam reached a hand toward Jack, but Jack just stared at it, a low growl rolling up his throat.

"Jack!" I elbowed him in the ribs.

Jack forced a smile, his jaw clenching and unclenching as he shook Liam's hand. I half expected to hear bones cracking. "I'm afraid I've heard nothing about you."

"Well, I haven't been in town long. And Angus... rather, Professor McKie, has been fairly busy with other things." Liam winked at me, making my mouth fall open.

Jack's eyes narrowed at Liam, and I could practically see the gears turning as he tried to puzzle together my father's motives. "It would seem you're correct about that. He's definitely been busy lately."

The testosterone flying between them was hot enough to set my skin on fire. I squeezed my thighs together to stave off the inconvenient cravings and tugged on Jack to leave before I dragged them both down onto the floor and had my wicked way with them. "Well, we'd better get going."

"Ivie?" Jack stood cemented in place. His eyebrows arched toward his hairline.

"Hmm?"

He nodded toward my fingers, still linked with Liam's. "You need to let go."

"Oh." I blinked. "Right." I wrenched myself free and immediately noted the loss of warmth.

Why did holding his hand feel so perfect?

Jack slammed the door, rattling the windows... and my nerves. Without a word, he stalked into the living room, chucking his phone and his keys onto the coffee table. He'd been eerily quiet on the ride home, but clearly, his anger bubbled just below the surface, and he was about to blow.

He paced over the carpet, hands weaving in and out of his hair, making it stand on end. With his mouth hanging open, Jack came to an abrupt halt in front of me. For a long moment, he stood wordlessly then closed his mouth and began pacing again. He completed the circuit a few more times before he finally decided to speak. "Please tell me how my fiancée manages to get arrested for destruction of private property, unlawful use of pyrotechnics, and what the hell was that last charge?"

I shrank away from his wrath, but my body hummed with pent-up sexual energy. "Trespassing?"

Jack barked out a hollow laugh. "How could I forget? Please tell me how you were arrested for trespassing... among other things?"

"Um..." My voice—not to mention my confidence—wavered. "My dad never actually got his university authorization reinstated?"

"Right. Your dad, the wizard—"

I frowned and crossed my arms. *That* went over the line. "Sorcerer."

He shook his head, letting out a humorless chuckle as he continued to pace. "Your dad, the *sorcerer,* has been doing unsanctioned experiments. Magic, I'm guessing?"

I winced and nodded.

"In a lab he doesn't have permission to use?" Jack's nostrils flared. He'd twisted his hair into a tangled mess. His perfect jaw spasmed with each muscle contraction.

I nodded again, biting back a grin. He looked positively delicious in a display of anger so impressive I couldn't help being a little—okay, *a lot*—turned on by it.

"And he dragged you into his *illegal* activities under the guise of what, exactly?" He stopped pacing to reach out and take a lock of my hair between his fingers. His touch sent a shock through me. "I'm guessing by this brilliant shade of red, you weren't just there for moral support."

My guilt resurfaced. It sounded so bad when he said it that way. "He needed my help?"

"Ivie, we talked about this." Jack sighed and gave my hair a gentle tug before releasing it. "You promised."

"I know, I know. I'm sorry. He's just... he's my dad." I perched on the arm of the sofa to pull off my boots and tossed each one aside. "He gave me the guilt trip. Then he told me his new apprentice had a spell he needed help with, and I'll admit the idea intrigued me. Dad called it a simple training spell. Apparently, they needed to channel my energy." I had no intention of sharing my suspicions about the mysterious nature of the spell—or the lasting impression it had left on me.

His eyes flashed at the mention of Liam. "And what happened after that? You looked awfully *chummy* with this so-called apprentice."

I gasped. "What exactly are you accusing me of?"

"I'm not accusing you of anything, but I know all too well what happens when you work magic." Jack went back to pacing and mangling his hair in his hands. "And the way he looked at you... I don't like it."

"Nothing happened, Jack." I stood and crossed the room to place a hand on each of his shoulders. "The police came within minutes of the windows blowing in. And even if they hadn't come, nothing would have happened. I'm engaged to you. I *love* you. Liam is nothing to me." Even as the words came out of my mouth, I knew they were lies. I didn't know what Liam meant to me, but whether I liked it or not, he meant *something*.

Jack wrapped his arms around me, and I melted into his warmth. "The thought of him touching you makes me crazy."

I shook off the unwelcome thought. "He didn't touch me."

"I saw you holding hands, Ivie. Your fingers were laced together." Jack leaned back far enough to stare into my eyes. "What am I supposed to think about that?"

The memory of Liam's hand in mine flashed unbidden into my mind, and a shudder ran through me. "You're supposed to trust me."

"I do trust you." He pulled me against his chest, resting his chin on the top of my head. "I don't trust your dad. Things have been strange since..." He didn't say it, but I knew what he meant. *Since you turned him back.*

Nestling into the crook of his shoulder, I breathed in his unique scent—a cross between soap, hay, and the outdoors. "It's just the wedding. I'm sure he's worried about the details. As the father of the bride, he feels obligated to pay for at least part of it, and I know he and Mom haven't been in a good way financially since he reappeared. Mom's been getting calls from the insurance company that paid out when Dad *died.* She's afraid they'll want their money back now that he's risen from the grave."

Jack sighed, his fingers drawing lazy circles on the back of my neck. "Your dad hates me. I sense it every time he looks at me."

My head snapped up. "He doesn't hate you. Remember how attached to you he was as a cat?" Memories of Karma curled up in Jack's lap caught me off guard. I missed that cat.

"No." He smirked down at me. "But I'm starting to re-member all the times I defiled his daughter in his presence without knowing it."

A loud burst of laughter bubbled out of me, reopening the delicious floodgates I'd fought to suppress. I squeezed my thighs together as a fresh shiver of need worked its way under my skin. "I'm pretty sure he left the room every time."

Jack chuckled. "He would've had to leave the neighborhood to escape the sounds we made."

"Mmm. That reminds me." I bit my lip and snaked a hand between us to stroke the zipper of his jeans, making him groan. "I *did* work a little magic today."

"So you did." His nose nuzzled along the length of my neck before he scooped me up and lifted me off the floor. "Shall we head to the bedroom? Or is my little witch feeling like a bathroom romp?"

I squirmed in his arms, a dull ache throbbing between my legs. "I think we're due for—" Heavy pounding on the front door cut off my thought. "Who the hell—" The shrill ring of Jack's cell phone cut me off again, and I dropped my head to his shoulder with a growl. "You answer your phone. I'll see who's at the door."

Jack put me down with a nod and reached for his phone where he'd thrown it when we came in. "Get rid of whoever it is, and meet me in the bedroom in five." He flashed a wicked grin my way. "Make it four."

I giggled. "Deal." The pounding continued as I hurried to the door. "Hang on. I'm coming," I shouted as I twisted the deadbolt. Before I'd finished turning the knob, my father shoved me aside as he and Liam barged in.

"Ivie!" My father panted. "Are you all right? We've been worried sick!"

"Dad?" His disheveled appearance shocked me. A wild tangle knotted his hair. His clothes were rumpled, the buttons misaligned, and on his feet were a pair of mismatched shoes with no socks. "What are you doing here?" I turned to Liam, a sudden flash of anger and attraction clouding my vision. "And you! What do you want? You've both put me in a very bad position."

"Has he harmed you?" Liam stepped around my father, molding his hot hand around mine.

My heart skipped a beat. "Has who harmed me? What are you talking about?"

Liam stroked the pulse point in my wrist with his thumb, and I suppressed the urge to purr. "The magician."

I tore my eyes from our joined hands and swallowed against the knot in my throat. "Jack? He's not a magician. He's a veterinarian. And of course he hasn't harmed me. He's pretty pissed off, but understandably so. I *did* promise to not work any magic."

My father shot a serious glance at Liam. "See? What did I tell you?"

Liam nodded. "It's worse than I thought."

Worse than he thought? What could be worse than finding myself inexplicably drawn to a man I barely know while the man I love waits for me—probably naked—in our bedroom? I daresay nothing.

"Ivie, you need to come with us." My father wrapped an arm around my shoulder, guiding me toward the door as Liam continued to caress my hand.

I tugged free, ducking under my father's arm, and took a few steps back. "I'm not going anywhere."

Faster than I could say "Sexy Scot on a stick," Liam spun me around. His fingers splayed over my stomach as he pressed into me from behind. "It's not safe here, lass." His lips whispered against my ear, making my already-racing heart flutter and my knees go weak. "Listen to your father. Come with us."

"Hey, sweetheart, who was at the—" Jack stepped into the foyer and froze midstride. "What the hell?"

My instincts told me to run—just bolt from the whole scene. I was young. Surely, I could lock myself in the bathroom before someone caught up to me. I attempted to wriggle free from Liam's gravitational pull, but if the expression on Jack's face was any indication, I'd failed. Miserably.

"This isn't what you think." My voice cracked. With each exhale, the heat of Liam's delicious breath fanned across my neck. He leaned into me—his lips all but touching my skin and his erection poking me in the back. I felt my self-control dangling by a thread.

"Get. Your. Hands. Off. My. Fiancée." Jack ground out the words, his fists balled at his sides, the vein in his forehead throbbing.

My already-thundering pulse jumped. His anger did delicious things to my insides.

"Now, Jack." My father draped an arm over Jack's shoulder. "We don't want any trouble here. I simply need my little girl to come with me for a bit. Her mother's been asking for her, and—"

Jack wrenched himself away and darted a glare between Dad and Liam. "Rose is welcome to come here to see Ivie. But she's not a little girl, and she's *not* leaving with *you*." His eyes locked with mine, and he reached a hand toward me. "Sweetheart, come here."

"*Jack...*" A soft whimper caught in my throat as Liam's long, agile fingers pressed into the soft flesh of my hips. A heady mix of confusion, indecision, and arousal muddled my thoughts. I'd never loved anyone the way I loved Jack, never wanted anyone as much as I wanted him. But Liam had somehow worked his way under my skin, quickly whittling away at my self-restraint.

"Leave with me, Ivie." Liam's lilting voice startled me out of his spell, and I pushed away from him, rushing into Jack's outstretched arms. My heart thrummed like a frightened bird.

"Go home, Daddy." I spat the words as I struggled to catch my breath.

My father exhaled a heavy sigh. "If that's really what you want."

I gave him a curt nod. "It is."

"So be it. But remember, I'm only a phone call away." He leaned in to hug me, but I melted deeper into Jack's embrace. "Now is that any way to say goodbye to your father?"

"I'm afraid we've worn out our welcome." Liam stepped in, the shadow of a smile on his lips as he took my father's elbow to guide him to the door. "Not to worry, Angus. There's still time."

My mind raced again as that now-familiar disconcerting feeling settled into my bones. *Time for what?*

Jack ushered my dad and his apprentice out the same way they'd come in then spun on his heels, his face an unreadable mask. "Well, *that* was enlightening."

"By enlightening, you really mean horrible and embarrassing, right?" I plastered a fake smile on my lips, but under my calm façade, a wave of panic threatened to take over.

Jack shook his head and turned to walk away. "Something like that."

"Wait. Jack, please." I held my breath and waited for him to turn around, but he didn't. He kept walking until I heard the hollow click of the bedroom door closing.

Chapter 4

MORNING DAWNED, AS COLD AND lonely as the night before. After tossing and turning restlessly on his own side of the bed, Jack slipped out before I woke. No kiss goodbye—not even a note to let me know he still cared. Hardly our first disagreement, but unquestionably our worst.

And what's a girl to do when her fiancé gives her the cold shoulder? Reach out to her best friend, that's what. But as I pulled into the school parking lot—almost thirty minutes late for class—the twenty-odd text messages I'd sent Chloe were, as of yet, unanswered.

Damned time difference.

With my hair flying behind me like a cape, I darted down the hall to my classroom and froze at the sound of brisk footsteps behind me.

"Late again, Miss McKie?" Dr. Alistair Clark, the new principal—and my new boss—whined in his upper-crust British accent. I suspected he faked it. He was probably from Hoboken.

I sucked in a breath and spun around to face him. "Al—uh, Dr. Clark. Hi. I know I'm a little late."

He tapped the dial of his gold-tone watch in time with my pounding heart.

"Okay, a lot late. But I had—"

His pinched nose wrinkled above a seemingly drawn-on mustache, forming what I liked to call his "stinky cheese" face. "Let me guess. Car troubles?"

My mouth, already open and prepared to formulate my latest excuse, snapped shut. For all of a nanosecond, I debated transforming him into a weasel so his appearance would better match his disposition, but I dashed the thought right out of my mind. Weasels were far too good for him. Instead, I conjured up a story on the fly, punctuating my lie with what I hoped was a convincing grimace. "Actually, no. *Female* issues."

"Ah, I see." As I'd anticipated, the mere suggestion of anything PMS–related had him backing up several steps as if I had the black plague. "Well, I do hope you feel—that is to say—I hope you're quite well."

Jackpot.

"I'm sure I'll survive. But thank you for your concern. I should really go before the, uh"—I hooked my thumb down the hall—"natives get restless."

"Yes. You do that." He spun on his fancy Italian loafers and power-walked in the opposite direction as if he couldn't get away fast enough.

Sort of like Jack this morning.

I ran the rest of the way to my classroom, where I found Sandy, one of the part-time aides, minding the store in my absence. I panted out a "thank you" and flashed her a grateful smile.

"No problem, Ivie." She winked, collecting her things from my desk. "I'm used to it."

After getting over her thinly veiled insult, I passed out some busywork for the miniature debutants and future CEOs and fell into my chair to check my text messages. Nothing from Chloe or Jack, but I did have several perplexing messages from a number I didn't recognize.

Unknown: Thoughts of you drive the melancholy from my day.

Unknown: Our time together was all too brief but undoubtedly memorable.

Unknown: My deepest apologies if I'm to blame for any difficulties you may be experiencing.

Liam.

I conjured his image, and a delicious ripple raced through me. I needed to unearth the reasons this virtual stranger had me so unhinged and why I felt so drawn to him. Try as I might, I couldn't shake him from my thoughts.

"Miss Key?" Robby Patterson, the adorable towheaded troublemaker in the front row, butchered my name. As usual.

"Yes, Robby?" I replied without looking up from my phone.

"A stranger."

My head snapped up to see Robby pointing at an all-too-familiar dark-haired figure in the doorway. "Liam! What are you doing here?" I jumped up, tipping my chair over in the process, and bolted to where he stood, leaning against the frame like a damn Calvin Klein model.

A crooked smile perched on his all-too-kissable lips. "I came to apologize for yesterday." His lilting brogue thrilled me to my core.

Tamping down my uninvited reaction, I cleared my throat, wiping the traitorous smile from my lips to scowl at him. "I'm at work. I really can't have visitors."

"Oh, of course. Sorry." He lowered his eyes, a faint blush stealing over his cheeks as he took in my appearance. "I thought it better to come here rather than to your home."

"Well, yes. Jack wouldn't—let's just say you're correct. But nevertheless..." I glanced behind me at my class. We had twenty pairs of eyes glued to us in rapt fascination. "I'm still at work."

Liam reached out to stroke the blue silk of my sleeve, leaving me mesmerized. "Perhaps I could wait for you—*after*."

"Wait for me?" I squeaked.

"I would very much like to take you"—his sapphire eyes met mine, and his lips curled up at the corners—"to *dinner*."

My heart broke into a sprint, and I clenched my thighs together. "I-I can't. I have a fiancé, you know. I love Jack." As much as I wanted to scream the words, I kept my volume low enough to hear the whispers and giggles from my class.

Liam frowned and gave me a curt nod. "So you say."

"I do—*say*, that is. It's true." A rush of heat crept up my neck. Why did he have to put me so completely on edge every single time I saw him? He might as well have been a teenage vampire. "I'm sure you're a perfectly nice guy, but I'm engaged. To be married."

A crooked smile reappeared on his handsome face, and he inched close enough for me to smell the pheromones he was giving off. "Ivie," he purred, trailing a finger from my wrist to my shoulder. He slid his hand into the hair at the base of my neck, holding my head in place as he skimmed the calloused pad of his thumb across my hot cheek. "Your skin is so lovely when you blush."

The words formed on my lips before I could stop them. "I get off at three-thirty."

"Chloe, I really need your advice. I have no idea what I've gotten myself into. I love Jack. I do. But for reasons I can't even begin to understand, I agreed to go to dinner with my father's apprentice. There's something about him. I can't explain it. And I can't seem to resist it, either. And it isn't helping that Jack hasn't returned my—"

An electronic beep sounded in my ear as Chloe's voice-mail cut me off.

"Damn it!" I threw my phone into my purse and sank into the faux black leather seat.

My anxiety level had reached DEFCON 1: meltdown imminent.

When I'd skipped out on the planning meeting, leaving the building the minute the last of the parents had reclaimed their young, I'd intended to go straight home. Instead, I ended up in the front seat of my Beetle with the motor running for nearly half an hour, dialing my way through my cell phone contacts. Every call I'd made had gone straight to voicemail. Jack, my mother, Chloe, all too busy—or unwilling—to take my call.

A quick glance at the clock set my heart on a collision course with my throat. Liam was due to arrive in less than ten minutes. I had a sudden urge for a cigarette, and I didn't even smoke.

Why am I still here? "Because I'm an idiot," I said out loud. "And apparently, I've also lost my mind since I'm now talking to myself." *You need to leave. You can't be trusted with the Scottish hottie.* Even my subconscious knew a bad idea when it heard one. With one last look around the parking lot, I threw the car into reverse and backed out. The vibrating phone on the seat beside me startled me. I snatched it up so fast I swerved into the on-coming lane for a moment. "Hello?"

"Ivie? This is your mother," she said, as if I wouldn't recognize her voice.

"Hi, Mom." Relief coursed through me. "I'm so glad you got my messages."

"What messages? I didn't get any messages. I'm calling about your father."

"Oh." Relief became irritation, and I gunned the engine. "I'm not speaking to Dad right now. He's trying to sabotage my relationship. Did he tell you what he did?"

"Yes." She exhaled into the phone. "But that's not why I'm calling. I need you to come over. It's urgent."

My hand jerked on the steering wheel. My parents' house was the last place I needed to be. "No way! Jack's already pissed off about yesterday."

For the first time since I had no idea when, my mother raised her voice. "Ivie Marie McKie! Your family needs you."

"Mom, my father got me arrested."

Her voice dropped to a whisper. "Well, if you don't get over here in a hurry, you may be bailing your *mother* out of jail."

"What?!" I drifted into the opposite lane again, making a quick course correction to right myself, but not before earning an impolite hand gesture from somebody's grandmother. "What the hell are you talking about?"

"The insurance investigators showed up. They're asking about your father's return from the dead. They have a file, Ivie. A file!"

"Tell them to talk to Dad."

"He—I have no idea where he is."

"Fine." Apparently, resistance was futile. "I'm on my way."

The instant my mother hung up, I dialed Jack's number. *Voicemail... again.* "Jack, I don't know if you're ignoring me or if you just haven't gotten my messages"—I took a deep breath then let it out—"but there's an emergency at my mom's house. I'm on my way over there. Jack, I'm—" I contemplated apologizing again but changed my mind. His jealousy had gotten ridiculous. He had no reason to distrust me. It's not as if he could read my mind. "Just, please call me."

I flung the phone into the passenger seat, ignoring the low-battery warning since nobody seemed to want to talk to me anyway, and made the first U-turn to head toward my parents' house.

A shiny black Chevy Suburban with dark-tinted windows sat in my mother's driveway, taking up both spaces and leaving me to park in the street. With a look that could terrify woodland creatures the world over, I scowled at the monstrosity and took the steps two at a time to let myself in the front door without knocking.

Two black-suited men made a synchronized turn in my direction and gave me the once-over, lingering on my cleavage. *Insurance adjusters, my ass.*

I stepped into the living room, where my mother held a plate of cookies out to the men. *She baked?* "Mom?"

Mom's head shot up at the sound of my voice. "Oh, thank goodness." Her shoulders sagged with obvious relief. "I'm so glad you made it."

"What's going on? I thought you said the insurance guys were here?"

Suit number one, a tall middle-aged man, who'd clearly avoided the sun for longer than even *I* had, took a half step toward me. He was a dead ringer for Agent Smith in the Matrix movies, right down to the sandy hair—parted to the side and slicked back away from his face—and the frosty demeanor. "We're with the FBI, ma'am. White-collar crime division." He enunciated each word in a smooth baritone.

Holy crap! He even sounds like Agent Smith.

"The FBI?" I shifted my eyes between the agents and my mother.

Mom stepped around Smith and his younger partner, who I'd dubbed Wesson in my head. "It's really a funny story." She chuckled, but I recognized the tremble in her voice. "Did you know the FBI investigates insurance fraud?"

"Insurance fraud?" It had never occurred to me that with Dad's sudden return from the dead, the insurance company would assume the worst.

"It would appear the FBI suspects we may have faked his death for the money." Mom cringed, and I could almost hear her heart fluttering.

"So? You just give back the money. It can't be that much."

Smith and Wesson snickered, and my mother flushed a deep red.

"It's not that easy, dear. I've *spent* some of it."

"It's okay. I can lend you some. How much did you spend? A few hundred? A thousand?"

"Five hundred."

"No problem." I reached into my purse and fumbled for my rarely used checkbook. "I've got at least twice that in my checking account."

"Thousand." Mom cleared her throat. "Five hundred *thousand.*"

My stomach plunged into my shoes. "What?"

She nodded, staring at the worn, avocado-green carpet. "Give or take a few thousand."

"What could you have possibly spent that much money on? The house and the car together aren't worth that much. And for Chrissakes, if you had that much money, why are you still driving the piece-of-crap Wagoneer?"

She looked up with a thoughtful expression. "Well, I didn't want to spend money needlessly."

"Of course." Because dropping five hundred grand with nothing to show for it *isn't* needless.

Agent Smith coughed into his fist.

Mom spun around as if she'd forgotten the two strangers standing in her living room. "Oh, my goodness, Agent Hunter. How rude of me." She turned back to me. "Dear, this is Agent Hunter and Agent Corrigan. Gentlemen, this is my daughter, Ivie McKie."

"Yes..." Agent Smith—err, *Hunter*, smirked. "We know all about Miss McKie. From her file."

"I have a file?" My pulse quickened, and the surface of my skin tingled.

"A quite-extensive file, actually." The strawberry blond, Agent Corrigan, spoke for the first time. His fresh-faced youthfulness belonged in a boy band, not the FBI. "I thoroughly enjoyed the *interesting* comments left by your former neighbor."

His mention of crazy old Mrs. Camp made me cringe. Hard to believe it was only six months ago that she'd made calls to the police accusing me of being a devil worshipper—or worse. She lived next door to my former fiancé: the chiropractor turned woodland creature. The entire situation with Matt had first helped me realize I was a witch.

Sorceress. I corrected myself then choked out a laugh. "Mrs. Camp is half senile."

"It's the other half we're interested in." Agent Smith turned to me with a raised eyebrow. "The police wrote her off as confused, but her recollection of the events intrigues me. You were, in fact, a fugitive from justice for nearly two weeks."

"Six days, and I didn't actually *do* anything. It was all a huge misunderstanding."

"Ninety percent of all convicted felons say the same thing," Agent Corrigan piped up, effectively changing my mind about liking him better.

"Well, I *wasn't* convicted or even arrested, for that matter. Matt explained the entire situation to the police, and the charges were dropped."

"What about the most recent charges?" Agent Smith sifted through several bright-colored folders before fishing out a printed document from a green one. "Trespassing, destruction of private property, and illegal use of pyrotechnics."

I blinked like a deer in headlights. No matter how often I heard the charges recited, they never failed to shock me.

He held up the page. "Was *this* just a simple misunderstanding?"

"Yes?" I whispered. "I-I ended up in the wrong place at the wrong time."

"So it would appear." Agent Smith tucked the paper back into the folder.

I inched backward and gulped. "Am I in trouble here?"

"You tell me? Are you?" He took a step in my direction like a lion stalking a gazelle.

A chill cut through me. "Maybe I should speak with an attorney before I answer that."

Before either of the agents could respond, the door burst open, and Liam strode into the room like a white knight on a horse. "What's going on?" His icy blue eyes locked on mine.

"I-I don't know. I think I'm being investigated by the FBI."

A twinkle of light flashed in Liam's eyes, and he reached out to clasp my hand. A surge of energy coursed up my arm and snaked its way through my core.

"Nonsense." Liam winked at me before turning his attention to Smith and Wesson. "Surely you can't think Ivie is a danger to society."

Agent Smith held his ground. "Miss McKie definitely has some explaining to do."

The tiny hairs on my arms stood on end, and the familiar sugary metallic taste settled on the tip of my tongue. I had no idea if I—or maybe Liam—had put the words into my head, but a spell had formed. My fingertips tingled with faint electric shocks, and I raised my hand toward Smith, trying to appear as nonchalant as possible while the barely visible blue flash arced between the two FBI agents and me.

Liam leaned in, his lips brushing my ear. "Ask them again," he whispered.

I pulled myself up to my full height before addressing the men in black. "Am I under investigation?"

The younger agent turned to his partner and shrugged.

Before my eyes, Agent Smith's stony expression softened. As if suddenly possessed by the Cheshire cat, he smiled. "Of course not. I think we've taken up enough of your time, Miss McKie. Agent Corrigan and I will be leaving now. Have a nice day." He scooped up his color-coded file folders, and the two of them marched straight out the front door without a backward glance.

I turned to Liam, dumbfounded. "What just happened?" Apparently, I'd Jedi mind-tricked two FBI agents into determining I wasn't the witch they were looking for. Amazing.

"You were brilliant!" Liam scooped me into his arms and spun me around. "You did so well."

"I did magic. Wait!" I wiggled out of his grip. "Did you help me? I felt your energy shooting through my arm."

He smiled. "I helped. But only a little. I let you draw from my power."

"Eeek." I spread my arms out at my sides and twirled until I got dizzy. "That felt so amazing. I'm still tingling." *All over, in fact.* I recognized the expression on Liam's face. He felt it too.

"Ivie." Liam groaned as he took a step closer, skimming his finger over my cheek. "You're so beautiful. I must kiss you."

I couldn't stop myself. I leaned in, letting him cup my face in his hands. He brought his lips down to mine, so close I could taste his minty-sweet breath. My eyes drifted shut as he closed the distance between us.

I froze. Well, on the outside. On the *inside,* my mind was a rocket sled, hurtling toward the edge of a steep embankment, with sharpened spikes waiting for me at the bottom.

What on earth am I doing? I love Jack!

"Stop!" With every ounce of strength I had, I pushed him away. "I can't. I have to go." I glanced at my mother. She fidgeted with a stack of magazines on the coffee table, pretending she hadn't just witnessed her engaged daughter all but kissing a virtual stranger.

"Ivie, wait." Liam took a step in my direction.

"No!" I threw my hands up in front of me like a wall. Taking one baby step at a time, I inched my way back toward the door, keeping Liam in my sights the whole way. "You stay right where you are. I can't be around you. You… you're dangerous." As soon as my foot hit the doorframe, I spun around and fled without looking back.

Chapter 5

"J ACK?" I SLAMMED THE FRONT door and skittered into the deserted living room, kicking off my black patent leather pumps as I went. My heart pounded against the walls of my chest like an intruder at the door. Liam had worked his way under my skin like a splinter, and I needed to pry him out. "Are you here?" I flung my purse and keys onto the coffee table and proceeded to peel off my blouse and skirt. They smelled like Liam, and I needed to strip the scent of him from my body—and quick—before I said to hell with it all and went back to where I'd left him. The horrifying reality of what had *almost* happened in the middle of my mother's living room haunted me, but somewhere in the back of my addled brain, I wanted to kick myself for walking away.

Leftover magic coursed through my veins like hot oil through a radiator, popping and sizzling as it made the circuit. The urge to conjure something—*anything*—fought against my need for self-preservation. If Jack walked in and saw me like this...

I didn't even want to imagine what he'd think.

A door slammed, injecting me with a fresh burst of adrenaline.

"Ivie?" Jack called out as he tore frantically through the room. He stopped cold when he saw me, his eyes wild as he sucked in a ragged breath. "Where the hell have you been? I've been worried sick. I tried to call you, but your phone's dead and—" He paced in front of me, gawking at my state of undress and letting his eyes roam from my chest to my toes and back again in slow motion. "What are you doing?"

"Just changing clothes." I went for casual, but my throat threatened to close on me. Yet somehow, I managed to choke out the words. "You know, rough day at the office and all that." I shrugged with a precarious smile perched on my lips then continued to undress, all too aware of his scrutiny. My hands shook as I unhooked the clasps on my peacock-blue lace bra—one of Jack's favorites—before dropping it where I stood, leaving me in nothing but the matching panties. "And I missed you."

Jack's puzzled expression softened, and the smile he reserved just for me lit his face. "I missed you too. So much." He took a tentative step toward me then stopped and let out a heavy breath. The weight of the world seemed to melt from his shoulders. "I'm a jealous idiot."

"Oh, Jack." I flung myself at him, wrapping my arms around his neck and my legs around his waist. I wanted to tell him he had no reason to be jealous, but the truth sat on my tongue like a fever blister, ready to pop. "I'm so sorry." Without giving him a chance to protest or ask questions, I peppered his face with kisses, my all-too-eager hips rocking against him in an attempt to quench the fire still burning inside me, thanks to my recent magical exploits.

Jack groaned, his fingers twitching as he gripped my hips in his large hands. The fragile hold on his control was slipping. I recognized the symptoms all too well. And maybe I encouraged it. Just a little. "What on earth has gotten into you today?"

I froze at the thought of what had *almost* gotten into me then shook my head to dispel it. Liam meant nothing to me. I barely even knew him. No. I wanted Jack. I *loved* Jack. I replayed the words in my head like a chant. *I love Jack, I love Jack, I love Jack.*

"It's been too long, and I *need* you." I exaggerated that last part and captured his face in my hands, locking my green eyes with his dark blue. "Take me. Right here."

My out-of-control hunger finally managed to drag Jack to the dark side, and before I knew it, he'd propelled me backward, flattening my back against the wall. Without a single hesitation, he tore the scrap of lace from my body and replaced it with his hand. "Mmmm. Sweetheart, you're so wet. Someone's been a naughty girl." He didn't say the words, but we both knew what he meant by that. *You've been doing magic again.* But as luck would have it, his erection trumped his outrage, and he nipped my ear with his teeth as his fingers worked me further into a frenzy. "Tell me you want me to take you right here against the wall."

A ripple of pleasure danced down my spine, setting every nerve ending in my body on fire. "Oh, God. I do. I want you. Please, Jack. Take me." I bucked my hips into his hand, driving his fingers deeper.

The pop of a button slipping through its opening, the metallic hiss of a zipper skating down, and finally the whisper of denim gliding over skin were my only warnings before Jack plunged his full length into me with a growl.

"So good," he murmured, dragging the words out before fastening his lips to my neck. He sucked hard enough to leave a mark—laying claim to me as he pulled all the way out only to thrust back in again.

On the verge of exploding all afternoon, my body thrummed at his touch. This was what I'd needed, what I'd been dying for all day. And while I was with Jack, I hadn't entertained a single thought about Liam. Or had I? I licked my lips and tasted sweet mint.

Get out of my head!

I shoved my confusing feelings for my father's apprentice into the dark recesses of my mind and concentrated on Jack's touch: his warm skin wrapping me from top to bottom, his soft lips brushing against mine, and his hard length hitting places only he knew as he moved within me.

"I love you," I breathed, pulling his clean scent into my lungs as he plundered my body over and over.

"Love you too." He moaned as we found our perfect rhythm.

I used to laugh when people said they saw fireworks during sex, but brilliant flashes of light stole my vision. My circuits overloaded, every nerve in my body exposed, waiting for the spark to ignite. Jack cupped my bottom in his hands and shifted his weight, hitting me in a new spot until I saw stars. My legs, still wrapped around him like a pair of hungry boa constrictors, shuddered as my body exploded into a million tiny pinpricks of light.

Jack followed right after, his hips jerking a few times before his fingers dug deeper into my hips, and his whole body stiffened. He burrowed his face into my hair, nuzzling my neck as he caught his breath. "Maybe we should fight more often."

I shuddered at the thought. "I'd rather not. Today was the worst day of my life."

"Speaking of your day, what happened?" He jostled my weight then unwrapped my rubbery legs from around his waist to ease them to the floor, never letting go of me. "You didn't reply to my text messages, didn't answer my calls. I drove by the school, but Helena said you skipped the meeting and left early."

"What are you talking about?" My mouth dropped open, and my heart lurched to a stop before the adrenaline kicked in again, this time for a completely different reason. "I did text you. All day long. And I called and left at least a dozen messages. You never called me back!"

He shook his head then rested it against my collarbone. "I didn't get any messages."

"Well, I didn't get any messages from you either." I couldn't help being angry. How had we managed to miss each other the whole day? It didn't seem possible.

"Chloe called me too. She said she's never gone that long without hearing from you. That's when I knew something was wrong. I called your mom, and she said you were there, but you'd already left. So I came home, hoping you'd be here." He pressed a quick kiss to my open lips. "And here you were. What made you go to your mom's today?"

My pulse picked up when he mentioned going to my mom's. I held my breath and hoped he wouldn't see the shame written all over my face. Finally, I pulled in a breath and forced a smile. "I, uh, just hadn't seen her in a while."

"How about we don't talk about your mom? Or Chloe. Or missed messages." Jack laced his fingers with mine and led me through the living room and the bedroom to the bathroom. He reached his free hand into the shower and twisted on the faucet. "And I definitely don't want to fight anymore."

"Well, that doesn't leave much." I schooled my features into a serious expression. "What do you want to talk about?"

"Talking is highly overrated." He grinned, then without missing a beat, Jack scooped me into his arms and stepped under the flow.

After several rounds of lovemaking, I should have passed out cold. But unlike Jack, I couldn't sleep. My mind kept going back to Smith and Wesson and the insurance money. I couldn't understand how my mother had managed to keep something like that a secret for so long.

As soon as Jack's breathing had slowed and given way to snoring, I crept out of our bed and pulled on one of Jack's T-shirts on my way to the kitchen to call Mom. She picked up on the third ring, and I didn't wait for her to say hello before launching an inquisition. "Why didn't you tell me?"

"Tell you what, dear?" If I'd taken her by surprise, her tone didn't show it. In fact, she was almost too casual.

"Don't play dumb with me, Mom. Why didn't you tell me about the money?" I slid onto the counter and fidgeted with a loose thread on the hem of Jack's shirt.

She sighed. "You were a child. It didn't seem appropriate at the time."

"But half a million dollars?" I had to fight to keep from raising my voice. All those years we'd barely gotten by, and she'd had money all along. "How could I have missed that? Even over the course of twelve years, surely I would have noticed. Your entire wardrobe couldn't have cost more than a few hundred bucks. How did you manage to spend so much?"

"I only spent a little at a time. And I managed to set some aside."

"Mom, your bank accounts are frozen. Having money set aside won't really help you now. What are you going to do?"

She didn't answer me, and I knew what that meant. "Mom, what are you keeping from me?"

I heard her moving around, but she didn't speak for almost a minute. "It's not important."

"Not important?" I shrieked then glanced toward the bedroom as I lowered my voice to a whisper again. "Are you kidding me?"

"There are some things you're better off not knowing." I had to give her credit. She kept her cool as if she'd been preparing for this moment for years.

"Better off—are you serious?" I sputtered out the words before reining in my temper again. "Mom, the FBI has a file on me. Me! And let's not forget I spent most of my life blissfully unaware I'm a witch."

"Sorceress, dear." She had the nerve to sound annoyed.

"Whatever. Sorceress." I wanted to scream at her that, according to Thesaurus.com, they were one and the same. "Listen, you told me my father died in a freak science experiment when in reality, he slept curled up on the floor of my bedroom until I graduated high school. Now I find out my mother burned through half a million dollars and didn't even bother to replace the same death trap she drove when she dropped me off for my first day of kindergarten?" How had I managed to make it to the quarter-century mark without realizing what a skilled liar my mother was?

"Fine." She took a deep breath. "I didn't actually *spend* the money. Of course, a few hundred dollars here and there for essentials, but I withdrew the bulk of it in small increments over time and locked it in the safe in the spell room."

"The spell room?" My father had charmed a room in the basement to appear as a dusty old storage space to anyone who didn't know the secret. "I didn't see a safe in the spell room."

"Well, that's because you didn't know it was there. Next time you're here, you'll see it."

"Does Dad know about the money?"

"Heavens, no. And don't you dare tell him, either. I have no idea what he might do with it. He's changed, Ivie. Don't get me wrong. I'll always love him, but he's not the same man he used to be. He's acting strange. First, there was the odd feline behavior—like eating tuna straight from the can."

I choked back a laugh. "Lots of people eat tuna from the can, Mom. Maybe he just likes fish."

"If there's one thing I know about Angus McKie, it's that he *hates* fish. But there's more to it." The line went quiet for so long I thought I'd lost the call. Then I heard the click of a door closing, and her voice came back in a low whisper. "I've caught him licking himself when he doesn't know I'm watching. I see him lapping at his hand then smoothing it through his hair. And every night, without fail, he sits on the side of the bed and scratches behind his ears. If I didn't know better, I'd say he has fleas."

"I'm sure there's a reasonable explanation."

"He caught a mouse."

"So?"

"With. His. Teeth."

Ew! I choked out a laugh as the image of my father dropping a mouse at my mother's feet flashed before my eyes. I'd seen him in action as a cat, and he was pretty good at catching ex-fiancés-slash-rats.

"But honestly, if it were only that, I could manage. His behavior has only gotten more bizarre since this apprentice of his arrived. The pair of them are always with their heads together. Your father has the notion the two of you would make a perfect match. He seems to have forgotten your engagement to Jack. And I see how Liam looks at you, as if you're a prize to be won. It worries me, especially after what happened today."

My insides twisted when she mentioned Liam. The odd happenings worried me too, but I wasn't about to tell her that. "What will you do?"

"I don't know. For now, I'll act as if nothing's out of the ordinary. But I'm telling you, don't let your guard down, Ivie. Something's going on, and I don't like the smell of it."

It took every bit of my self-control not to say it was *fishy*. "You be careful too, Mom."

"And if you know what's good for you, you won't let Jack get wind of all this. That boy wouldn't know what to do if he found out you were on an FBI watch list."

"Speaking of Jack, I'd better go back to bed before he realizes I'm gone."

"Okay. Goodnight, dear."

"'Night, Mom." I ended the call and tucked my phone back into my purse.

I heard Jack's bare feet shuffling across the floor before he made it all the way into the room. He had one hand in his hair, and the other rested just under the waistband of his gray plaid boxers. "What are you doing in the kitchen?"

"I'm sorry if I woke you. I couldn't sleep. I thought maybe I'd make some warm milk."

"Forget the milk, and come back to bed." A sexy smile lit up his face. "I know just the thing to make you sleep like a baby."

Chapter 6

"**D**ID YOU SEE ROBBY PATTERSON?" Helena sidled up to me on the edge of the playground where I stood, watching over my young charges. "I swear he's trying to knock out the rest of his front teeth before break."

I leaned in to whisper, "He almost knocked out two of Max Young's teeth on the slide a few minutes ago."

"He might single-handedly help the tooth fairy hit her quota for the year." Helena bumped me with her shoulder and giggled. "We need to get in on that action. Tooth fairy gets the teeth, we get a ten percent cut of the cash."

I bumped her back. "I guess it's a good thing his parents are rich."

As per usual on the Friday before spring break, the schoolyard resembled a Wild West outpost. The rambunctious five – and six-year-olds dashed from the swings to the monkey bars with barely contained energy, as if their internal clocks were set to detonate precisely at three p.m.

"Hey, are we still dress shopping Monday?" Helena asked.

"As far as I know. I still haven't heard from Chloe." The growl of an approaching engine drew my attention away from the playground in time to see a shiny red sports car race toward us. It skidded to a stop, sideways across two parking places, and sat idling.

"Who's that?" Helena leaned forward, staring at the car as if trying to see through the tinted windows.

"No clue."

The passenger door opened, and a familiar head of red-streaked hair popped up. The rest of him followed as he stopped to scan the playground, and my stomach reintroduced itself to my toes. His face lit up, and he waved at me like a circus chimp.

Helena tilted her head to the side, shifting her gaze from my face to the car. "Hey, isn't that your dad?"

"You mean I'm not hallucinating?"

She laughed. "Nope. Pretty sure that's him. What's he doing here?"

"I have no idea, but mark my words, it can't be anything good." I glanced over at the kids on the swings. "Can you watch my class for a few minutes? I need to see what he wants."

"Sure, go ahead." She gave my shoulders a shove then gasped. "Oh, hey. Who's he?"

I spun around to see Liam climb out of the car. My traitorous hormones perked at the sight of him. "That's my father's, uh—teaching assistant."

"He's—wow." Helena fanned herself. "I wouldn't mind him teaching *me* a thing or two."

"Stay away from him," I snapped. "I mean, he-he's trouble." An uninvited ripple of jealousy tore through me, and I tamped it down. Why on earth would I be jealous of Helena? Over Liam? I pressed my palm to my forehead. The flu. It had to be the flu. But delirious or not, I needed to deal with my father. "I—uh—I'm just going to go talk to my dad for a minute."

"Stay strong. Don't cave." She giggled.

"Yeah. Famous last words." I barked out a laugh. She had no idea.

As I crossed the distance between Helena and my father, Liam jogged over to me.

"Ivie." He beamed. "I hoped I'd get to see you again."

Stupid sexy sorcerer, messing with my insides. But I had no intention of giving in to his charms. "Well, I *do* work here."

He gave a nod but said nothing.

"Ah, my bonnie lass, I'm so glad we found you." My dad bounded in my direction and scooped me into an awkward hug.

I wriggled free and took a few steps back, bumping into Liam's warmth. "Daddy." I tried to keep my voice chilly, despite the many conflicting emotions stirring within me. I wanted to rip into him for my FBI file and the problems he'd created with Jack. But mostly, I wanted to scream at him for bringing Liam into my life because, try as I might, I couldn't imagine life without him anymore. I tried to ignore Liam's crooked grin and focused on my father's guilty face. "Why are you here?"

"You know I wouldn't bother you at work if it wasn't an emergency."

I crossed my arms and raised an eyebrow.

"Okay, so maybe I would—but not today. Today, it's an emergency."

"I'm waiting." I locked my eyes on his.

Dad snuck a glance at Liam. "It's about those gentlemen who visited your mum the other day."

"You mean Smith and Wesson?" I uncrossed my arms and took a step closer.

Liam turned up the volume on his grin, his whole face lighting up. "Smith and Wesson?"

"I don't remember their names." I glared at Liam, steeling myself against his charms before giving my father my full attention. "But you're talking about the two FBI guys, right?"

"Yes. They showed up at the house again today, a little confused about their last visit but no less determined to find your mother guilty of insurance fraud. And they'll use every underhanded method in the book to do it, including dragging you into the whole sordid mess."

My mouth dropped open, and I couldn't decide where to look: at my father's grim expression or Liam's hopeful one. "B-but I didn't know you were still alive. All those years, I thought you'd *died!*"

Dad nodded. "Yes, of course you did. And your mother—God bless her—she knew, of course, but she didn't think there was any hope of bringing me back. I don't think she filed the claim on the life insurance until I'd completely disappeared."

I hadn't known it then, but the trusty Irish wolfhound that slept at the foot of my childhood bed until I drifted off to sleep had actually been my father. Then one day, I came home from school to discover my dog had vanished. Run off. But of course, he hadn't gone far. Dad had simply managed to transform into another animal form and had found his way into my life again as the cat I'd named Karma.

"Dad, what are we going to do?"

"It's going to be all right, Ivie." Liam stepped up, grasping my arms in his strong hands—strong hands I had no trouble imagining sliding across my bare skin.

I wrenched my arms out of his grip and backed up. "How? How will it be all right?"

"I have a plan!" My father thrust his index finger in the air to strike a pose.

I'd heard that one before.

"We need to attempt a spell. Unfortunately, it won't last forever, but it'll buy us some time while we figure something else out."

"Forget it!" I spun on my heels, ready to march right back to where Helena stood, watching us from the corner of her eye.

"Ivie, wait!" My father caught my elbow, turning me around to face him again.

"No, Dad. I'm not sticking around for this. I promised Jack no more magic." I yanked my arm back, this time getting a few steps away before turning to him. "You'll have to work your spell without me."

"You don't understand!" My father shouted. "We need you. This will only work if we channel your power. If we had a lock of hair or something personal from one of the agents, maybe—but the only thing we have is your memories of them from the other day." He fisted his hair, pacing in front of the red car, mumbling incoherently.

I heaved out a sigh. "What about Liam? Or Mom? They were both—"

"No! It has to be you." Dad's eye twitched. "You're the one they're after."

"Dad, I'm sorry. I can't risk ruining my relationship with Jack. I just can't." I turned my back on him again and darted toward Helena and the playground.

"Your dad sounds pretty upset." Helena furrowed her eyebrows, stealing glances at my father and Liam, still loitering in the parking lot.

I tried to flash an easy smile, but my stomach was wound tighter than pantyhose in a dryer. "Understatement."

"Ivie Marie McKie. You get back over here this instant!" My father's voice echoed through the clear air. "I did not raise you to turn your back on your parents."

The entirety of the playground stopped to stare at my father's outburst.

"Oh, my God, what does he think he's doing?" I gaped at my dad stomping around the parking lot, talking to himself. "I'd better go calm him down. I'm sorry. Watch my class again?"

"Better hurry. We only have"—Helena turned her wrist to check the time—"ten minutes left in recess."

"Thanks. I owe you." I gave her a quick hug before dashing back to the red car.

Dad continued his frantic pacing with Liam keeping up with him, stride for stride. Based on the bits and pieces I heard of their conversation, Liam's attempts at calming Dad down had failed.

"Damn it, Dad. You're going to get me fired!" I whisper-yelled as I got closer.

Dad froze at the sound of my voice. "Ivie! Thank goodness." He rushed over to pull me into a hug. "I knew you wouldn't disappoint your family."

I wiggled until I could put my hands on his chest then pushed free. "I'm doing this for Mom."

He nodded. "Of course." His eyes lit up, and he grabbed my hand as if I were a small child. "Come 'ere. I wanna show you something."

I reluctantly allowed him to lead me to the back of the car and waited while Liam released the trunk latch.

Sandwiched between several thick coils of rope and a gray wool blanket sat a small, rusted cauldron filled with crystals, an assortment of incense and candles, and a few colorful ribbons.

"You brought me here to see Liam's magical toolbox?"

"No." My father scoffed. "I brought you here for *this*." He reached into the trunk and pulled back the blanket to reveal a tattered old book. "My first spellbook." Dad lifted the book from its hiding place and cradled it as if it were an infant.

I reached out to glide a finger over the brittle binding and feared the cracked leather would crumble at my touch. "This doesn't look like the book I used to change you back."

"Oh, no. It's not. This is my very *first* spellbook. From my schoolboy days."

I scoffed. "Are you trying to tell me you went to Hogwarts?"

Liam gazed at me with a crooked grin. "Sorcerers don't go to Hogwarts, Ivie. That's wizards."

I held back an unladylike squeal. "Hogwarts is real!" The ten-year-old me had been desperate to go to Hogwarts.

Both Liam and my father doubled over in laughter.

"Not real then?" Right. *Nice going, Ivie.* I narrowed my eyes at Liam as he stood and pulled himself together. *Could that have been any more embarrassing?*

"Don't feel bad." He brushed a piece of hair from my eyes. "I believed in Hogwarts as a boy—convinced I'd go there one day—only to have my hopes dashed as a young teenager."

I crossed my arms. "Well, I'm a grown woman. I shouldn't have fallen for an obvious joke."

"Ivie, it's almost time to go in." Helena's voice gave me something else to focus on.

"Be right there." I waved at her then turned to my father. "I appreciate you showing me the book. Maybe I'll take a closer look one day soon, but recess is just about over."

"Wait." Dad grabbed my arm. "Give us just five minutes more. We need to work this spell immediately. We've wasted enough time as it is."

I glanced at the playground. The kids darted around, burning off the rest of their nervous energy as they lined up to go in. "You've got two." I gave them the sternest look I could muster and held a hand out to each of them.

Before I had time to take a breath, the magic crashed over me like an angry wave in the middle of a hurricane. From the fingers laced with Liam's to the hand clasping my father's, the current flowed through me as if I'd touched a live wire. The words of a spell echoed around me in stereo as they chanted, over and over, in a language I recognized but didn't speak. *Gaelic.*

My skin tingled, hotter and sharper, until the sensations became almost painful. Wind rushed around me, swirling my hair around my face. A tornado of power surrounded us, reaching out farther from my body with each pass. "Dad?" I heard the alarm in my own voice. My tongue burned with peppery sweetness.

He didn't answer, but Liam squeezed my hand. His unique touch comforted me in the midst of a tsunami.

Then the air stilled—the rush of electricity drained out of me, taking my breath for an instant—just before the windows in the shiny red sports car exploded and with them, every window in every car around us.

I screamed, folding in on myself as Liam swept me into his arms to cover my body with his—protecting me from flying glass. *Again.* The sudden urge to rub my backside against him like a cat in heat overwhelmed me. And yet— *don't ask me how*—I managed to resist.

A hint of ozone tinged the air, pricking my nose. "What the hell was that, Dad? How is it things blow up every time you do magic?" I shook glass from my hair as I stood to scan the parking lot. Not a single car had escaped the destruction, not even my own.

Dad shrugged, his ears tinged red. "Maybe a bit too much of the white sage." He pinched the air in front of him.

Liam nodded.

"Too much white sage? *Too much white sage!*" My feet crunched on broken glass as I paced over the concrete. "You destroyed an entire parking lot! And you—" I shook a finger at Liam. "Why do you keep helping him? Mom was right. I should have listened to Jack. How do I get myself into these things?" The sound of children screaming brought me back to my senses. "I need to get back to my class."

I sprinted across the distance but came to a screeching halt right in front of Dr. Clark. His eyebrows formed a sharp V, and his nose twitched, making his penciled-on mustache dance above his thin lips. "Miss McKie. Why am I not surprised to see you in the thick of all this chaos? You do have a penchant for destruction of private property, don't you?"

My mouth fell open as I struggled for words. Why wouldn't he be surprised? Sure, I'd been late a time or two. And okay, so I had a history of calling in sick when

I wasn't. But destruction of private property? *What?* "Dr. Clark, I-I don't know what to say. My father..." I turned to where my father and Liam had been, but they were gone. Nothing was left of the red sports car but a trail of broken glass. *Liam and his stupid disappearing act. How does he do that?*

For the second time in a week, I found myself sitting in the back of a police car. The smell of vomit and body odor permeated every square inch and had probably soaked into my Rag and Bone jeans, and my Betsy Johnson shoes were undoubtedly ruined, thanks to the assorted shards of glass embedded in the bottoms and whatever sticky substance had glued them to the floorboards. And while I sat, hands cuffed behind my back—yet again—my father and Liam had vanished into thin air.

"I saw her talking to two men in the parking lot." Helena's voice managed to carry over the sounds of the police radio and the sirens in the distance. "She yelled at them to leave school grounds, and when she turned to come back to the playground, everything exploded. Ivie couldn't have had anything to do with it." Once she'd finished telling her side of things, I caught Helena's eye through the bulletproof glass, and she winked.

I bit back a smile. It wouldn't do, in my current predicament, for me to look so pleased. But I owed her a few drinks and probably a pair of Manolos.

The door wrenched open, and a middle-aged policeman with what looked like a bun in the oven—but most likely a few dozen donuts—reached in to pull me to my feet. "Well, teacher lady, looks like you're free to go." The jangle of steel as he uncuffed my wrists was music to my ringing ears. "If I were you, I'd steer clear of any more explosions for a while. Got it?" He flashed me a smile.

I returned it with one of my own. "Got it."

Dr. Clark cleared his throat. "Am I to understand it was your *father* who blew up the parking lot? Would that be the same father who mysteriously returned from the dead after blowing up his science lab, only to blow up another one after his resurrection?"

That would be the one. "He—it's—*technically* yes. But he didn't actually blow up the parking lot. I'm sure there's a perfectly reasonable explanation." I exhaled a sharp breath.

"A reasonable explanation?" He swished his mustache from side to side. "The men from the FBI said you might say that. *Tsk, tsk*, Miss McKie. Blaming your circumstances on chance?"

"The FBI?" My heart thundered in my ears. For the first time in ages, I wished my father were here. He needed to fix his own mess for a change.

"Yes, the gentlemen were kind enough to visit my office the other day. I, of course, gave you the benefit of the doubt. What sort of person would I be if I hadn't? But as they predicted, your true nature has shown itself."

"As they predicted? My true nature? But I didn't even get arrested this time. I didn't *do* anything." I was dumbfounded. Smith and Wesson had set me up. Sort of. They couldn't have pulled it off without my father's unwitting *help.* "Dr. Clark, there really has been a terrible misunderstanding. You can ask Helena—"

His sweaty palm shot up in front of my face. "Ms. Ferrell said she saw you speaking with your *father* on school grounds—a violation in and of itself—right before the explosion. I have no doubt he played a large part in the destruction. As I understand it, he has a history of these things. However, I cannot discount your hand in it. I'm afraid I'll have to let you go."

"Let me go?"

He nodded, his twitchy little nose wrinkling.

"If you would collect your things and leave, I'll see to it your final check is sent to you."

"You're firing me?" A spark of fury bubbled up in me, and the fleeting image of Alistair Clark in weasel form danced through my mind. But before the idea raged out of control, I tamped it down. I already had enough problems to deal with without transforming another jerk into a woodland creature.

"Yes. Should I spell it out for you?" He leaned in until I smelled the gorgonzola on his breath. "You're F-I-R-E-D."

"Fired." I mouthed the word, willing it to sink in.

"And really, Miss McKie. Look at you. You don't fit in here." His face twisted into one of distaste as he stared at my hair. "How I failed to notice that obnoxious shade of red is a mystery." He turned his face to the clear blue sky before locking his beady eyes on mine. "It must be the natural light. But no matter. I think you'd be better suited in the public school system, where they embrace *individuality* in their teachers. But I'm afraid we're a bit more—"

Snobby? Stuck up? Arrogant? Pretentious?

Dr. Clark tapped a long finger against his chin, and his face lit up with a smile. "Selective."

All of the above.

Chapter 7

FTER WALKING MORE THAN THREE miles from the bus stop—including a slight detour to the local beauty supply store—I lugged my bedraggled carcass up the steps and through the front door, kicking off my shoes before I'd made it across the threshold.

Home. I thought I'd never make it. My poor Betseys—definitely not suited for long walks—were doomed to forced retirement. But with a little luck, I'd have my hair back to normal before Jack realized it'd turned red. *Again.*

I heard his voice before I saw him step around the corner. "Ivie, is that—?"

His startled expression froze me in place, and I shrank into myself. He'd caught me red-handed, so to speak.

He marched toward me, his hands heading straight to my hair, his fingers weaving into the tangled strands. "What the hell happened?" He took his time roaming my face with his eyes as his hands skimmed over my shoulders and down my arms. "Are you hurt? You look like you walked for miles to get here."

Three point four miles, to be exact. But who's counting? I shook my head but said nothing. I wasn't sure what to say that wouldn't leave me with a guiltier conscience than I already had.

"Helena called. She was worried about you. She said your principal fired you, but your car's still in the school parking lot. What happened?"

I swallowed my fear and lifted my head high. No more hiding behind hair dye and misdirection. "My dad showed up during recess."

Jack frowned as he slipped a hand into my hair again, studying the color in the light. "I figured he had something to do with this."

"He—he said he needed my help." I flinched at the steel in his gaze. "That *Mom* needed my help. They're investigating her for insurance fraud. And I can't let them arrest her, Jack. I just can't." I blinked, and the tears brimming in my eyes spilled over.

Jack dropped his hand and stalked away from me. "How many times is he going to pull you into one of his crazy schemes? What happens when a spell goes so wrong it can't be fixed?"

"I know." I collapsed into the supple leather of the sofa. "God, I know. You were right."

His head snapped up, his expression wavering between cautious optimism and outright shock.

"Living as an animal for the past twelve years has changed him. He's not stable. I see that now. I just wish—" I stopped myself from telling him about the spell book and the utter bliss rushing through me when I did magic, especially when I did magic with Liam. *That* would not go over well. At. All. "I feel like I owe him something. He's my father."

"You don't owe him anything, Ivie. If anything, he owes you for putting you through hell all those years."

"It was supposed to be an innocent little shield spell." I let out a sigh. Even I didn't believe what I'd said.

"There's no such thing as an 'innocent little spell.'" Jack made air quotes then flopped into the sofa beside me. "So why'd you get fired?"

I pulled my bottom lip between my teeth and debated exactly how much of the truth I should tell him. "The, um, spell backfired. The energy must have spiked or something.

I still don't understand the mechanics involved, but whatever happened caused the car windows to blow out."

Jack tilted his head to the side. "W-what car windows?"

"All of them?" I winced and waited for him to respond, but he just sat there, eyes wide and mouth hanging open. "Yeah. Exactly. Every car in the parking lot."

Jack made a choking sound in the back of his throat, and if he hadn't motioned me to go on, I would have stopped there.

"The, uh, same thing happened at the science lab. A-all the glass blew up, and shards went everywhere." My animated gestures seemed to make him uncomfortable, so I tucked my hands under my legs before continuing. "Well, it blew in at the lab, but in the parking lot, it was as if we'd attracted every car in a hundred-yard radius—like a giant glass magnet or something."

"You could have been killed." He dragged me into a crushing hug.

I burrowed my head into the crook of his neck. "Um, Liam—h-he saved me—again."

Jack jerked back, all his fears for my safety swirling down the proverbial drain. "Liam? He was there? Why didn't you say that right away?"

"I-I guess I forgot?"

"You forgot?"

I nodded.

"About the six-foot-three-inch male model strutting around the parking lot like a damned prized rooster?"

I choked back a giggle. Liam didn't strut. Well, not much.

"It's not funny."

"I know. I'm sorry."

"I don't like it. I don't like him. And I sure as hell don't like the idea of my fiancée spending time with a man who has an obvious crush on her. He wants you, Ivie. He's made no secret of that. And when you do magic..." Jack huffed out a breath then pushed a hand through his hair as a horrified expression took over his features. He raked his eyes over me as if he were searching for something in my disheveled appearance. "Geezus. You didn't...?"

"Didn't what?" I studied Jack's face until his meaning sank in. "What! Of course not. How could you even—I wouldn't do that. Jack, I love you." Even as I protested, my skin tingled at the thought of it.

He wrapped his arms around me. "I know. I know. I'm sorry. He just makes me crazy. And it's not just the sexual energy. After what we went through last time, I worry about you doing magic. I'm afraid you'll end up like your dad. Who's going to change you back if you transform into a cat?"

"I won't turn into a cat." I melted into his chest. I wanted to tell him Liam meant nothing to me, but I couldn't. "Everything'll be okay. You'll see."

"I can't bear to think of anything happening to you. Please promise—"

"You don't even have to say it. I know. My father has problems, but I can't help him with his issues anymore. I'm done. He's managed to *almost* get me arrested enough times in my life. I'm finished."

"Do you mean it?"

"I do. I promise." I only hoped I wouldn't have to go back on another promise.

Bright and early Monday morning, I jumped at the honking of a horn outside. "That's my ride!" I smoothed my hands over my gray pencil skirt and matching silk blouse then snatched my purse and keys from the coffee table. Before I reached the door, Jack caught me, wrapping his arms around me from behind.

He spun me around, dipping me toward the floor as he pressed his lips to the pulse point in my neck. "Have fun.

But don't stress over finding the perfect dress." He yanked me upright again and cupped my face in his hands to lock his eyes with mine. "Just remember, I'd marry you in a towel if it came to that."

A rush of emotion hit me, and I blinked back the tears. After a weekend spent in bed with Jack, I looked forward to shopping for wedding gowns with Chloe, Mom, and Helena, but I almost dreaded leaving the sanctuary of our home. "I love you, Jack."

"I love you, too, sweetheart." His lips captured mine in a toe-curling kiss as the horn blew for a second time. Jack gave me a few more light pecks before releasing me. "Now go before Chloe wakes up the entire neighborhood."

I grabbed my things and bounded out the door and down the front steps. Cyndi Lauper's feminist anthem blared from the bright-blue rented convertible idling at the curb. I laughed at Chloe dancing in the driver's seat, singing along with the rousing lyrics.

"Hey, shopaholic!" I shouted as I rounded the vehicle and hopped into the passenger seat with a giggle.

"Ivie!" Chloe squealed, pulling me into a hug. "Are you ready to shop?"

Ready or not, a-shopping we would go. "Of course I am. Lay on, Macduff."

"You're so weird." Chloe gunned the engine as she left the neighborhood. "Your mom and Helena are meeting us at Colette's."

I sucked in a huge gulp of air and choked on my own saliva. "Colette's? In Buckhead?" My pulse jumped. "I can't afford a garter from there, let alone a dress."

Chloe glanced at me then back to the road as she zigzagged through the morning traffic. "Oh, please. You're marrying a *Blake*. That family is made of money. And Jack *is* the baby. You know his mother would rather give up her weekly manicures than see her son get married in anything less than style."

My heart nearly stopped at the mention of Jack's mother. I'd only met her once, and the thought of her accompanying us sent ice through my veins. Thank heavens she was still in Europe for the *season*. "Well, *my* family isn't made of money. And I certainly can't afford anything from Colette's, especially now." My stomach twisted into a knot as I did a quick mental calculation of everything in my combined bank accounts. Even with one last paycheck coming in, the money would disappear before I knew it. A fleeting thought of the money my mom had stashed in the spell room came and went. "Can't we just go to the Bridal Outlet?"

Chloe gasped, swerving into oncoming traffic then jerking the car back into our lane. "Bite. Your. Tongue." She shot me a death glare. "I refuse to allow my best friend to buy an off-the-rack gown. Besides, you owe me."

I wracked my brain to remember a lost bet or promise made but came up empty. "How do I owe you?"

She looked at me and rolled her eyes. "You know how badly I wanted my Big Fat Chic Wedding." A horn blast brought her to her senses, and she turned back to the road. "But instead, I got married by a big fat freak Elvis in a chapel off the strip."

And oh, what a wedding it was! I wasn't there, but I'd watched the video on YouTube. Jon even had some Hollywood mega movie star as his best man. "So? You eloped. How is that my fault?"

"Fault, schmalt. You're my BFF. My dreams are your dreams. And if I couldn't live the fantasy myself, I should at least get to live it vicariously through you."

Despite her faulty logic, I sort of understood her point. "Fine. Colette's it is. But I'm telling you right now, I can't afford the sales tax on a dress from there."

Chloe's face lit up in a wide grin. "Let me worry about the dress. You just worry about looking amazing in it."

When Chloe had told me to "dress the part," she wasn't kidding. She hopped out of the rented Mustang and smoothed the wrinkles in her pleated Gucci dress. She stuck her chin in the air and flipped her blond hair over her shoulder like a vanilla cape over the dark-orange silk. "Come on, Sabrina. It's show time."

I followed her through the glass front doors as if part of a royal procession. All she was missing was the tiara. No one would dare argue Chloe's princess status when she put her mind to it. She sidled up to the reception desk and put on her serious shopping face. "We have a nine o'clock appointment with Françoise."

The bored stick figure behind the dainty French table flipped through a red leather ledger. "*Oui.*" Her French accent was about as authentic as my Scottish one. "Françoise is in zee *Chocolat Salon* today."

The Chocolate Salon? I inched forward and dared speak to her haughtiness. "How many *salons* are there?"

Stick Figure sighed, fanning out her fingers to inspect her harlot-red nail polish before holding up three fingers. "Zere are *trois*: zee *Chocolat Salon,* zee *Aubergine Salon,* and zee *Rouge Salon. You* are in zee *Chocolat Salon.*" She pointed to a mahogany door with swirly brown letters spelling it out for me.

"Come on, Ivie." Chloe hooked her arm with mine and giggled. "Let's head to zee *Chocolat salon.*"

As Chloe reached for the handle, the door swung open, and a stunning older woman greeted us from the other side. She wore a body-hugging black sheath and had a sleek black bob with matching streaks of platinum blond framing her narrow face. She was just one spotted-fur coat away from being Cruella DeVille.

"Ah, *bonjour,* ladies! Come in." She leaned in and kissed the air to each side of my cheek as I held my breath to keep from choking on her cloying perfume. "I am Françoise, your stylist." Her accent, at least, sounded authentic.

"*Bonjour*, Françoise." Chloe gave her air kisses while I soaked up the scenery like a tourist.

I'd driven past Colette Bridal Couture more times than I could count, but I'd never stepped foot inside the door. As I twirled around, taking in the lavish surroundings, I had to swallow back the urge to squeal like a kid in Chuck E. Cheese. From the shimmering lights dancing across the shiny black ceiling to the gleaming mahogany floors, the place oozed glamour. Glossy chocolate walls and sparkling crystal chandeliers added to the opulence. Two matching button-tufted settees upholstered in brown velvet floated like islands in the center of the room.

But *nothing* could compete with the rows of satin and lace. Rich brown velvet curtains framed the dresses, and a glass display case housed an array of glittering headpieces like diamonds in a jewelry store. The polished finish on the floor reflected everything like a mirror. The grandeur locked me in a stunned silence.

A chorus of shrieks interrupted the quiet as my mother and Helena bounded into the salon like a pair of giddy schoolgirls.

"This place is amazing." Helena spun around. "I feel like I'm inside a treasure chest."

Mom eyed the gowns from a distance. "It is lovely, but it looks a bit pricey."

Finally, someone agreed with me. Even without checking the tags, I knew I could buy a car for what one of those dresses would cost.

"Oh, please." Chloe waved a dismissive hand. "A girl only gets married for the first time once."

"That's horrible!" Helena swatted Chloe's arm then accepted a bubbling champagne flute from François. "Oh, mimosas!"

"Thank you." Mom took her sparkling drink then plopped down on one of the settees. "Well, I suppose it's a good thing I've set some money aside."

I coughed and sputtered at my mother's comment. Agent Smith's face flitted into my thoughts. If only he could hear my mom offering up the insurance money for a couture wedding gown. "Um, no thanks, Mom. I'd rather not spend *that* money."

"But a few thousand dollars won't—"

I shot her a stern look. I had enough to worry about without taking a dime of that money. Françoise held out a crystal glass for me, her glossy hair swinging above her shoulders like a curtain as she moved. "No thanks." I waved her off. Any way you looked at it, champagne for breakfast was a bad idea.

"Oh, no you don't." Chloe snatched up the glass and shoved it into my hand without spilling a drop. "We're celebrating, and I refuse to let you be a party pooper."

"But—"

"No buts." She flashed her perfectly white teeth in a glittering smile. "Trust me, after an hour of trying on dresses, you'll be glad I made you drink."

"Good point." I gave a little salute then tossed back the contents of the glass in a single gulp, much to the delight of my party. They clapped and cheered as if we were at the bachelorette party, not the dress shop.

Off to the side, Françoise scowled at our *uncivilized* display before stepping forward, one penciled-on brow arched in a comic expression. "Mrs. Blake, would you like to begin? Or shall I give your group time to settle down before bringing out your selections?"

I flinched at the name and looked over my shoulder for Jack's mother before remembering Chloe was actually the Mrs. Blake in question.

Chloe flashed her far more impressive bitch brow in response. "No, I think we're ready." She turned to me with a smile. "Right, Sabrina?"

I snagged a second champagne flute from the tray and brought it to my lips. "As I'll ever be." I poured it down my throat with a shudder.

"Excellent." Chloe grabbed the empty glass from my hand and shoved me forward, forcing me to follow Cruella through an arched doorway into the bowels of the glitzy dress shop.

Chapter 8

CHLOE WAS RIGHT. AFTER AN hour of trying on dresses, I'd lost track of how many mimosas I'd downed. My tongue felt like a rolled-up piece of deli ham in my mouth, but I couldn't imagine going through the process without the benefit of alcohol, especially the horror of having a total stranger dress and undress me—all but giving me a breast exam as she shoved me into the dresses Chloe'd picked out. My nipples had been practically rubbed raw from all the action they were getting.

My faux-Parisian stylist, Françoise—or Cruella—or *Fifi*, as my numb brain had renamed her, strapped me into yet another whipped-cream confection and led me into the main salon—or "Hall of Mirrors" as I'd decided to call it—like a Christian to the Coliseum.

"Oh, I like this one!" Helena held up her glass, repeating the mantra she'd started around dress number three with the enthusiasm of a drunk woman at a male strip show. I half expected her to start shouting, "Pull out your penis!"

"Oh, I don't know. Don't you think it's a bit too...?" My mother joined in with her own favorite phrase. She wouldn't finish the sentence until Chloe had chimed in with her opinion.

As for Chloe, she stood silently tapping a French-tipped fingernail against her chin as she studied the dress from every angle. "No. I don't think that's quite right for you. I don't mind the neckline, but with all the ruffles, we can't even see your impressive cleavage. And while I do like the frothy skirt, I think it might be too fluffy. It makes you look like a Barbie cake."

Helena nodded. "Chloe's right. Definitely a cake. Hey, do we have cake? We should order cake."

"Hmm." Mom tossed back another drink. "It does remind me a little of a dessert."

Wonderful. Another dress that made me look like food. With my luck and the way things were going with the magic lately, I'd end up looking like a cherry-topped sundae at the top of my own wedding cake.

Fifi nodded her agreement then turned to Chloe. "Shall we try again?" They seemed to forget I had a functional grasp of the English language, treating me like nothing more than a dressmaker's dummy.

"Yes. But this time, less coconut meringue, more Cinderella." Chloe barked orders from her perch on the settee. I half expected her to shout, "Off with her head!" but that might have been the champagne talking.

Fifi's face lit up. "Oh, I know just the gown."

With my shoulders slumped and my spirit broken, I waddled back to the dressing room and held my arms up for Fifi to remove the offensive dress and replace it with something more fitting for a Disney princess.

Once she had me in my knickers, she hauled an ornate confection from the nearby rack. Chloe would be pleased with the plunging neckline. In fact, everyone within a hundred-yard radius would be delighted with the amount of recently acquired cleavage I would be flashing—but the skirt? I doubted I could even walk on my own while wearing that monstrosity. I'd need a crane to carry me up the aisle.

"Wait!" A flash of white silk caught my eye, and I lit up like a kid in a toy store. "What are these?" I scooted past her to examine a rack of gowns unlike anything I'd seen so far. The instant my fingers brushed the buttery fabric—like heavy cream spun into silk—I knew I had to have one.

"Oh, you wouldn't be interested in *those, mademoiselle.*" Fifi's attention shifted from the weighty satin in her arms to me to the hidden collection. "Mrs. Blake was very specific about—"

"Oh, can I try on this one? No, this one." I couldn't decide on just one. I wanted to try them all. I couldn't tear my eyes away from the dresses, each one more beautiful than the last. I continued to fondle my way through the rack then stopped when I came across the holy grail of wedding gowns. I'd never seen anything more perfect. My lips tugged into a full-blown smile. "You've been holding out on me, Fifi."

"Fifi?" She scoffed then snatched the hanger from my hands. "I don't think this—"

I tugged on her sleeve and pouted like a little girl. "Please?"

My fake French stylist sighed then, with a nod, swapped the heavy monstrosity with the delicate dress. "If you insist."

I gave a squeal of delight and raised my arms for her to lift the luxurious fabric over my head. She twisted and tugged the ruched silk bodice until it wrapped around me, hugging me from my ample bust to my shapely hips. The flowing tulle skirt flared out from a row of clustered pearls at the dropped waist to puddle around my feet.

My heartbeat picked up as I stared at my reflection. "It's beautiful," I whispered and took a quick steadying breath before letting her drag me back to the Hall of Mirrors.

"I said Cinderella, not the Little Mermaid." Chloe arched a brow in a fierce expression and flung her hair over her shoulder.

Helena raised her glass with a giggle. "I like this one!" Then she gulped down the last few swallows.

"Thank you, Helena." I pulled her into a hug. "I like it too."

Mom tilted her head to one side. "It does seem a bit *plain* compared with the others."

"Plain?" Fifi blurted. "This is the finest silk taffeta money can buy!"

"It's nice, but I had something more *fabulous* in mind." Chloe sighed. "It's just not regal enough. You *are* marrying a Blake. Go back, and try on the—"

"But I like this dress." I grabbed hold of Fifi's arm to keep from tipping over in my stilettos. "I've tried on every froufrou dress you dragged out for me, and you know I would have been just as happy shopping at Goodwill."

Fifi gasped and pressed her perfectly manicured hand to her chest. "*Sacrebleu!*"

I blew a lock of hair out of my face and grumbled at the stylist. Her accent grated on my nerves. "Oh, give it a rest."

"Ivie Marie McKie, you take that back!" Chloe shrieked and stomped her foot. "I refuse to allow you to get married in a Goodwill wedding gown. You're going to wear the dress I've dreamed about since I was six!" The instant the words tumbled out of her mouth, her hands flew up to cover it, and she froze.

The rest of my group gaped at her outburst.

I threw my head back with a burst of laughter then dropped to the floor in a heap, the tulle skirt pooling around me.

"You can't—" Fifi whipped around to glare at Chloe. "She can't sit on the *floor!* That's a Colette original!" she huffed out, her fake accent faltering slightly.

Chloe took one look at Fifi's face and let loose with a laugh of her own before turning back to me. "I'm sorry. I keep forgetting this is your wedding, not mine." She reached down to wrench me from the gleaming mahogany. Despite Fifi's objection, I suspected we could eat off the shiny surface.

"I really like this dress." Once on my feet, I twirled in front of the closest mirror. "It's pretty, and it doesn't make me crave fattening desserts."

Chloe rolled her eyes. "Fine. You can get this dress."

I cocked an eyebrow and scoffed. "Thank you for giving me permission to spend the entirety of my life savings."

"How much is it?" Helena asked, shattering my brief fantasy.

"Um, I'm afraid to look." I fidgeted. Would I even be able to afford a "Colette original"?

"I'll do it." Chloe took a deep breath, grabbed my shoulders, and spun me around, searching the back for the price tag. I knew she'd found it when she gasped. "Holy shit!"

Fifi smirked at me, her stick arms folded over her flat chest. "I *did* say you wouldn't want one of *those* dresses."

"Wait. What do you mean by *those* dresses?" I narrowed my eyes at her pinched expression.

Her pointy chin jutted into the air. "Colette originals are the most sought-after wedding gowns in all the world."

"In all of Atlanta, maybe," I said under my breath then turned around in time to see Chloe pull her hands away from her face and tip her lips into a phony smile. "How much is it?"

"It's a *bit* over budget." She held her thumb and finger so close they were almost touching.

I took a gulp of air. "Coming from you, that scares me."

She let out a nervous laugh and shrugged. "It's just, well, maybe if we had them make it in rayon instead of silk?"

Fifi shook her head, and I wanted to slap the smug smile from where it perched on her cherry lips.

I flitted my eyes from Chloe to Mom and then Helena. She was in the process of raising another mimosa to her lips, and I snatched it away, downing it in one gulp. I wiped my lips with the back of my hand and screwed up my courage. "Okay, give it to me straight. How much are we talking?"

"Uh…" Chloe winced, shrinking back from me like a deflating balloon. Her voice came out in a barely discernible whisper. "Um… *fortnyhousan?*"

I stuck a finger in my ear and wiggled it around. I couldn't have heard her correctly. "Come again?"

She cleared her throat, annunciating clearly this time. "Forty-nine thousand."

"Forty-nine *thousand?*" My voice came out in a shrill squeak. "Oh, my God, Chloe. I can't afford that!" I reached for another drink on the tray and chugged it without taking a breath. My head spun, and I wasn't sure if it was from the shock or the champagne. I took a few wobbly steps in an attempt to pace. "Even if I *had* a job, I wouldn't be able to afford almost fifty thousand dollars for a wedding dress."

"I didn't even know they carried dresses that expensive. The Cinderella dress was just over three thousand—" Chloe glared at Fifi. "Would you mind giving us a few minutes?" Fifi stalked off with an impressive huff, and Chloe giggled. Then she grabbed my arm and pulled me to the side. "You love this dress, right?"

I nodded. Heaven help me, but I did. It was perfect. My imagination had already built an entire ceremony around that one article of clothing.

"Okay, good. Wedding dress problem solved."

Problem solved? I opened my mouth to object, but she put up a hand to stop me.

"You just need to—" She glanced over her shoulder at Helena, who was staring at her reflection in the floor, then back to me to whisper. "Wiggle that nose of yours, and make a dress just like this one."

"What!" I snapped my mouth shut before I said something I would regret. Her suggestion of magic as an option infuriated me at the same time as it intrigued me. A flicker of delicious power licked at my fingertips, followed by a cold chill down my spine. If Jack knew I'd even entertained such a ridiculous thought, he'd blow a gasket. I could almost *see* the vein in his forehead throbbing.

"Come on." Chloe nudged me with her shoulder.

"Uh." I snapped my mouth shut as quickly as I'd opened it. Maybe she was right. What harm could a tiny little spell cause? It's not as if I'd be messing with anyone's life. *Hmmm.*

"It's just a little wiggle." Chloe rested her finger on the tip of her nose and shifted it to one side.

A bubble of nervous laughter worked its way up my throat. "First of all, my nose does *not* wiggle. It takes a whole lot more effort than that to conjure something. Secondly, do you have any idea what you're suggesting?"

Chloe's lips curled up at the corners like the Grinch in the Whoville town square. "You're actually thinking about it, aren't you? Come on, Ivie. If the cosmos didn't want you to work magic, you wouldn't be a witch."

My mind raced with the possibilities. Visions of silk and tulle flashed through my thoughts like an out-of-control slide show. "Well, it wouldn't be an *entirely* bad idea, I suppose."

Sure, Jack would hate it, but since the groom isn't supposed to see the bride before the wedding, he'd never be the wiser.

As if she'd eavesdropped on my thoughts, Chloe nodded. "Like I said, problem solved."

I faced the mirror to memorize every detail of my dream dress, from the careful folds of the pleated bodice to the bottom of the ruffled tulle skirt. Every inch of imported silk branded itself into my brain.

"It is a lovely dress." Fifi sidled up to me to stare at my reflection over my shoulder. Her overpowering floral perfume stung my nose like a giant bee. "And I suppose your frame fills it out well enough. But since we've established you can't afford it, I'm going to need you to take it off. I'm sure we have *other* dresses available within your means.

And if not, perhaps you would prefer one of the bridal consignment stores on *your* side of town." For the second time since we'd arrived, her French accent faltered, and I distinctly heard the hint of a Southern twang.

I clenched my fists at my sides and struggled to keep my voice from shaking. "Who do you think you are? You aren't even French!"

"How dare you!" Fifi barked, and her washed-out complexion flushed until I swore I saw smoke curling out of her ears. "This is precisely why we need to screen our clients. Among the four of you, you've consumed enough champagne to pay for an entire trousseau. And you're drunk. Thank goodness I didn't waste a superior vintage—not that you would have noticed."

Cheap champagne? That would explain my spinning head.

She looked down her nose at me, her face pinched as if she'd gotten a whiff of her own perfume. "I have no idea how you managed to get through the screening process. Our clientele is as exclusive as our gowns are. And an unemployed *Goodwill* shopper certainly doesn't belong in Colette Couture."

Her incessant yipping continued, sending ripples of heat through me. *Who does she think she is?* Nothing more than a fancy French poodle, that's who.

What started as a faint prickle grew until I could sense the entire room. A gust of wind whipped my hair around me, and hot oil flowed through my veins. I knew the feeling well, and my entire being tingled with giddy anticipation. Fifi's red-rimmed mouth moved, but my racing heart thundered in my ears, drowning her out. The lights flickered for an instant... and she was gone.

Chapter 9

"**W**HOOOA! DID FRANÇOISE JUST TURN into—" Helena shot upright, gripping the arm of the settee to keep from spilling onto the floor. A fit of giggles came over her. "Nah, don't mind me. I think I may have had a few too many of those yummy little drinks."

"Are you okay, dear?" Mom shot me a death glare as she staggered over to check on my inebriated friend. Helena wasn't the only one who'd had a few too many of those "yummy little drinks."

"A poodle? Really?" Chloe took a step back as the little dog leaped toward her. "Ivie, I said a *dress*, not a dog! Haven't we already had enough trouble with dogs to get us through the rest of eternity?"

I pressed my hands to my mouth to hold back the laughter as I slithered away from the scene. "Oops?"

Fifi barked—this time she actually *barked*—at me, baring her tiny white teeth in a vicious snarl.

My mother fell into the seat beside Helena and shook her head at me. "Haven't you learned your lesson when it comes to dogs?"

"Um... guess not?" I tried to smile but couldn't get my face to cooperate. I imagined my snarl was almost as impressive as that of the little poodle at my feet.

"What are you going to do now?" Mom whisper-shouted at me.

"She's going to turn her back." Chloe's eyes stretched so wide I could see white all the way round her irises. "Right, Ivie?"

"Sure." I giggled as Fifi continued to jump in the air like a circus pooch. "I'll simply turn her back." I'd done it before: twice, in fact. After multiple failed attempts, I'd finally figured out how to change my former fiancé Matt from a dog to a human again. And I'd changed my dad back from a cat. Surely, I could fix the pretentious French poodle in front of me.

"Easy peasy, right?" Chloe coughed out a laugh as she scooped up the dog. "Where shall we do this?"

"Uh, here's fine." I eyed Helena, still slumped on the velvet sofa. "Mom, can you stay with her and keep her... uh, *occupied*?"

"Of course, dear." I didn't miss the sarcasm dripping from her lips. "What are mothers for?"

"Here goes nothing." I put my hand on the dog's head and concentrated on envisioning the wretched woman who'd insulted me. Her human image flitted unfettered into my mind. "From bitch to bitch, a hasty curse. A simple trick I must reverse..."

A light gust rushed through the room, ruffling my hair and the satin gowns around me. Fifi yapped at the static charge flowing between us.

I glanced at Chloe, who waved at me to keep going.

My eyes flitted around the room as I scraped the bottom of the proverbial barrel for the next line of my makeshift spell. I knew I had to fix the stupid dog, but my heart wasn't in it. Rows of sprinkler heads, dotting the black background of the ceiling, caught my eye, reminding me of the tin stars worn by lawmen in the old west. Which made me think of Woody from *Toy Story*, which made me think of Jack and his magnificent—

"Oh, my God." Chloe bit back a grin. "Did you just say you wanted to ride Jack until his 'morning wood' burst into flames?"

"Uh..." I blinked at her a few times while I pulled my thoughts out of the gutter. "Did I?"

A blast of laughter burst from her lips. "Yes you did. You two go at it like rabbits. Can you even imagine sex so sizzling you'd actually ignite?"

Yes. Yes, I could imagine it. In fact, I *was* imagining it as we spoke. My lady bits were on fire, and I'd broken out in a hot sweat. I'd gotten so warm I smelled smoke. Fifi, the French poodle, must have smelled it too because she started frantically barking at me.

"Is something burning?" My mother jumped off the couch, sniffing the air as she scurried toward us.

"Maybe the candles—" A loud wail cut me off, making me jump. The electronic shriek of the alarm echoed off the walls as heavy metal doors rolled down from a seam in the ceiling, caging in the dresses just in time for the sprinklers to douse everything—and everyone—with an icy shower.

An older woman in a violet pantsuit and contrasting flame-colored updo burst into the room, her face frozen in comic horror. Or too much Botox. "What on earth?"

An inappropriate giggle forced its way out of me.

"What happened in here? Where is Françoise?" She mashed her hands into her sides, making water squish out like a sponge.

"I-I think she ran to get help." Chloe hip-checked me, staring at me with her eyes stretched so wide I could see all the way around her blue irises. "Right, Ivie?"

Purple Lady gasped and turned as white as a slice of Wonder bread. "Is that one of our *original* gowns?" Her bony hand flew up to cover her horrified expression.

I opened my mouth to speak as Fifi splashed her way over to us, barking her ridiculously coiffed head off.

"Not only have you destroyed some of the finest silk in existence, but you brought a-a...? This is positively outrageous." She pointed a shaky finger toward the drenched poodle. "You can't have that *dog* in here!"

I couldn't help it. I laughed. As it happened, Fifi was the least of our worries.

"Who called the five-oh?" Helena staggered over to us, still sipping from her empty flute, trying to suck every last drop of champagne condensation from the inside of the glass.

"That would be the fire department." The purple lady huffed. "You've set off the alarm. How exactly you managed to do *that* is still at question, but thank heavens for our dress protection system." She eyed the steel doors before turning her glare on me.

"*I* didn't set off the alarm." Not on purpose, anyway. "As far as I can see, there isn't even a—"

"So where's the fire?"

I spun around at the soft, lilting cadence of Liam's Scottish brogue, and my traitorous skin pebbled at the sound.

He eyed me up and down, desire reflecting in his baby blues. "Nice dress."

"Ohhh, you again." Helena ran a finger along Liam's forearm, and he jerked away from her touch. "Will someone *please* tell me, who *is* this delicious creature?"

I fisted the front of his cornflower-blue chambray button-down, pulling him to the side, well aware of the four pairs of eyes gawking at us. "How'd you get in here? Better yet, *why* are you here?"

Fifi let out a pitiful whine, her front two paws scratching at the ruined dress hanging from my body.

Make that five pairs of eyes.

Liam leaned in until his warm breath washed over me, making my knees weak. "I sensed that you needed me. So here I am."

"You *sensed* that I needed you?" I whispered out of the side of my mouth as I took turns studying Liam and the dog through narrowed eyes. "Exactly how does that work?"

"Is that really important right now?" He scooped up the agitated poodle with a smug grin. "You're getting wetter by the minute, and the sirens are getting closer."

My thighs clenched at the way he said *wetter* and the incendiary look he gave me. "Fine." I exhaled with a groan. "Let's do this before I end up in handcuffs again." *Or end up in a dressing room with my legs wrapped around the Scottish hottie.*

"Aren't you going to introduce us?" Chloe's jaw flexed as she glared at me.

"Uh, sure. This is Liam. My dad's apprentice. Liam, this is Chloe, my best friend."

"Nice to meet you, Chloe." Liam extended a hand then dropped it when she didn't reciprocate.

"Well, that explains absolutely nothing." Chloe blinked at him a few times before turning back to me. "What's he doing here?"

I fidgeted. "He's going to help me fix my little situation."

She grabbed my arm, towing me toward a large display case. Liam trailed not far behind. "That would be an excellent idea, the first useful thing you've said since you wiggled your—"

I leveled an icy glare her way.

"Ugh, fine. No wiggling. Now hurry up and change her back before the six o'clock news team gets here. And try to stay out of sight until the deed is done, okay?" She didn't wait for a response. She spun around, splashing her way back, hopefully to do a little damage control. If Chloe was good for anything, it was damage control.

"I've done this before." I sighed, pressing my fingers into my temples. "I have no idea what went wrong this time."

Liam cupped my cheek and caught my eyes with his. "You just need to focus. Pay attention to the dog spell only the dog. Come on. You can do it." He set Fifi down in front of me and took each of my hands in his. "Concentrate on turning her back."

I closed my eyes and imagined Fif—*Françoise* standing in front of me in all her disingenuous glory. "From bitch to bitch, a hasty curse. A simple trick I must reverse. No more barking. No more fur. No memories of what you were. No matter how it all may seem, to you it feels like just a dream." A warm gust ruffled my hair, the static current raising goose bumps on my arms as I forced myself to focus on the transformation.

Françoise's human form exploded out from the tiny poodle like an egg in a microwave. She looked a little worse for the wear as she sat cross-legged on the floor between us, drenched from head to toe.

She opened her mouth to speak and stared up at us. "What happened? Why is it raining in here?" Her French accent appeared to have washed away with her makeup.

"Something set off the sprinkler system." Liam winked at me, giving my hands a squeeze, sending a jolt straight to the apex of my thighs.

"Oh no, the dresses! Is that Gertrude? Oh, my stars, she must be furious. I'd better see if I can help her." Françoise jumped up from the floor and hurried to the purple lady's side.

"That's one problem solved." I blew out a breath and stepped back from Liam, trying to escape the heady sexual tension between us. "I, uh, I should probably take off this dress."

A slow grin crept across his face, and he glanced at the water droplets pooling in my cleavage. "It's a beautiful dress, even soaking wet. But if you feel the need to take it off, don't let me stop you. In fact..." He reached toward me. "Please, allow me to help."

I swallowed the lump in my throat and took another step back. "Liam, don't. Please don't look at me that way."

He crept toward me in the downpour like a lion stalking his prey. I think I even heard him growl. "What way?"

"Th-that way. Like you want to eat me." I stole a glance down his body, freezing as I discovered his zipper straining against the massive bulge in his Dockers.

"Maybe I *do* want to eat you." He closed the distance between us, leaning in to whisper his lips across my ear. "One. Bite. At a time."

A zing rushed through me, and I lunged, hiking the dress up to wrap myself around him like a vine and crushing my mouth against his in a heated kiss. As if I'd freed the beast from his cage, Liam whipped me around, pressing my back into the wall, holding me captive with his hips as his greedy mouth attacked, keeping me breathless and panting in his arms.

Where kissing Jack had always been a mutual give and take, kissing Liam was nothing but take—and he did all the taking. I struggled to catch my breath as he held my face in his hands, devouring my mouth as the spray rained down on us. Every bit of it—the length of his body pressing against me, the apples-and-cinnamon taste on his full lips, even the delicious way those lips molded to mine—felt wrong. But I couldn't seem to make myself stop as my body waged war with my brain.

"Ivie!"

Chloe's frantic voice snapped me back to my senses, and I released my hold on Liam, sliding down the wall until I stood on my own two unsteady feet. I shoved his chest, and he staggered backward.

My best friend snatched my arm in hers, dragging me through a shallow puddle from a stunned Scottish hottie. "What the *hell* was that? You are *so* lucky Jack wasn't here to see you practically raping Liam. What on earth has gotten into you?" She stopped walking and shook her head, sending water droplets everywhere. "Never mind. I don't want to know."

Oh, my God. Jack! A jolt of panic twisted my insides. "You won't tell him, will you?"

She wheeled on me with fire in her blue eyes. "I would *never*. But you'd better get a handle on this whatever-it-is you have going on with that guy." She hooked her thumb in Liam's direction. "I'm not the only one who noticed your little lip lock. Just be glad Helena is three sheets to the wind, and your mother understands the whole 'magical Viagra' thing." She shook her head again. "No wonder Jack doesn't want you working spells when he's not around. You. Are. Out. Of. Control." She punctuated each word by poking a finger into my sternum.

This time, I stopped dead in my tracks. "My mom saw?"

Chloe rolled her eyes. "*Everyone* saw. I'm pretty sure a few firemen will be using your little display as spank bank material tonight."

I gasped and dropped my face into my hands. I'd turned myself into masturbation fodder. "Could this day possibly get any worse?"

"Don't jinx yourself. Just be glad Jack wasn't here to witness your little meltdown." Chloe giggled and bumped my shoulder. "So did you see where Françoise scampered off to after you... you know?"

"I'm right here."

I picked up my head, staring openmouthed at the bane of my morning. Without the perfectly coiffed hair and artistically applied makeup, and minus the penciled-on eyebrows that either didn't make it through the spell or washed off in the sprinklers, she didn't look nearly as intimidating. Even her expensive clothes were soaked through and dripping into her shoes. I'd outdone myself this time. Under different circumstances, I might've been impressed.

She pushed a damp curl out of her face. "You were right."

I studied her resigned expression. "About what?"

She blinked a few times as she shifted her gaze between Chloe and me. Her shoulders slouched, and she leaned against the wall beside me. "You said I wasn't French. Well, I'm not. I'm from Muncie, Indiana. My name isn't even Françoise. It's Frances. My friends call me Frankie. Colette absolutely *insists* we use French accents."

My guilt meter shot straight to the red line. "Yours is really good, unlike the girl at the front desk."

"Some of us are better than others." She shrugged, and her lips formed a sad smile. "Colette thinks it makes the experience more exclusive."

"Oh, it does." Chloe nodded. "I would have never guessed you weren't French."

"Thanks." Frances flashed a genuine smile then turned to me. "I'm sorry I was rude to you. You look beautiful in that dress. Your fiancé is a lucky man." She glanced over at Liam, having what appeared to be a heated conversation with my mother.

"That's not her—"

I glared at Chloe before forcing a smile for my frazzled stylist. "Thank you, Frances."

"Call me Frankie."

"Thank you, Frankie." Someone finally shut off the water, and I glanced down at the sodden silk clinging to my skin. "I'm sorry about the dress. I think it's ruined."

She shrugged. "It happens. I'm sure the insurance will cover it. Believe it or not, this isn't the worst disaster to strike Colette's. We cater to celebrities too. I could write a book about the crazy things I've seen in here."

"Really? Like what?" Chloe rubbed her hands together as she prepared to soak up some fresh gossip.

Frankie's face lit up. "Well, there was this one time..."

My attention drifted from her wild story to catch Liam's eye as he attempted to extricate himself from my mother. "I'll be right back." My lips still tingled from his kiss as I made my way across the room. "Mom, can you excuse us for a minute?"

"Are you sure that's wise?" She stepped in front of Liam, effectively blocking him from view, and gave me the dirtiest look.

I twisted my hair in my hands, squeezing out at least a half gallon of water. "I'm sure, Mom. I just need to have a few words with Liam before he leaves."

She crossed her arms. "Fine. I'll be over there." She pointed at the spot where Helena had lined up empty champagne bottles and was trying to bowl, using an expensive white satin purse.

"I'm sorry," Liam and I said at the same time.

"You go ahead," he said.

I kept my eyes trained on my feet. I knew if I dared to gaze into his blue stare, I'd be lost. "I shouldn't have kissed you."

He hooked a finger under my chin, tipping my face up, and that simple contact left me even more confused and wanting more. "That's the one thing I'm *not* sorry about."

"Liam..." I stepped back, and he dropped his hand. "We can't."

"Why?"

"Because I love Jack."

His lips twisted into a grin. "You keep saying that, but it doesn't seem to stop you from being drawn to me."

"It's just a side effect of magic." *And you're too damn sexy for my own good.*

He took a step closer, and I froze. "Hey, I'm not going to hurt you."

"I don't even know who I am around you." I groaned.

"Maybe you're finally allowing yourself to be who you really are. You're a sorceress, Ivie. And a sorceress should be with a sorcerer. That's how nature intended it."

I glanced back at Mom, who was wrestling the expensive purse from Helena's hands. "My mother isn't a sorceress, and my parents are very happy."

"Perhaps, but that doesn't change the fact that your father was meant for someone else. He chose to break the covenants, and he's accepted the consequences of that decision. I would hate to see you suffer because you denied the connection we share."

Covenants? Consequences? Connection? "I have no idea what you're talking about." I turned to walk away.

"Ivie, wait." Liam captured my wrist, holding me in place. "Ask yourself what you feel for me. And be honest. I know you feel something."

"I-I *can't*." I wrenched my arm free and splashed my way across the room. Being so close to him had scrambled my thought process. I needed to get out of there before I did something else I'd regret. And I had no doubt I'd regret every glorious moment I'd spent with Liam.

Chapter 10

W HAT HAD STARTED OUT AS one of the happiest days of my life had turned into nothing but a series of catastrophes, and I wasn't interested in lingering in the burning wreckage. After changing back into my own clothes and convincing Chloe to surrender her rental car's keys, I made my escape. I snuck out the back, avoiding Liam and steering clear of the inevitable conversations I knew I'd have to have with my mother and Helena at some point in the near future. I had no idea how to explain my actions to anyone else when I didn't understand them myself.

What the hell had I been thinking? Kissing Liam had been a horrifying—yet deliciously toe-curling—mistake, a mistake I had no intention of ever repeating. I'd lost track of how many times I'd nearly destroyed my relationship with Jack since my father had introduced me to his apprentice.

Jack was right. No matter how many times I'd tried to convince myself otherwise, I had no business doing magic, despite how right the power flowing through me felt. I knew that, instead of running away from the situation, I should have confronted it head on, but I didn't care. I needed to get home.

Driving with the top down dried my hair into a chaotic mess, but nothing short of a dye job could eradicate the thick ribbons of red threading through the dark. My options were limited: either make a detour to my favorite hair salon for a quick color treatment or head home to face the music. For once, I opted for the honest approach.

"So as I'm sure you can imagine, I couldn't *possibly* let the dress shop burn to the ground without at least *attempting* a spell to put it out." I finished my elaborate fabrication then took a deep cleansing breath. *Where's the harm in a little white lie?*

Jack's mouth hung open. He hadn't spoken a word since I'd started talking. "You put out the fire with magic?"

Interesting word choice. More like magic stoked the flames. "Yep," I squeaked. "Thanks to me—and a state-of-the-art sprinkler system—Colette Couture is still in business." *Okay, a few little white lies.*

"Wow." Jack fell back into the couch cushions and blew out a breath. His dumbfounded expression told me I'd managed to pull off the ruse. "It never occurred to me that your abilities could actually come in handy."

"Amazing, right?" *Liar, liar pants on...*

"Fire, huh? Do they have any idea what caused it?"

Guilt climbed up my throat, threatening to choke me. "I, uh, think it was the candles?"

Jack tugged me into his lap, shaking his head. "My little witch saved the day. Who would have guessed?"

A nervous laugh burst out of me before I could push it back. "Not me, that's for sure."

"So I suppose that means you're all... *worked up* now." His lips curved up at the corners as he gazed at me with lust in his eyes. He could pretend all he wanted, but deep down, he loved what magic did to me. "Have a little energy you need to work off?"

Jackpot! That was exactly what I needed to get my mind off Liam. "Hmm, maybe I do." I shifted in his lap, feeling him swell beneath me. "What did you have in mind?"

He thrust upward, sending delicious tingles through me.

"Oh, that?" I gulped down a mouthful of saliva. "I-I think I could be convinced."

He chuckled. "Since when do you require convincing? After one of your spells, I'm surprised either of us is wearing clothes right now."

Excellent point. I hopped up from his lap, unbuttoned my blouse, and slid it from my shoulders. I toyed with the idea of working a quick spell to get us both out of our clothes but decided against it. The odds weren't in my favor after the day I'd had.

"Here"—he reached around my waist to unzip my skirt—"let me get that." The gray linen pooled at my feet, leaving me in nothing but my delicate lace underthings. Jack's eyes followed the contours of my body from head to toe, and he licked his lips. "Beautiful."

Before I had a chance to formulate a reply, his insistent mouth was on mine, steering me back to the cushions until I was sprawled out beneath him. He slid a hand down my stomach, into my panties, and his long fingers spread me apart, teasing me into a writhing, desperate mess. "Jack, *please.*"

"Oh, don't you worry. I have every intention of pleasing you." He slipped a finger in. "More than once." Then two. "But not yet." His weight disappeared from above me as he removed his shirt and jeans to stare down at me.

I whimpered at his naked form, and his muscles twitched at my perusal. I wanted—no, *needed*—him to be inside me.

With a mischievous smile, he pulled me to my feet and helped me step out of my panties before sliding my bra straps down, trapping my arms at my sides. "Patience, little witch. You're *always* in such a hurry." He wrapped his hand around his hardness, stroking a few times before releasing it.

I licked my lips in anticipation. I longed to taste him, to feel him fall apart from my touch.

"Turn around." He gripped my shoulders with a grin, guiding me as I spun away from him to face the sofa.

I waited with butterflies teeming in my stomach while he unfastened the hooks and let my bra fall to the floor. "Now, bend over, and grab on." His tone was harsh and his demeanor abrupt, but his touch was gentle as he eased me forward until I was holding the back of the couch. Without further preamble, he dug his fingers into my hips and thrust into me from behind with a growl.

I held on for dear life as he slammed in and out of me like a man possessed. I didn't know what had come over him, but especially after the morning I'd had, I wasn't complaining.

Jack leaned in to brush his lips across my ear. "Touch yourself."

I hesitated for half a second before reaching between my legs to seek out my slick center. My earlier arousal had barely diminished, so it didn't take long to bring me to the edge. Images of Liam forced their way out of my subconscious, and I fought to send them back to where they'd come from. I refused to fantasize about my father's apprentice with Jack inside me.

"That's it," Jack purred as he sank his teeth into my shoulder. "Faster."

My fingers swirled over my heated flesh, matching his rhythm stroke for stroke, until tingles sparked over my skin. My entire body screamed for release. I bit my tongue to keep Liam's name from crossing my lips. "Oh, God," I panted out the words as he shifted his hips, making me see stars again.

"Come with me." He shoved his hand into my hair, wrapping his fist around a clump and pulling me upright as I shattered around him.

I twisted my head around to meet his lips in a searing kiss. My heart ached with how much I loved him, and tears filled my eyes as I considered how close I'd come to destroying everything we had, how close I came every time thoughts of Liam distracted me.

"Hey..." Jack slipped out of me and captured my face in his hands. "Are you crying?"

I turned the rest of the way around and laid my forehead against his. "I just love you so much."

"I love you too, sweetheart." He brushed his lips to mine again before scooping me into his arms. "In fact, I'm going to take you to our bed and show you exactly how much."

The afternoon sun streamed through the slats in the blinds as I stretched my deliciously sore limbs. I rolled toward Jack's side of the bed, reaching out for him, but my fingers came up empty. I heard him breathing, but his spot had gone cold. "Jack?"

"Were you *ever* going to tell me?" He stood with his back against the doorframe, arms folded across his bare chest, unforgiving eyes trained on me.

I sat bolt upright and untangled myself from the sheets, fear twisting my insides as I gaped at his icy expression. "Tell you?"

"The truth."

Oh, God. I couldn't begin to guess which of my secrets he'd uncovered. Before my father had come back, I'd had no trouble keeping to the straight and narrow, but since his return, it seemed as if I told one lie after another. I couldn't keep them all straight. "I—I don't know what you—"

He slammed his fist into the wall, making the windows vibrate. "Damn it, Ivie! Stop lying to me."

"I've been doing magic?"

"You've been doing magic? That's all you're going to say? I already know *that*. It's written all over your hair. Why don't we start with the most recent lies and work our way back?" He pushed away from the wall and stepped closer to the bed. "What really happened at the bridal shop today?"

A flash of heat rippled over my skin, and my mouth went dry. I had to squeeze my hands into fists to keep them from shaking. The words tumbled past my lips, barely making a sound as I reluctantly confessed my sins. "Chloe made me try on every dress in the place. They plied us with champagne until I wasn't thinking straight, and I-I turned the stylist into a poodle. But in my defense, she *was* a horrible person. And I *did* turn her back."

"And what about the fire?"

I bit my lip. "I may have started that too. By accident. I don't know exactly what happened. One minute, I was trying to conjure up a copy of the wedding gown, and the next, the sprinkler system had gone off."

"I see." He pulled his phone out of his back pocket and fiddled with the buttons. "And when did Liam show up?"

I sucked in a gulp of air. "Liam?"

Jack shifted back on his heels, popping up an eyebrow.

Flashes of Liam's lips on mine clouded my thoughts, and my stomach clenched for an entirely different reason. "He, uh, just showed up after the sprinklers went off, while I was trying to change the stylist back."

Jack frowned down at me for a long moment, the wheels turning behind his eyes until I wanted to shout at him to get to the point. "Convenient."

I almost asked him how he knew, but since he still hadn't addressed the worst of what happened, I wasn't going to bring it up. Instead, I sent up a silent prayer to the gods that he'd never find out what really happened.

As if he'd read my mind, his face twisted until I could almost feel his pain. "Was it worth it?"

"What?" A twinge of something unfamiliar gripped my insides: an overwhelming sensation of dread. "Was what worth it?"

"I got an interesting email while you were napping." He tossed the phone onto the bed beside me. "It came with an eye-opening video attachment."

It took me a moment to recognize the sounds coming from the device. *Is that my voice?*

"Liam, don't. Please don't look at me that way."

"What way?"

"Th-that way. Like you want to eat me."

My blood ran cold as the reality of what I was hearing sank in. "Where did you—"

Jack's eyes flashed with fury, and I bit my tongue.

"Maybe I do want to eat you. One. Bite. At a time."

"Pick it up," Jack snapped before smoothing his features into an eerily calm smile. "You don't want to miss the next part."

I reached out but stopped just short of grabbing the phone. I knew exactly what happened next and flushed at the memory. "Jack—"

"Save it." He snatched up his phone and held it out for me, but instead of looking at the screen, I watched his tortured face. "Make me understand, Ivie. Give me *one good reason* for what I'm seeing here."

"It..." I swallowed back a sob. "It wasn't me. Not really. It was the spell. You know what happens when—"

"Are you saying the magic made you do it?" He shook his head. "That's a lousy excuse."

The sob broke free, and I clutched the sheets in my hands. "I don't know what came over me. I didn't mean—"

"Don't say you didn't mean to do it. I've watched the video at least a dozen times. You kissed him." He leaned down until his hot breath slapped me across the face. "*You.* Kissed. *Him.*"

"I know." I swiped at the tears running down my cheeks. "I'm so sorry."

"I told you magic was dangerous." His jaw flexed like an elastic band stretched to the breaking point. "I begged you not to work spells."

I worked to get my breathing under control but failed. "I tried to stay away from it, but it's... it's part of who I am."

"Well, I can't be around that part of you right now." Jack grabbed a shirt from the floor and yanked it over his head.

"Wait!" A jolt of adrenaline spiked through me, and I leapt off the bed. I reached for him, but he flinched away. He was leaving me. The reality of the situation sat like a block of ice in the pit of my stomach. "Where are you going?"

"Anywhere but here." Every drop of emotion drained from Jack's eyes until he seemed to stare right through me like I wasn't even there. "And do me a favor. Don't be here when I get back."

Chapter 11

"I DON'T *KNOW* WHO SENT HIM the video," I whined into the phone as I navigated Chloe's rented convertible through the congested midday traffic. An ancient yellow Cadillac, plastered with blue and red Atlanta Braves bumper stickers, cut across two lanes, nearly taking off my passenger-side mirror and making me miss my exit. *Why did it have to be baseball season?*

"Well"—Chloe huffed—"I have a pretty good idea."

I let out an exaggerated sigh and took the next off-ramp, looping around until I came to a stop at the light. "You think it was Liam."

"Who else had a motive for sending Jack a YouTube video of you climbing Liam like a beanstalk? Hell, who else would have even known the footage *existed*? It's not as if you made the twelve o'clock news. Not that flooding the most exclusive bridal salon in Atlanta isn't newsworthy— that was truly epic. But really, Ivie, of all the embarrassing recordings that could have been made of you over the past year, this one doesn't even rate. It *must* have been Liam, and he did it specifically so Jack would find out."

I opened my mouth to speak, but she beat me to it.

"And I'm sorry to come at you like this, but you only have yourself to blame. What the hell were you thinking, kissing the guy in a public place? While wearing a wedding gown, no less."

I winced. "I have no idea what I was thinking. It's as if I'm in a trance whenever Liam's around. At first, I thought it was just an innocent crush or something. I mean, he's cute, but I don't love Liam. I love Jack."

"I'll admit it, the guy's gorgeous. I'd probably do him, too."

"Chloe!" I frantically checked my mirrors as if the cars around me could hear what she was saying. "I didn't *do* him." *Though the thought did cross my mind. More than once.*

A scruffy guy in a mud-covered red pickup pulled up beside me and blew me a kiss. *Gross!* The instant the light turned green, I gunned the engine and squealed tires as I pulled through the intersection, leaving my not-so-secret admirer far behind me. Was I suddenly giving off super pheromones?

"Hey, I just meant I *would* have... if I was single." She barked out a laugh then cleared her throat to cover it. "But I'm not, and neither are you. And let's face it, as cute as he is, he's not hot enough to send you into a tailspin at the mere sight of him."

Chloe's words reverberated in my brain. She was right. It wasn't *only* his looks that drew me to Liam. It was as if the guy was a high-powered tractor beam, drawing me into his personal space station. Maybe *he* was the one giving off super pheromones, not me. "Then there's something wrong with me because, ever since that first day my dad introduced us at the lab, I haven't been able to get him out of my head."

"Wait." Several seconds ticked by before she finished her thought. "When you say *the first time*, do you mean before or after your dad blew up the lab?"

"I don't know. Why is that important?"

"Just think about it. When your dad introduced you, did the guy make you weak in the knees, or did that happen *after* all the hocus pocus and broken glass?"

"After? Maybe? I'm not sure." I wracked my brain to remember the events leading up to my short stint in the slammer. The car behind me honked, and I realized I'd stopped moving. I jerked the car forward. "Yes, I think it was after."

Chloe's breath came out in raspy puffs. "Do you know what this means?"

"No, what does it mean?"

"You really need to pay attention. I think your father did something to you during that spell. It's like they roofied you or something."

"No..." I groaned.

"Oh my God! Ivie, that's it!"

I let out a breath. "I'm telling you, my dad wouldn't do—"

"No! Listen. I'm not talking about drugs. I'm talking about magic. Can't you see? They put a spell on you." Her voice climbed an octave, excitement oozing from her every word. "You said the guy keeps showing up at the most inopportune moments. And you can't stop thinking about him. And you're drawn to him like a swan to a vampire. There's really no other explanation."

"But that's my dad you're talking about. He wouldn't do something like that to me."

"Sweetie, your dad was a house pet for twelve years. There's no telling what he might do." I could practically hear the gears turning in her brain. "You need to tell Jack."

Jack. My eyes welled up with tears. "Why? He basically dumped me for kissing Liam."

"True, but that was before we found out about the spell."

"Alleged spell. I still can't believe my father would use dark magic on me." *Would he?* This was the same man who'd read me bedtime stories and tucked me in at night until I was twelve.

"Didn't your mom tell you he was acting strange? Well, maybe this is why."

"I don't know." I pulled up in front of Chloe's three-story brick townhouse and cut the engine.

She waved from where she waited for me on the front steps. I could see her mouth moving as she spoke into her phone. "Ivie, if you won't tell Jack, I will."

"Chloe, please don't. Give it a few days. I haven't even talked to my dad yet." Once we were close enough for me to hear my voice in stereo, I ended the call.

"Oh, look. My line's finally free." She punched Jack's number into her cell then switched the call to speaker.

I followed her through the front door, waiting with a lump in my throat for Jack to pick up.

"What is it, Chloe?" His brusque tone sent shivers down my spine. Any thoughts of him forgiving me evaporated like a water droplet on a hot skillet.

She glared at Jack's smiling face on the caller ID display. "Well, it's nice to talk to you, too, Houdini."

"What do you want? Just cut to the chase." His voice cracked, and I could almost see him tugging on his hair.

Chloe rolled her eyes. "I'm calling about Ivie."

"Why am I not surprised?" He blew out a breath. "I don't want to talk about her right now."

I paced around Chloe's *House Beautiful*-worthy living room with my stomach twisting into knots. I snatched a silk throw pillow from her white linen sofa and was tempted to use it to knock the phone from her hand. I knew Jack was angry, but I wasn't prepared to hear him sound so ambivalent.

"Fine, then just listen." Chloe perched like a dainty little bird on the arm of the sofa. "Whatever's been happening between Ivie and Liam isn't her fault. We're fairly certain her father put some sort of spell on her."

A burst of hollow laughter came through the speaker. "Oh, really, more blame shifting? Well, I guess it all comes down to the magic factor, doesn't it?"

"I'm serious, Jack." Chloe's cheeks flamed. "I don't think she has any control over what's happening."

"Come on, Chloe. We all know Ivie can't control her urges when she's doing magic. But that hasn't exactly stopped her, has it?" Venom dripped from his voice, and the sound broke my heart.

"I don't think you understand what I'm saying." She exhaled then flashed me a sad smile.

"Oh, I understand perfectly. Ivie knows what happens when she does magic, but she still can't seem to resist the draw." He growled through the line. "She's like an addict."

Chloe winced. "Come on, Jack. Don't you think it's odd that Liam always seems to be around when she's doing magic? It's not as if she calls him. He just seems to materialize at the perfect moment."

"I don't know what to think anymore. In fact, I don't want to think about it at all. I'm sorry, Chloe. I know she's your friend, but I need some time to process everything."

"Jack, wait!" Chloe yelled, but it was too late. The line went dead. Just like my relationship.

After riding to Jack's house with Chloe to retrieve my car and every other worldly possession I owned, I cranked up the romantic playlist Jack had created for me on my iPhone, flopped down on her guest bed to stare at the ceiling, and broke down in tears.

Chloe burst through the door with a bottle of Fireball and two matching floral teacups. "Okay, I've had just about enough of you feeling sorry for yourself. You're a grown-ass witch, for crap sake. Now drag your carcass out of this bed and deal with your troubles like an adult." She poured a cupful of the cinnamon whisky and shoved it into my hand.

"I've decided being an adult is overrated." I threw back my drink with a shudder, letting the burn warm me all the way down, then fell into the fluffy duvet to search for cracks in her perfect ceiling again.

She refilled my cup. "A few more of these and you won't even remember Houdini's name."

"Maybe I don't want to forget his name. Maybe I don't want to forget a single moment I spent with him. I miss him so much." I watched her in my peripheral vision.

Chloe poured herself a shot and tossed it back. "Don't worry. The memory loss is temporary, but trust me, well worth it."

"Maybe Jack was right. Magic is a curse."

"Don't listen to him." She scoffed. "Magic is part of your heritage, and as much as you might want to pretend you're just a normal twenty-something, unemployed schoolteacher, you're not."

"Gee, thanks for reminding me." I held out my cup, and she refilled it.

Chloe giggled, clinking her cup to mine before bringing it to her lips. "Don't mention it. Now, drink up!"

Half a bottle later, we lay facing each other on the pink duvet with the smell of cinnamon heavy in the air around us. "I feel better already," I slurred. My tongue felt like a wad of bubble gum in my mouth—a wad of spice-flavored bubble gum.

Chloe groaned. "Well, I feel like shit. And I miss my husband."

"Hey, where *is* Jon?" I spun my head around as if I expected him to be hiding behind the curtains or something. Hey, weirder things had happened. The guy *was* a magician.

"I left his ass in Vegas. And if he doesn't get his act together, I won't be going back."

I gasped and tried to pull myself to a sitting position, only to flop backward. "Why didn't you tell me?"

"What's to tell? I hate the groupies, and he won't stop flirting with them."

I reached out and squeezed her hand. "I'm so sorry, Chloe. And here you are, dealing with my ridiculous issues when your marriage is at stake."

"Pfft." She waved her hand, clipping herself in the nose. "My problems will still be there when I get back. I'm just glad I didn't sell my house, or we'd be shacking up at the Red Roof Inn."

I rolled onto my back and cracked up. "We both know you wouldn't be caught *dead* at the Red Roof Inn."

"True." Chloe cackled beside me. "Besides, five-star hotels may be nice, but I really like my bed."

I exhaled. "I really liked Jack's bed."

"Oh, sweetie. If he's anything like his brother, I'm pretty sure you're thinking about the things he *did* in that bed."

"Hey!" I gave her a little shove, almost sending both of us over the side. "You're supposed to be cheering me up."

Chloe snorted out a laugh. "Sorry. I'm drunk."

"Yeah, me too." I swallowed the last of my mirth and sank into the mattress.

"I'm heading to bed." She bumped my shoulder. "Awful Waffle in the morning?"

"Deal." I didn't wait for her to leave the room before rolling into a ball on my side with the pillow clutched in my arms like a teddy bear. I'd been through worse things than losing Jack. I'd almost gone to jail for murder. If Jack hadn't been there...

A sharp pain spiked through the center of my chest. To hell with being a strong, independent woman. I didn't want to think about the rest of my life without him.

I drifted in and out of a fitful sleep, unable to turn my mind off. My thoughts were torn between memories of Jack and images of Liam. And Chloe's words continued to loop through my brain on repeat. *They put a spell on you.* But no matter how things might have appeared, I couldn't believe my father would do something so completely unforgivable.

Moonlight spilled in through the window, and I watched, mesmerized, as shadows danced across the floor. The shapes moved and shifted until I could swear I saw Liam's outline in the darkness.

"Ivie..."

I sat bolt upright, my stomach leaping into my throat. "Liam? Wh-what are you doing here?"

The bed dipped as he sat at my feet. "I felt as if you needed me."

"You said that earlier. But I don't understand. How can you *feel* when I need you?" I gripped the sheet in my fists to keep from reaching out to him.

"My senses are always on high alert when it comes to you."

Confusion flowed through me like hot maple syrup over pancakes. "But why?"

"Because we're connected." He scooted closer until his fingers brushed my hip. "Why can't you see we're meant to be together?"

I shivered at the contact. "*Liam*, I've told you already, I love Ja—"

"*Jack*. Yes, I know." He brushed a stray lock of hair from my face then cupped my cheek. "But you have to admit to yourself—if no one else—you feel something for me too."

Despite myself, I melted into his touch. "I'm so screwed up; I don't know what I feel."

"Stop fighting it." He leaned in until our lips were all but touching, and the hammering of his racing heart filled my ears. "I know you want me as much as I want you. Just this once, give in."

I swallowed back a moan. "All I've done since I met you is give in."

He tensed before latching his lips to mine as if he were drowning, and I was his only source of oxygen. With gentle pressure, he guided me against the mattress as his weight settled over me. "Is this okay?"

I gave him a faint nod, seeking out his lips again. A giant switch flipped in my brain, and every minute fiber of my soul shifted its focus to Liam. His kisses sobered me up only to intoxicate me again. I clung to him, struggling to stay quiet for fear of waking Chloe, only a few rooms away, while roving hands slipped under my threadbare T-shirt, leaving a fiery trail in their wake.

I was going straight to hell, and I would've been lying if I said I gave a damn.

Thundering hearts and soft groans, coupled with the whispered sounds of our clothes falling away, seemed deafening in the dark night. Once we were skin to skin, I could have sworn dual electric currents zipped below the surface, waiting to ignite.

His lips grazed my earlobe. "If we do this, there's no going back."

I gulped then nodded, unsure if I was ready, but unwilling to stop something that felt so right. So... *necessary*.

Liam lined himself up at my entrance. "I've waited my whole life for this moment." Then with a gentleness I didn't expect, he entered me.

Unfamiliar warmth spread out from the spot where we joined. The distinct flavor of his magic coursed swiftly through me like wind, engulfing every molecule in my body until his butterscotch-and-hot-pepper taste filled my senses. Sex with Liam was like nothing I'd experienced before. I knew it wasn't love. I couldn't even be sure it was real affection. I struggled to put a name to the emotions swirling around my veins.

Possession. Plain and simple.

A twinge of something familiar swept through me—the same tugging sensation I'd felt that first day in the lab— as if my very soul had ripped free, and something foreign had taken up residence in its place. Panic set in, and I was desperate to pull away, yet unable to release my hold on him. He was a magnet, and despite my love for Jack, I found myself inexorably drawn to him.

Pleasure—so intense it bordered on pain—swelled, and I struggled to form words. "Liam, what's happening?"

His arms tightened around me in a bear hug, and his thrusts grew impatient. "Our binding is almost complete." His lips found mine again, and he used his tongue to part them, darting it into my mouth to stop my protests even before I'd decided to voice them.

This was more than sex. As he moved within me, I felt him in my blood. Every beat of my heart was for Liam. Every breath I took made me want him more. With one last violent shudder, Liam grunted out his release then stilled as another wave of pleasure spiked through me. I didn't think my orgasm would ever end.

For several minutes, neither of us spoke. We just lay there, catching our breath in the darkness. Then he rolled off me and pulled me into his arms. "You're mine now."

My head throbbed, and I squinted at what could only be a floodlight pointed directly into my eyeballs.

"Wake up, sleepyhead." Chloe's artificial-sweetener voice made me want to lash out at her with whatever limbs I could convince to move.

Wait. Chloe?

"Where'd he go?" I sat up and winced. The ticking time bomb in my head counted down to the big BOOM.

"Where'd who go?"

I untangled myself from the blankets to discover the clothes I'd worn the night before—or rather was *still* wearing. *As in not naked.* And for someone who'd supposedly had sex fairly recently, my nether regions felt awfully cold and unused. "Something really weird is going on."

Chloe chuckled. "And you're just discovering that now? Where have you been?"

"Right here. All night long. But I was sure I wasn't alone. I thought... I mean, maybe I dreamed it, but it seemed so real. Liam. He was here, and he told me I was his now."

"How'd he get here?" Chloe looked around the room, peeking under the bed and behind the curtains. "And where'd he go?"

"That's just it. I don't think he *was* here. Not really. But I don't think I dreamed it either." I watched the wheels turn in Chloe's head until her eyes popped wide, and she flopped onto the bed beside me.

"Are you saying...?"

"I think you're right. I think Liam and my dad put a spell on me."

Chapter 12

"EXPLAIN TO ME AGAIN WHY we're halfway to North Carolina?" Red streaks etched across the evening sky as day slipped quietly into night, and I slumped into my seat to stare at the trees whipping past the window. If my life hadn't spiraled so completely out of control, I might have enjoyed the mountain views.

Chloe's pale-blond hair billowed around her as we raced northward on the rural highway with the top down. "You need someone who can figure out what sort of hold Liam has on you."

The sound of Liam's name on her lips sent a shiver through me. Memories of his hands on me came flooding back. But they weren't really memories, were they? Why couldn't I shake the feelings he stirred in me? "And you're convinced we need to travel three hours from home to do that?"

"I'm certain you need an intervention, and I only know of one place within driving distance with the kind of tools we need."

I couldn't help the sound that forced its way out of my throat—a cross between a laugh and a groan. "Come on, Chloe. Where are we going, really?"

Chloe angled her face toward me and rolled her eyes before tucking a loose strand of hair behind her ear. "We're heading to Ratz in the Attic. And before you ask: no, it's not a secret lab conducting unsanctioned medical experiments on the unsuspecting offspring of sorcerers. It's a blues bar."

"Oh, well, that's a relief. Seriously, Chloe!" I gaped at her, completely dumbfounded. If we hadn't been going nearly eighty, I would have considered bailing out of the moving vehicle. "In the midst of my worst crisis to date, we're going to listen to music?"

She flashed me a sweet smile and nodded. "Among other things."

I waited for her to laugh, but her serious expression didn't waver even a little as she stared at the road. We were going way too fast for the hairpin turns ahead—more proof that my best friend was completely nuts. "Okay, all kidding aside. Where are we going?"

She furrowed her perfect brows. "I thought we'd already covered that."

I grabbed hold of my seatbelt like a lifeline and waited for her to elaborate. She wasn't getting out of this that easily.

"Listen, it's not like we can waltz into an urgent care facility and ask them to remove a spell. You need a specialist."

I choked out a laugh. "A specialist. And what? I'm sup-posed to believe we'll just *happen* to run into this special-ist at a random bar in the mountains?"

She snorted. "Of course not. I called ahead. He's ex-pecting us."

The bluesy music assaulted me the minute the door swung open, a combination of hot guitar licks, the rhythmic *ratatatat* on the drums, and crashing cymbals. The bass thumped so loudly I felt it in my bones, and I had to shout to be heard. "Why are we here?"

Chloe scanned the room, her eyes settling on a large man on a stool on the stage, practically swallowing the mic as he belted out the lyrics in his heavy Cajun accent.

She gave him an enthusiastic wave, and he smiled. "There he is!"

I sidestepped a petite brunette carrying a tray filled with drinks. "There *who* is? You aren't seriously going to tell me you drove me to the middle of nowhere to talk to a musician?"

Chloe rolled her eyes, tucking a strand of her pale-blond hair behind her ear. "You're a"—she leaned in to whisper—"witch. You clearly need a *witch* doctor."

My mind raced as I tried to put two and two together. Chloe wasn't just run-of-the-mill crazy. She was certifiable. "What are you talking about? What witch doctor? Have you and Jon been smoking peyote in the desert?" I bit the words off and spit them at her.

"No, I haven't been smoking anything, illegal or otherwise. I met Daddy Whatnot in Vegas. He came backstage after one of Jon's shows. He's a fascinating guy—a voodoo priest, also known as a witch doctor."

Daddy Whatnot? Voodoo priest? Witch doctor? I planted my feet on the sticky floor. The silicone in her boobs must have leaked into her bloodstream. Or the bleach from her highlights had finally soaked into her brain. Either way, she'd lost her mind. "I'm not talking to a-a-a whatever he is. That's crazy!"

"No crazier than hallucinating the Scottish hottie in your bed. You said it yourself. You can't understand your own feelings. *And* you said it all started with that spell in the chem lab. None of this makes sense, and you can't go on like this forever, unless you're ready to walk away from Jack."

I refused to admit she had a valid argument. And walking away from Jack was too painful to contemplate. "What if it's not a spell? What if I'm just attracted to Liam?"

She came to an abrupt halt, making me crash into her from behind. "Are you really asking me that? Ivie Marie McKie, you love Jack."

"Yes, I love him with everything inside me, but I just can't believe my father would do something so..."

"Dirty and underhanded? Well, believe it, because I don't believe for one minute your feelings for Liam are real. He's cute and all, but that doesn't explain why you'd risk everything less than eight weeks before your wedding."

Chloe was right. I was on the razor's edge of ruining the best thing that had ever happened to me, and the only solution that made any sense was staring me in the face. I just refused to accept it.

The song ended, and the band set their instruments aside as the mellow tones of classic Bob Marley came through the speakers. Chloe ran onto the stage, squealing as she wrapped her tiny arms around the hearty bass player. She looked like a doll in his massive embrace. He had to have been as wide as he was tall, or close to it. But for a man of his proportions, he moved like a cat, spinning her around as if she were a ball of yarn that weighed nothing.

"As I live and breathe." His voice boomed out like a cannon blast as he pulled away from her embrace to scrutinize her. He smiled behind his heavy salt-and-pepper beard. "Chloe Blake! How the hell are ya, sugar?"

She beamed at him. "I'm good, Daddy. But look at you—you're fabulous!"

"Well, of course I'm fabulous. It's about time you noticed." He laughed, and the thunderous sound startled me. "So have you come to your senses and decided to dump that fancy husband of yours for a real man?"

Chloe giggled. "Not quite yet, but I'll keep you posted if I change my mind."

"So if it isn't *amour*, what brings you to my neck of the woods? And who's the lovely lady you've brought with you this evening?"

I must have looked like a frightened deer when he turned his intense gaze on me. Daddy Whatnot's overwhelming presence rendered me speechless, not that I would have known what to say, anyway. Were there some sort of rules of etiquette when dealing with a voodoo priest witch doctor? Was I expected to curtsey? I had no clue.

"This is my best friend and soon-to-be sister-in-law, Ivie McKie. She has a delicate situation she's dealing with, something your *special* expertise might help out with."

When I didn't respond, Chloe elbowed me.

"N-nice to meet you." I forced a smile and reached a shaky hand toward the man. He grasped it in both of his giant paws.

"Well, I'll be. Jon's little brother gonna marry this pretty lady? He made a good choice, he did." His Cajun accent seemed to fade in and out according to his excitement level.

"He did," Chloe agreed somberly. "But, Daddy, Ivie's *situation* could ruin the whole thing."

"That bad, huh?" Daddy Whatnot pulled the flat cap off his head and scratched the bald spot hiding under it. "Well, lay it on me."

Chloe scanned the room then pointed to a table in the back and led the way. Once we'd settled in, I gave Chloe a nod, and she started from the beginning, bringing the witch doctor up to date on my dilemma.

She barely paused to take a breath as she told him everything from the first minute I found out I was a witch, right up to the minute she'd tricked me into getting in her car to drive deep into Appalachia this afternoon. She let out a sigh. "So there you have it. Ivie's under a spell, her father's up to something, and Jack broke off the engagement because she kissed Liam."

"That's quite a predicament to be in." He nodded, eyeing me as if I might turn him into a skunk or something. And in truth, I could do it if I wanted to. I'd gotten much better at controlling the magic. "I've got to play another set here any minute now, so you girls order a drink on me, sit back, and enjoy the show." He patted my hand then scraped his chair across the old pine floorboards as he got up. "As soon as I'm finished, I'll do what I can to fix you right up."

"A love spell, huh? That's serious business." We sat in the back of the bar, and Daddy Whatnot gulped down his second Lemon Drop in a row.

"Can you fix it?" Chloe asked.

"I can try." Daddy Whatnot laughed and looked me, his expression turning serious. "But I have to ask: are you sure you're not just conflicted about your feelings for the younger Blake?"

I stared into his chocolate eyes. "I'm not conflicted. I love Jack."

"Okay, then." The teddy bear of a man stood and reached his hand toward me. "Let's see what's goin' on in that head of yours, shall we?"

He led us through the back and down a quiet hallway to an unmarked door. He didn't say a word as he worked the lock and pushed the door open, motioning for me to go in ahead of him.

The room was barely big enough for the three of us to squeeze in and shut the door behind us. The smell of cigars and stale beer hit me right away. I also detected a hint of something sugary sweet—cherries maybe—but I couldn't quite make it out.

"Okay, *cher.* You get comfy on the sofa. I'm gonna grab something really quick." The voodoo priest disappeared into the hallway we'd just come from, while I eyed the rust-colored upholstery, searching for recognizable stains. I tried not to imagine the assortment of bodily fluids that might or might not have soaked into the heavy tapestry fabric over the years.

Daddy Whatnot wedged himself back into the space, carrying a worn leather bag in his arms like a baby. One of the handles had rotted clean through and hung loosely to the side, while the other appeared almost new. "Go on now. Lie down, and stretch out like a cat ready for a nap in the sun."

The image of a raggedy black cat flickered in my head before being replaced by my dad. Had he really done something to me to draw me to Liam? Could I forgive him if he had?

I slipped out of my sandals and eased back onto the sofa until my head nestled against one end and my toes brushed the other. The scratchy fabric rasped over my bare arms, and I tensed. "What now?"

"Now you relax and let Daddy do the rest." He smiled down at me, his lips vanishing under his heavy beard as he showed his teeth. "Close your eyes, and count sheep or something."

Chloe snorted out a laugh. "Count goats."

"Am I supposed to fall asleep or something?" I glared at her.

"Nah, nothing like that. But you're wound up tighter than a virgin on prom night." He squeezed my shoulders in his giant hands and spoke to me as if I were a small child about to face a firing squad. "Come on now, you need to uncurl those pretty pink toes of yours. And relax your fingers before they break off. I promise, I don't bite, not unless you ask real nice." He chuckled again.

I tried to follow his instructions, closing my eyes and counting fluffy white bunnies as they jumped out of a magician's hat behind my eyelids while Daddy Whatnot shook what sounded like salt into a circle around me. I heard the distinct sound of a match as it scraped the side of a box and ignited, leaving the biting scent of sulfur in the air.

The air around me shifted, and I flinched.

"Now don't be so jumpy. I'm just gonna light a few candles so we can get started," he whispered, and even the soft sound sent chills through me.

The hair on my arms rose up to meet his outstretched hands as Daddy Whatnot passed them over me. He never once touched me, but I felt the heat and electricity coming off his skin.

The temperature in the small room dipped as he chanted something under his breath. Goosebumps erupted over my exposed flesh. He passed his hands over me again, and it was as if giant magnets pulled at the life force inside me, drawing answers out through my pores.

Chloe muttered something, but he hushed her, and she immediately quieted. He raised his voice, and at the same time, his hands moved faster over me, not touching but still drawing strength from within me. The tugging grew stronger, almost like cramps spreading through my entire body. He whispered curses under his breath, and his large hands captured my face.

He was so close, his lemony breath swept over my lips as if he were about to kiss me. The kiss never came, but the unbearable urge to squirm fought to break free as he held me still. My eyes snapped open.

Daddy Whatnot hovered over me, steam oozing from his sweaty skin and his face so close it blurred out of view. "Someone's gone and put a binding spell on you, *cher*." I sucked in a quick breath, and he released me, hopping up like a jack-in-the-box and taking the other chair.

Chloe found her voice first. "A binding spell?"

"Nasty things, those binding spells. Powerful magic. But it would seem they missed a step, or maybe..." Daddy Whatnot struggled to catch his breath, using the front of his shirt to mop his face as he studied me from his chair. "Maybe something *else* got in the way. If they'd managed to complete the spell, you'd have no desire to be free of it. I'd say that makes you one of the lucky ones."

"Lucky ones?" I shook my head and forced a laugh. *Lucky my fiancé dumped me? Lucky I couldn't control my feelings?* I didn't consider it to be *lucky* at all.

"Sure. It's not too late for the spell to be broken."

Hope blossomed in my chest. "Can you break it?"

"Who, me?" Daddy Whatnot leaned back in his chair and crossed his feet at his ankles. "Nah, I'm afraid that's above my pay grade, *cher*. A binding spell can only be broken by the one who placed it."

Chapter 13

AN HOUR LATER, CHLOE AND I sped through the pitch-black night on our way back home. We'd barely spoken a word since leaving the blues bar. I didn't know about her, but I was numb, operating on autopilot. I had no other explanation as to why my heart continued to beat in a perfect rhythm or why my lungs sucked in breath after breath.

I'd been in shock ever since Daddy Whatnot had explained the principles of the binding spell as he understood them. I was no expert, but it sounded a whole hell of a lot like the magical convergence Jack and I had attempted that first night in the woods, the night he'd tried to convince me he—a total stranger—was the answer to all my magical prayers. I'd long since forgiven his deception, but looking back, it would seem we'd created more than one kind of magic that night. And since neither Jack nor I had known what we were doing, reversing the spell would be next to impossible.

Unfortunately, the witch doctor agreed.

Imagining my life without Jack in it made me physically ill. I loved Jack with every fiber in my being, but how much was real, and how much was the spell? And what about his feelings for me?

As the significance of that revelation sank in, tiny tremors of guilt danced down my spine. I had no idea how my life had spun so spectacularly out of control. Just a few weeks ago, I had been madly in love and planning a wedding. Now I had to figure out what my next step would be and how to remove whatever magic had inextricably linked me to not one but two men.

The threat of fresh tears burned behind my eyes. "How am I going to explain this to Jack? He'll never forgive me."

Chloe opened her mouth then clamped her lips together and shook her head. That was the closest thing to an answer I'd gotten from her since we'd left the voodoo priest.

"I wish I could pretend I didn't know." I turned to stare into the darkness outside my window, watching shadowy trees whip by in a blur. "I wish I could just have Liam's spell removed and go back to being happy with Jack. But I can't. Even if I never told him, *I'd* know. And I know him, Chloe. If I tell him about the spell, he'll end things. He *hates* magic now." *He hates me.* "He won't want anything to do with me when he realizes I accidentally bound him to me."

"Hey." Chloe broke her silence. "Don't forget there were two of you out in the woods that night. If you *did* bind yourself to Jack, he helped. In fact, it was his idea, as I recall."

She had a point. Jack *had* suggested the magical convergence in the first place. But at the time, all he wanted was an excuse to see me in my underwear—and out of my underwear. And dear God, that'd worked out spectacularly too. "It-it was an accident."

"Accidents happen, sometimes even happy accidents. You and Jack could live happily ever after if you would just accept that your love started out as a minor case of magic gone wrong."

I spun in my seat to face her, nearly strangling myself on the seatbelt. "I can't do that! How would you feel if you found out Jon only married you because of magic? Could you live with that?"

Chloe's grip tightened on the steering wheel until her knuckles went white. "I guess not."

"You know what the worst part of this is?" I sniffled.

She shook her head before whispering, "What?"

"I have like seven texts and twice as many missed calls from Jack." I scrolled through the messages on my phone, alternating between staring at Jack's handsome face smiling up at me from the display and reading his heart-wrenching pleas.

"How's that the worst part?"

"He says he believes me about the spell." I choked back a sob. "And that he's sorry. God, he's begging me to forgive him because he has no idea he only loves me because I somehow hocus-pocused him into a relationship."

Chloe scoffed. "You don't know that for certain."

"You heard what Daddy Whatnot said. That has to be why the second binding spell wasn't completed. The first spell wasn't finished because we didn't know what we were doing, and the second one was left open because of the first. So there's a distinct possibility that I'll spend the rest of my life trying to decide which one I want more."

Chloe's mouth dropped open. "You still can't decide?"

"It's complicated." More so since I realized the magnitude of the situation.

My phone buzzed in my hand as the first chords of "Magic Man" played.

"Jack?"

I nodded.

"Well, go on! Answer it."

I shook my head, staring at Jack's smiling image on the display. "I have no idea what to say."

"How about, 'I need more time'?" A sad smile curved her lips. "At least text him. He's probably going out of his mind."

"You're right." I keyed out a quick text letting him know where we were and when we expected to be back then powered my phone down and tucked it into my pocket. "I'm not ready to talk to him yet. It's all too much at once."

With Jack, Liam, and the whole thing with my dad, it was no wonder I was overwhelmed.

For several long minutes, the roar of the engine and the rushing wind were the only sounds inside the car. Then Chloe cleared her throat. "You know, maybe you're looking at this the wrong way."

"What do you mean?" She had my undivided attention.

"I mean, you need to approach the problem from a different direction, you know, like that old saying about eating an elephant."

"I have no idea what you're talking about. What does my love life have to do with eating an elephant?"

I couldn't see her eyes, but I'd known her long enough to know she'd rolled them. "No, no. Listen. It goes like this: how do you eat an elephant?"

"Fine, I'll bite." I blew out a breath. "How *do* you eat an elephant?"

Chloe laughed. "That's exactly it! You eat it one *bite* at a time. You need to tackle your problem the same way. You need to start at the end and work your way backward. Solve what's going on with your dad, get him to remove the spell with Liam, then you can figure out what's going on between you and Jack. If you can fix the one, the other may just fall into place."

The beginnings of a smile tugged at my lips. "I know I'll regret saying this, but Chloe, you might actually be a genius."

"I think I might be." She beamed. "So since you can't fight two wars at once, no talking to Jack until you figure out what's going on on the other battlefield."

"Sounds like a good strategy to me."

Game on!

We pulled into Chloe's driveway just after two in the morning, and I dragged my frazzled carcass from the car with one goal in mind: sleep. I wanted nothing more than to collapse into Chloe's guest bed and sleep. For as long as she'd let me.

"Ivie!" The hair on the back of my neck stood on end as a disheveled Jack hopped up from the front steps and practically ran to my side.

"Jack." Seeing him again make my insides flutter. His calloused fingers brushed my cheek, and my pulse jumped. "Wh-what are you doing here?"

He rested his forehead against mine, and his warm breath caressed my face. "I missed you, sweetheart."

So much for battle strategies. I melted into Jack's arms, sucking in a greedy lungful of sweet hay and mint soap. His scent was nearly my undoing. The inexplicable draw I felt toward him erased every worry lodged in my short-circuiting brain. "I've missed you too."

"Hey, um, I'm gonna head inside. You know where I am if you need anything." Chloe slipped past us and into the house, taking her brilliant plan with her.

"Thanks, Chloe," Jack said over my shoulder before turning his full attention back to me. "I've been a complete ass. I went to see your father and—"

"Wait. What?" I froze and pulled my lips from his throat. The butterflies in my stomach took off and left a churning mess in their wake. "You went to see my dad?"

He coiled a lock of my hair around his finger and used it to tug my face back to his. "I had to find out if you were right, if he'd actually do *that* to his own daughter."

I untangled my hair from his hand and stepped back. The mention of my dad brought me back to the present. "By *that*, you mean the spell?"

He nodded and gave me a sheepish grin.

"So you didn't believe me until my dad confirmed it?" My temper spiked, and I took another step away from him, watching his face as the weight of my accusation hit him.

"No." His eyebrows knitted together, and he shook his head. "No, Ivie, that's not at all what happened."

I crossed my arms and waited. *Let's see him dig himself out of this one.*

"Your dad told me I was being ridiculous. He said he'd never do something like that to you. Basically, he told me you'd fallen for Liam because you could be yourself with him. And I've gotta tell you, that hurt." Jack flexed his fingers as if he wanted to reach for me, but he tightened them into a fist and dropped his hand to his side.

I let out a breath, my shoulders deflating. How could I be mad at him for not believing me when the truth was so ridiculous that I didn't believe it myself? "Jack."

"No, wait. Don't you see? Your dad was right. I haven't been fair to you. At all. Magic is part of who you are, and I've been such a dick about making you give that up." He took a step in my direction, his eyes pleading with me. "Sweetheart, I love you. Every part of you. And if that means your hair turns red or your sex drive cranks up a notch, I'll have to learn to live with it. Honestly, there are worse things in life than having a wife with a ridiculously high sex drive." His smile lit up the night.

My head spun from information overload. Nothing made sense anymore. "I don't understand. How did that revelation make you suddenly believe me about the spell?"

He moved closer, reaching his hand out to cup my face. "Because you've always been honest with me. You've never held any part of yourself back, and I was stupid to think you would start now. Whatever's going on with you started the day you went to the lab to help your dad with that damn spell. It has to be the reason for all the craziness. I don't know what happened, but I know you haven't been acting like *you*. And magic is the only explanation I can come up with that makes any sense. I'm so sorry I didn't believe you when you first told me."

Jack leaned in for a kiss, but I backed away, shaking my head.

"Ivie?" A whisper of pain etched across his face, and I would have done almost anything to erase it.

I covered my face with my hands. The one thing he needed right then was the one thing I couldn't, in good conscience, give him. *Why couldn't things be easy? Why couldn't everything go back to the way it was?* "Please don't look at me like that. This is way more complicated than you realize."

"Ivie?" The soft, lilting voice startled me, and I spun away from Jack to gawk at Liam's smug grin.

My already-churning insides twisted into a pretzel, making me suck in a sharp breath. "What are you doing here?"

"I've missed you." His words echoed Jack's, and the feeling of *déjà vu* hit me like a pair of Louboutins to the skull.

"You..." An uninvited zing ripped through me, and I fought back the urge to move toward him. Something was seriously wrong with me. It was as if Liam was the Death Star, and he'd caught me in his tractor beam. "*You're* not supposed to miss me."

"I completely agree." Liam ignored the dangerous expression on Jack's face and stepped between us. "You should never be so far away from me."

I took a quick step back, tripping on one of Chloe's stepping-stones. Both Liam and Jack reached out to catch me. "Stop! Both of you, please." I steadied myself then pressed my fingers into my temples to force back the impending headache. They had me so confused. Tough decisions had never been my forte.

Jack growled on my left side, and on the right, Liam scoffed.

"Can't you see Ivie and I are meant for each other?" Even though he'd directed them at Jack, Liam's words sliced through me. "She should be with someone who embraces who she really is, not someone she has to hide that side of herself from."

"Ivie knows she doesn't have to hide herself from me." Jack shouldered Liam out of the way to take my left hand.

He seemed buoyed by the sparkling diamond on my ring finger.

"Things have changed." Liam turned to me and raised an eyebrow as if waiting for me to say something.

I darted my eyes from Liam to Jack then back again. "What?"

Liam flashed a shy smile. Even the darkness couldn't hide the pink tint staining his cheeks. "Well, after last night, I sort of expected you to agree with me."

"Last night?" Jack dropped my hand and stepped back. It was as if the three of us were working out a new dance—an angry tango, by the looks of it. "What happened last night?"

I glanced at Liam and wanted to slap the smirk from his lips. "*Nothing* happened."

"Then what the hell is he talking about? And don't fucking lie to me. Did you...?" Jack reached up and grabbed a fistful of his own hair, his voice ratcheting up an octave as he paced the lawn. "Did you sleep with him last night?" The way he said *sleep* told me that wasn't his first choice of words.

"No! God, no, of course not. You can ask Chloe. I was here all night long. Alone!" I glared at Liam, but he'd locked his icy-blue eyes on me as though he could see straight into my soul. His lips curved up at the corners in a knowing smile, and the bottom fell out of my stomach. "Oh, my God." I threw up my hands and paced in a small circle. "It was a *dream!*"

"You dreamed about having sex with him?" Jack shouted, and I wasn't sure what made me more anxious, the anger in his voice or his horrified expression.

"It wasn't my fault! It's the spell!" I shrieked back then turned to Liam. "How did you even *know* about that?"

Liam shrugged, his smug smile cracking his face in two.

Jack stormed over to his silver SUV and climbed in, slamming the door behind him, only to get out again a few seconds later. The wild look in his eyes as he approached Liam made my stomach bottom out.

He jammed a finger into Liam's chest. "Who the hell are you? Where did you come from? Why did you have to come here?"

"Who I am and where I come from is none of your concern. Why I'm here is the only thing that matters."

"Then enlighten me." Jack threw up his arms. "Why *are* you here?"

"I thought that was obvious." Liam's eyes zeroed in on mine, holding me hostage in their icy-blue depths. "I'm here for Ivie."

Jack's teeth clenched so hard I was sure they'd shatter. "Ivie doesn't want you."

Liam chuckled. "I think it's pretty obvious she does if she's having dreams like the one last night."

I flinched at his accusation.

Jack's hand tightened into a fist an instant before he threw his arm forward and punched Liam square in the jaw. Liam's dark head snapped back, but before Jack could get another punch in, Liam disappeared, reappearing behind him. *How does he* do *that?*

"Jack!" I tried to warn him before Liam sucker-punched him in the kidney, dropping Jack to his knees. Red-hot fury tinged the air, and heat blew my hair back as if I'd stoked a raging fire within me. I felt the magic resting like a hard ball in the pit of my stomach, just waiting for me to wield it. I'd never felt so in control of my own powers before. "Stop! Both of you."

Liam must have felt it too. He held perfectly still, his hands squeezed into tight fists at his sides. With the faintest of nods, he flexed his fingers and pointed at Jack, jutting out his chin like a petulant child. "He started it."

I almost laughed at him before reminding myself that same *nonchild* had repeatedly used magic to get into my head and would likely do it again anytime it suited him.

The air whooshed out of my lungs like a tire running over the mother of all spikes. Exhaustion had finally caught up to me. "Go home, Liam."

His face registered shock. "You want *me* to leave?"

"Yes, please."

"Fine. Since it's late and you look ready to drop, I'll go. But I'm not giving up on you, Ivie." Liam glanced at my lips, and I knew he wanted to kiss me, but I wasn't about to give in this time. "I'll call you tomorrow."

I wanted to say, "Please don't," but instead, I nodded and avoided eye contact until he was safely ensconced in his rented sports car and driving away.

Jack slid his eyes in my direction and sucked in a breath. Pain twisted his features, and I doubted it had anything to do with the hit he'd taken. "How upset would you be if I killed that guy?"

My mouth opened and closed like a fish on the deck of a boat. We both knew Jack didn't stand a chance against Liam's advanced sorcery skills. "Please don't kill him. I-I can't afford bail."

Jack threw his head back and laughed, but as soon as the sound died down, his teeth came together with a snap, and the muscle in his jaw flexed. He pulled himself to his feet and turned to me, pleading with his eyes. "Come home with me, Ivie. Please."

"Jack..." I closed my eyes and took a deep breath before opening them again. I wanted to. I really did. But if Daddy Whatnot's suspicions were true...

He didn't wait for me to find the words before nodding. "You can't."

"I can't."

He reached a hand toward me but curled his fingers into his palm at the last second and dropped it to his side. "Will you tell me why?"

"As soon as I have everything figured out, yes." Though even I didn't have a clue how long that would take.

With another nod, he pressed his lips to my temple as if he could somehow fuse us together that way. I felt rather than heard his words. "Take care of yourself, Ivie."

The hollow expression in his eyes gutted me, and hot tears rolled down my cheeks before I could stop them. "Jack, wait."

"You know where to find me." He didn't turn around once as he stalked to his car and backed onto the quiet street. Then he was gone.

Chapter 14

FTER ADJUSTING MY PILLOW FOR the umpteenth time, I rolled over to stare toward the window. The first few rays of morning light filtered through the cracks in the blinds, and I grabbed my phone from the nightstand to check the time.

Only six fifty-two and already three new texts from Jack.

Excitement faded into dread as my finger hovered over the first message. Was I ready to read what he had to say? I'd already spent most of the night tossing and turning, unable to fall asleep for more than a few minutes at a time. My overworked brain wouldn't shut off. Images of Liam and Jack fighting over me plagued my subconscious. If push came to sorcery, Liam would destroy Jack. And I couldn't allow that to happen.

I needed to fix things before talking to Jack. And by *fix things*, I meant confronting my dad. I shoved my phone under the pillow and buried my face in the lofty goose down with a groan. The absolute last thing I wanted was to see my father, but deep down in the pit of my stomach, I knew the voodoo priest was right. Dad was at the center of the binding spell, and I had no choice but to confront him if I ever wanted to be free of Liam's hold.

I rolled out of bed and made my way to the bathroom to shower and get dressed, mentally preparing myself for what I had to do next.

What if Dad refused to remove the spell? Would he force me into some kind of magical showdown to get what

I wanted? And after everything was said and done, would Jack even want me?

My phone pinged with another incoming text from Jack. *He still wants me.*

Once I'd tamed the wild mess of red hair sprouting out of my head and dressed in something befitting a mediocre sorceress—a pair of black Rag and Bone skinny jeans paired with a black-and-gray silk tank—I set out to find Chloe's keys, hoping she wouldn't hate me for stealing her car.

"If you're looking for condoms, I keep them in the kitchen. In the flour canister."

I picked up my head to gape at Chloe. She'd staggered out of her room wearing nothing but a loose-fitting Viva Las Vegas T-shirt with her usually-coiffed blond hair swirled around her head in a wild nest. "The flour canister?"

"Well, I used to keep them in my *Hello Kitty* lunch box, but my mother found them, and that was just..." She sounded as if she were caught somewhere between choking and laughing. "And really, like my mom would ever bake?"

I gave her a quick once-over then went back to pawing through her Gucci bag. "So you're up early."

"I heard noises." She yawned behind her hand. "I'm glad it's just you looking for... breath mints?"

"Who else would it be? And no, my breath is fine."

"I don't keep money in my purse. And lately, it could have been just about anyone. I was almost certain I'd have to kick a sexy sorcerer in the balls with my bare feet." She shuddered. "Definitely not something I wanna do before breakfast."

"Well, you're in luck." I fished out her keys with a triumphant smile. "No sorcerers here this morning. Your foot is safe."

She nodded and made her way to the kitchen. She opened the fridge, and the top half of her body disappeared inside. "So why are you stealing my car?"

"I'm going to kick a sorcerer in the balls for breakfast."

My mom's Wagoneer wasn't in the driveway when I pulled in, but a familiar shiny black Suburban with dark-tinted windows occupied her spot. I slid Chloe's sleek rental into the spot beside the hulking Chevy and climbed out. Chloe's keys sat heavy in my hand as I practically vibrated with the urge scrape them over the pretty paint job.

"I trust you weren't plotting the destruction of government property, Miss McKie." Agent Smith-err-Hunter's smooth baritone caught me off guard, and the keys slipped out of my hand, hitting the pavement with a clank.

I scooped them from the driveway and spun to face him in all his inhuman glory. "What are you doing here?"

Hunter flashed a frosty smile. "My job."

I smashed my hands against my hips. "You mean harassing citizens? Good to know my tax dollars are well spent."

"*Your* tax dollars? Didn't I hear you were unemployed?"

Hunter's strawberry-blond partner, Agent Corrigan, stepped forward. "Yes, fired for destruction of private property, wasn't it? Your track record is quite impressive for such a tiny little thing."

Tiny little thing?

A burst of adrenaline spiked, and I shoved back the magic rising in me.

"As I recall, Bonnie Parker was a tiny little thing too." Agent Hunter stepped forward and pinched a lock of my hair between his fingers. "Though, based on the photos I've seen, she wasn't as pretty as you."

I shook my head until my hair fell from his fingers then backed up. "You never answered my question. Why are you here?"

"We haven't completed our investigation, though we've uncovered some intriguing new information."

I was dying to ask, but Hunter's smirk told me he was baiting me, so I kept my lips zipped. "That's nice for you. If you'll excuse me, I need to see my father." I sidestepped the men in black and made it halfway to the front door when Hunter's vibrating monotone froze me in place.

"If you're looking for Mr. McDougall, he isn't here."

I whipped around to face him, confusion lacing my voice. "Mr. McDougall?"

"Liam?" Corrigan bit back a grin. He was definitely the more animated of the two.

"W-why would I be looking for Liam?" *And why didn't I remember his last name was McDougall?*

The two agents volleyed looks between them, but Hunter kept his expression flat as he inched his way toward me. The man must have been an amazing poker player. "I couldn't help noticing the two of you have a tendency to gravitate toward one another."

"You couldn't help noticing?" I moved within striking distance, squeezing my hands into tight fists at my sides as heat licked at my palms and electricity raced to my fingertips. "We've met once. Liam happened to be here. That's hardly a pattern."

"I'm referring to his presence at the school the day you were fired, not to mention your joint trip to the bridal salon and your heated debate last evening in front of Mrs. Blake's house, in addition to the times we've already discussed." *Point to Hunter.*

My face went up in flames at the same time an icy chill zipped down my spine. "You were *spying* on me?"

"Not spying," Corrigan said with a straight face. "Investigating."

"Why are you investigating *me*?" My voice climbed an octave, and I fought to get my emotions under control. The last thing I needed was to turn the two of them into lab rats. *Then again...*

"Because I find you fascinating. First, you're accused of killing a fiancé who miraculously reappears just as the authorities are about to arrest you. Then you turn up like a terrorist in the middle of a series of unfortunate explosions you claim to have no connection to. You're a chameleon..." Hunter drew me in, flicking at my hair again as he circled me like a spider in a web. "A siren with two markedly different men hanging on your every move. You take day trips to visit voodoo priests in the mountains. Disaster after disaster follows in your wake, and yet here you are, miraculously unscathed." His teeth came together with a crack as his unflappable mask split down the middle, allowing his pent-up resentment to show through. "I know you're hiding something, Miss McKie. And I'm going to get to the bottom of it if it kills me."

I flinched away from him, backing slowly toward the door. "I-I don't know what you're talking about. I'm not a terrorist! I'm a kindergarten teacher—*was* a kindergarten teacher." I tripped over a crack in the sidewalk, and when I looked up, Hunter's smirk was back.

"You can run, Ivie. But you can't hide. I'll be watching you."

I turned around and ran the rest of the way to my parents' front door, closing and locking it behind me. I watched through the peephole until Smith and Wesson backed out of the driveway and disappeared around the corner.

"What on earth are you doing?"

"Gah!" A scream ripped out of my throat, and I spun around, ready to lash out at... *my mother.*

"Ivie? Are you okay, dear?"

"Don't scare me like that! Don't you know what I can do? I'm a horrible witch with absolutely no self-control!" My heart pounded like a scared rabbit's, and I slammed my back against the door, sliding down until I sat cross-legged on the floor. "I didn't think you were home. Your car isn't in the driveway."

"It's parked in the garage. I finally convinced your father to clear out those old boxes of his. Almost everything ended up at Goodwill. Even the things that fit him were out of style. Can you believe he still had that dusty-blue, disco-era jumpsuit? It had bell bottoms and zipped from the crotch to the scooped neck. If memory serves, he wore platform shoes and a hideous brown-and-cream paisley shirt with it."

"No! Not Dad."

"Yes! He actually wanted to *keep* that. The one bright spot after being a domestic pet for so long was his lack of weight gain over the years. He could still fit into most of his old clothes. But I wouldn't even consider allowing him to donate *that* one. I was too afraid he'd go back and buy it all over again."

"What'd you do with it?"

She bit the insides of her cheeks to keep a straight face. "Burned it in the back yard."

Laughing helped ease my pulse back toward normal. Then I remembered why I'd gotten upset to begin with. "What were the Men in Black doing here?"

Her casual facade cracked. "You mean Agents Hunter and Corrigan?"

I nodded.

Mom couldn't look me in the eye, which meant whatever had gone down before I showed up wasn't good. "They were here to see your father."

"Insurance fraud?" The words turned to dust in my mouth. I don't know why I thought the whole thing would go away after I'd mind-tricked the agents at our last meeting. My luck didn't work like that.

"Among other things. Oh, Ivie. I have no idea what your father's gotten himself into. He asked me to leave the room while they were here, but of course, I listened at the door. I didn't hear everything they were saying, but I heard enough. And whatever no-good he's up to, he's managed to drag you into it. You and that apprentice of his."

Color me shocked. Not. I was beginning to realize that, like my dad, Liam always seemed to wind up at the center of everything.

"That's why I'm here, actually. I need to talk to Dad about Liam."

If Mom knew what I was referring to, she didn't let on. She flashed an easy smile. "Okay, dear. He's in the basement. Would you like me to go get him for you?"

I gave her a hug. "No. I'll go down. I need to talk to him in private anyway."

"That's a good idea." She pressed her lips together and stepped away. "I'll be in the kitchen, whipping something up for lunch."

I stole a glance at the clock. *Ten fifteen.* "Isn't it a bit early for lunch?"

She waved my comment away like dust motes in the air. "Lunchtime comes early in the McKie household. You should know that."

With one last furtive peek at my mother, I headed down the dark basement stairs.

I found my dad tinkering in the spell room. Before discovering the room had been hidden by a concealment spell my entire life, I'd been terrified of the dark corners and thick cobwebs. Now I saw it for what it really was, a sunny room filled with jars of potions and nectars.

Dad stood at the window, watering the neat row of potted herbs lined up along the sill. Beside him, the counter was filled with snippets of dried plants, and a yellowed sheet of parchment lay open. I stepped closer, trying to read the words scrawled across it.

"It's not polite to sneak up on people, you know." Dad's back stiffened as he paused in his task, but he didn't turn around.

I cleared my throat. "Sorry. I, uh, didn't want to disturb you."

"Yes, you did. You came down here with the express purpose of disturbing me." He placed the watering can in the sink and wiped his hand on a towel before turning and giving me a warm smile. "Otherwise, you would have stayed upstairs with your mother."

I crossed the small space and leaned against the counter. I didn't have it in me to beat around the bush, so I got straight to the point. "What did the FBI want?"

He chuckled and went back to his recipe. "Don't you worry about them. I can handle those two bumbling idiots. Now, do your dad a favor and hand me the black salt."

I searched the shelf until I found the jar filled with what looked like granulated ash. "What's this for?"

Dad took the bottle from my hand and waved me off. "Never you mind about that. Some things are best left to the seasoned professional."

I gasped as his off-hand comment tripped my defenses and glared at the back of his head while I pulled my thoughts together. "Oh, you mean like *binding* spells?"

He fumbled the bottle, spilling about a teaspoon's worth of black salt onto the polished wood floor. He swiped at it with his foot, focusing his attention on anything but me. "What do you know about binding spells?"

"Well, thanks to Daddy Whatnot, Chloe's witch doctor friend, I—"

"Jack, now isn't the best time to speak with Angus. He's in the middle of—" Mom's frantic voice came from the top of the stairs just before Jack bounded down the steps.

"Unless he's in the middle of a coma, he's going to hear what I have to say." He came to a screeching halt directly in front of me, and the air whooshed out of his lungs. "Ivie."

"Jack." I tucked my arms around my middle to keep myself from wrapping them around him.

"What can I do for you, Jack?" My father stepped around me. He looked relieved to have a distraction from our conversation.

Jack's nostrils flared as he came toe to toe with my dad. "You can remove the fucking binding spell you put on Ivie."

The relief drained from my father's face, along with every drop of color.

"Yeah, that's right. I know about the binding spell. I haven't figured out your reasons yet, but I know you want Ivie with Liam. And I'm here to tell you, that'll only happen over my dead body."

"I'm fine with that." Liam danced down the steps with my mother close on his heels.

"I'm sorry, dear. He just *popped* in." She snapped her fingers, and I knew she meant he'd apparated into the house—a trick I still hadn't figured out.

"It's okay, Mom. Liam isn't planning on staying."

"I'm staying as long as he's here." He nodded toward Jack.

"I'll give the three of you some privacy." Dad hurried past Jack and Liam. "Rose, I need to have a word."

My parents disappeared up the stairs, leaving me alone with Jack and Liam. Their mutual rage vibrated like a living being.

"Did you know?" Jack ground out the words directed at Liam.

Liam crossed his arms and raised an eyebrow. "I know a lot of things. You'll have to be more specific."

Jack let out a growl. "Did you know about the binding spell?"

Liam grinned, and I took that as confirmation.

"You knew?" Betrayal burned my throat.

The grin slid off his face, and he turned to me. "You don't understand what's at stake here, Ivie." He threw a heated glance toward Jack. "And you don't know what the *magician* is capable of."

"What *I'm* capable of?"

"Liam, I think you're confused." I laid my hand on his arm and tilted my head to gaze into his eyes. "Jack's a veterinarian."

"Jack's a lying son of a goat."

"Who's calling who a liar? You've done nothing but lie to her since you got here." Jack shoved Liam toward the steps. "Taking advantage of her weakness after doing magic... Pushing your way into her dreams..."

"Ah, and what wonderful dreams she has," Liam purred as his eyes practically licked my body from top to bottom.

The muscle in Jack's jaw ticked right before he reached out, taking me by surprise and wrapping an arm around my waist to pull me against him. He spoke to Liam, but his eyes never left mine. "I hate to tell you, buddy, but even the best dreams come a sad second to reality." He had me caught in his net as he bent down and pressed his lips to mine.

"You. Know. Nothing!" Liam bellowed so loud the jars along the wall trembled, clanking into each other. "I reside within her. With every breath she takes, I'm there, under her skin. No matter where she is, or what she's doing, I feel her. You may have had her body—though I shared every touch, every glance while you did—but her soul is mine."

Chapter 15

"**Y**OU SONOFABITCH." JACK STALKED TOWARD Liam, hands balled into tight fists at his sides.

Before my brain even registered what was happening, he'd shifted his weight from one foot to the other and thrown a fist toward Liam's face—or rather where he'd last seen Liam's face. Liam disapparated before Jack's arm completed the full motion, making Jack stumble over his own feet.

"What the hell?" Somehow, he managed to catch himself before falling, but Liam reappeared in front of him, taking advantage of Jack's disorientation by sucker-punching him in the gut. Jack doubled over, going down like a ton of bricks.

"Jack!" I rushed to his side, but he waved me off, coughing and sputtering for me to get out of his way.

Jack staggered toward Liam again. "Stand still, you fucking wizard."

"Sorcerer," Liam taunted.

"Liam, don't." I shoved Liam from behind, but he ignored me and went after Jack. "Leave him alone!"

Jack brought his fist up again, throwing all his weight into an uppercut that never connected. Liam disappeared then reappeared an instant later, punching Jack square in the face.

I screamed, and my hands flew up to cover my mouth. Even the ringing in my ears couldn't block out the sickening sound of bones cracking as Liam's fist connected with Jack's cheek.

I tried to reach Jack before he hit the floor, but without Liam's vanishing trick, it was hopeless. Jack slumped to the ground in a heap, barely conscious with blood oozing from a cut below his eye.

"Look what you've done!" I yelled at Liam, and a loud pop sounded from inside me as fury bubbled over, and the magic blew out like a backdraft, shattering glass all around us.

My parents came flying down the stairs as if the house were on fire. And maybe it was. I didn't notice anything outside my little field of view.

"Ivie!" My mother grabbed a damp rag from the sink before dropping to her knees beside me. "What's going on? What happened? Why is Jack bleeding?"

"They fought... and Liam. Too fast." Sobs choked me as I cleaned Jack's cut. I stared up at my father through the blur of tears. "Will he be okay?"

"I'll take care of it." Liam bent down toward Jack.

I flinched away from him, covering Jack's body with mine. "Haven't you done enough?"

"Please let me help, Ivie." Liam held out his hand again, and I didn't know why, but I took it, letting him pull me to my feet. He took my place beside Jack, laying his hands along Jack's face as he spoke words I couldn't comprehend. Less than a minute later, Jack pulled away from Liam and hauled himself to his feet.

We all stood frozen in place as my mother crossed the room with a purpose and shoved a finger into my father's chest. "Angus Donald McKie, I'm only going to say this once. It's time for the secrets and lies to end. This has gone on long enough. You need to tell her the truth." Mom gave him one last jab then planted her hands on her hips. She glowered at Dad for a long moment before shifting her focus to me and flashing a sad smile. "For my part in this, I'm sorry."

"Mom?"

"Come on, boys. We need to leave them alone to talk." She didn't leave a whisper of room for argument in her tone, and both Jack and Liam nodded, following her up the stairs.

Liam was gone before I'd reached the top. And when I reached for Jack, he shook me off.

"Jack... I'm so sorry."

"Talk to your dad, sweetheart." He flashed a sad smile. "I'll call you later."

Mom pulled me in for a quick hug then patted my cheek but didn't say another word before turning and walking out the front door behind Jack.

As soon as they were gone, I wheeled on Dad. "What did she mean by, 'it's time for the secrets and lies to end'? Aside from the binding spell, what *other* secrets have you been keeping from me?"

My father pulled out a dining room chair and waved me over, his face a mask of grim determination. "Sit down, Ivie."

I crossed my arms and turned my back on him. "I think I'd rather stand."

"I *said*..." My father's tone went from pleading to exasperated in a flash. "Sit. Down!" He scraped a dining chair across the floor with a loud screech.

Like a mindless robot, I followed his instruction, closing the distance between us and sitting in the chair he held out for me. Dad waited for me to get situated before taking his seat and folding his hands in front of him. The fourth finger on his left hand bulged around his plain gold wedding band, and I wanted to reposition it for him. It looked uncomfortable.

He caught me staring and shifted his hands. He studied me across the table for a long moment before speaking. "I know you're angry with me, and I don't blame you. I haven't exactly been forthcoming with information as of late."

I opened my mouth to wholeheartedly agree, but he held up a hand to stop me.

"Believe me, I've had my reasons, flawed as they may be." He pressed out a remorseful smile, and I noticed a new crop of wrinkles forming around the edges of his mouth. "But your mother's right. You're a grown woman, and you deserve the truth."

My fingers tingled, and my leg bounced under the table as pent-up energy fought to break free. Wanting to know the truth and actually listening to his confession were two different things. I wasn't sure I was ready to hear what he had to say.

"Where shall I begin?" Dad tapped a finger against his lips in a nervous habit I recognized all too well.

I cocked an eyebrow and leaned forward, resting my bare forearms against the cool table as I stared into his seaweed-green eyes as if I could pull the information out of their murky depths. "Why don't you start with the spell?"

"Ah, yes. The spell." He chuckled. "I should have known you would figure that out. You were always an incredibly bright girl. But I admit, I never expected you to seek out a shaman. Our kinds don't normally run in the same circles."

"Come on, Dad. Can we try to stay on task here?"

"Of course. Sorry." He didn't look a bit sorry. His eyes danced with amusement, as if he took some sick pleasure in dragging this out. And if I wasn't mistaken, a little spark of pride glowed in there as well.

"Why would you put a love spell on me, binding me to someone else, when you knew how I felt about Jack?" Even thinking about Jack made my heart break all over again. What if it was too late to remove the spell? What if I was doomed to spend the rest of my life in love with two different men but unable to commit to either? My insides twisted into painful knots.

"Why? Well, that's the most difficult question to answer sometimes, isn't it? Why do any of us do the things we do? Why does your mother put up with me after all these years and all the trouble I've brought her? Why do you continue to dabble in magic when you're unwilling to take the time to truly learn your craft?" He held my attention for a moment longer than was comfortable.

"Daddy, *please.*" My voice came out in a whine, making me feel like a small child again.

"Yes, yes. Of course." He reached out to give my hand a squeeze then pulled it back just as quickly. "In order to explain the various whys, I have to go back to the time before you were born."

I waited while he collected his thoughts then sat back as he launched into what was bound to be a protracted history lesson.

"The sorcery clans in Scotland have a long-standing tradition of arranged marriages. For centuries, the clans have engaged in careful planning to determine the best matches to strengthen the bloodlines, oftentimes reaching out to distant clans as the best way to ensure the continuation of our kind. Where one clan has a weakness, another may show strength, and by combining the gene pools, the clans basically create the perfect sorcerers. "

The back of my neck prickled. "You talk as if this practice is still going on."

"Aye. 'Tis, especially in the more powerful clans. It is rare indeed to find a pairing not preordained by the—"

"Like you and Mom?" I interrupted his story. "Your marriage wasn't arranged. I mean, Mom isn't even a sorceress."

Dad sputtered for a moment, reaching for a glass of water I hadn't even noticed. He took a sip then cleared his throat. "Yes, your mother and I went against the norm. But for most, it starts from the moment a babe is born. An immediate plan is set in motion to find their perfect match— sometimes, even further back than that. Some marriages were arranged when their parents were still children.

"But once the matched couple reaches maturity—traditionally this occurs around age twelve or thirteen years—"

"You mean puberty?" My mouth hung open as what he'd said sank in. In what world would a twelve-year-old ever be considered mature?

"Yes, I suppose that's correct. Once they reach puberty, they're brought together to begin bonding. Then upon reaching adulthood, they're joined in the traditional binding ceremony—much like a wedding. This is where the couple is bound together for eternity. Even death cannot separate them."

"Arranged marriages? Binding ceremonies? I'm not sure what any of this has to do with me, Dad. I'm an American. We don't do that here. As far as I know, we don't even have sorcery clans or covens in this country." And I'd never been happier to be a US citizen.

"You are correct. There are no clans in America. But just because this is your home, that doesn't change your heritage. As early as conception, you became one of us. You *are* part of the Scottish clans. And from the moment you were born, you were betrothed to Liam."

Betrothed to Liam?

My mouth opened, and my lips moved, but the words wouldn't come.

My dad continued as if he were reciting a grocery list. "Of course, he was just a baby himself back then. But a promise is a promise."

A promise is a promise? Was he kidding? My heart clawed its way into my throat, making my head spin. If I hadn't been sitting, I would have dropped to the floor in a heap. "I don't understand. How could I be promised to someone an ocean away? Why would you and Mom allow something like that? And why wasn't I told that I'd been *betrothed* to someone before I was even born?"

"Believe me, I never thought I'd have to have this conversation with you."

"What, you were just going to spring it on me on my wedding day?"

"No, of course not." He jumped up from his chair to pace. "That's not at all what I meant."

I would have followed him to my feet, but my legs had turned to rubber. "Then please, enlighten me. What did you mean? When *were* you planning on telling me about this 'forced marriage' scenario?"

Dad's upper lip curled as if he smelled something foul. "*Forced* is such a strong word. We prefer 'arranged.'"

"Well, just so you know, I'm not okay with an arranged marriage either. But that doesn't exactly explain why you put a spell on me."

"Ah..." His face became more animated. "I had no choice in that matter."

I leveled a bitter scowl at him. "There's always a choice. You could have chosen to let things be—let me have my happily ever after with Jack." If the whole binding spell had never come up, I would have never known my entire relationship with Jack was based on nothing but magic. I could have lived a long and happy life, blissfully unaware.

"I tried that. Believe me, I did. You have no idea what I've sacrificed for your happiness!"

"What you've..." Red-hot anger spiked through me, and I quickly tamped it down before I did something I'd regret. "Are you kidding?"

"Why do you think your mother and I fled Scotland?" Dad couldn't even look me in the eyes. He focused on an arbitrary spot on the wall behind me as he continued with his explanation. "We'd chosen to live outside of the clans, but the minute you were conceived—the moment I discovered your mother was carrying you—I packed up everything we could carry, and we hopped the next plane to America. Your mother's family—God bless them—took us in until I could find work. I had absolutely no intention of letting my baby girl get wrapped up in any of that old-world nonsense."

I finally found my sea legs and dragged myself out of my chair. "So if you and Mom left Scotland and the clans behind, why are we even having this conversation?"

My father slammed his fist against the table so hard the windows rattled. "Because no matter how hard I tried to protect you, the clans are part of your heritage. I knew it would only be a matter of time before they came for you."

His sinister tone sent a ripple of fear down my spine. "Came for me?"

"It didn't take long for me to know you'd inherited the sorceress gene. Your poor mother was clueless, of course, but the signs were obvious to anyone who knew what to look for. Of course, I'd always known there was a better than fifty-fifty chance of our child inheriting my magical powers, but I'd still held out hope that it would skip a generation. But we weren't that lucky. When your powers began to emerge, I had no choice but to block your magic at every turn. And the closer you got to your twelfth birthday, the more frightened I became. I knew the clans would be keeping track of you through me. And unfortunately, my fear spilled over onto your mother. She begged me to do something. So I did the only thing I *could* do. I attempted something that would prevent them from using a locator spell on me." He let out a breath in a loud whoosh.

"What happened?"

Dad scratched his head with a chuckle. "I ended up as an Irish Wolfhound."

I fell back into my chair. "That's how you turned into a dog?"

He dropped his eyes to his feet and gave a solemn nod. "It was the only way to ensure your safety. I'd bound your magic and hidden myself in a way that would make it impossible for them to find us by scrying."

I reached out to him, taking his hand in mine and giving it a squeeze. "But why, Dad? Could you just have told them no? What could they possibly do to us all the way in Georgia?"

His eyebrows came together in a deep furrow. "They wouldn't have let it go. They would've come for you once you reached puberty. They would've expected you to go live with Liam's family until the ceremony." He shook his head emphatically. "And I couldn't allow that. I couldn't let them take my baby girl."

"But your spell backfired." It wasn't a question. I'd lived through the aftermath. I knew the toll that spell had taken on our family.

"That's a good way of putting it. But worse than that, I'd failed to cloak you properly. When your magic finally broke free, I wasn't there to help you through it. And the power emitting from you was like a giant beacon in the sky, pointing them right to you." Dad seemed to melt into the chair across from me.

"But you *were* there." I gave him a weak smile. "As my cat."

"I could only do so much in feline form. I'd been watching you from the shadows. I saw the telltale signs that your powers were about to break through. But when you turned your idiot fiancé into an animal, I knew I needed to find a way back into human form before the clans discovered you."

"But you didn't. Did you?"

"No. I didn't. By the time you changed me back, things had already been set in motion. Liam's mother had already made plans to come for you. Thankfully, he convinced her to let him go on ahead of her. He couldn't wait to meet you."

"You still haven't explained why you chose to keep this all a secret from me. Why didn't you tell me what was happening?"

"I saw how you were with Jack. I knew you wouldn't just walk away from him without a fight. The only way I could see you agreeing to bind yourself to Liam was if I gave you a little nudge."

"A little *nudge*? Dad, you screwed with my emotions! You... you broke my heart."

The roar of an engine approaching the house had us both turning toward the door.

"Speak of the devil."

I spun back around to gape at my father.

"It's just an expression, dear. Liam is hardly the villain in this story. I knew the minute I met him that bringing you together would make for a far better future than hiding would. He's a good man. And I'd be proud to have him as my son-in-law." Dad got up and walked away from the table.

"But—" I jumped up and followed him. I wasn't even close to finished with this conversation. And I wasn't about to roll over and allow the clans to win. We were living in the twenty-first century, and I was a modern witch with a mind of my own.

Dad glanced at the door before gripping my shoulders and locking his eyes with mine. "We're done talking about this for now, but listen to me, Ivie. Marrying Liam is your only chance for happiness. I've done all I can to protect you. We've run as far as we can go. But it would seem destiny has caught up to us. It's time to accept your fate."

Chapter 16

ITH ONE LAST SQUEEZE, DAD let his hands drop. "What do you mean 'accept my fate'?" He didn't answer. Instead, he focused his attention on the thundering footsteps outside. "Dad?"

Before I could demand an answer, Liam burst through the front door as if an army of demons chased him. And with the way things had been going, I only partly dismissed the possibility. A light sheen of sweat coated his skin, and his cheeks were pinker than normal. It was the first time I'd actually seen him with even a single hair out of place, and I had to admit, disheveled looked good on him. Almost too good.

"What is it, boy?" Not for the first time that morning, my father sounded exasperated.

Liam pulled in a deep breath. "My mother."

A spark of hope lit up my father's face. "Has something happened to your mother?"

Liam shook his head and quickly pulled himself together. "She's coming. The entire clan is coming."

"Well, that changes things." The light in Dad's eyes dimmed, and he wrung his hands together. "I thought her plans were set for next month. And bringing the entire clan? That's... unprecedented."

Liam's face darkened, and he shook his head again. "She heard..." He shot a pained look my way then turned back to my father.

Dad raised his eyebrows and motioned for Liam to go on.

Liam sighed. "Mother heard about Ivie's reluctance to bond with me. She's furious. She swore she wouldn't let you do this to her again." Liam slid another glance toward me. "She doesn't trust anyone else to handle the situation. She's coming to make sure things proceed as promised."

"I see." Dad nodded, but I caught a flash of something in his eyes that set my nerves on edge. He looked almost *worried*.

"Dad? What's going on?"

My father grimaced. "I had hoped to delay things has long as possible, but it would seem we'll be having the binding ceremony a bit earlier than anticipated."

"What?" My legs gave out, and I sank to the floor with a thud. I wasn't ready for the clans to show up and throw a wrench into my entire future. My mouth dried up like a grape under a heat lamp, and my heart pounded like stampeding pachyderms. "You only explained everything to me today. I thought I'd have more time to decide, more time to prepare. I don't even know what's expected of me, let alone if I can go through with it."

Liam directed a soft smile my way, and the anger from earlier evaporated. He reached down and helped me up from the floor, his gentle touch making my bones go soft. He held tight to me even after I managed to find my footing. "It'll be fine. My mother likes to bluster, but she's not all bad. And she'll adore you. You'll see."

"She's coming here? As in *here* here?" I pointed to the floor at my feet, and they both nodded. I shot a panicked look to my father, but he darted his eyes away at the last moment. *Traitor.*

Liam gave my hand a squeeze. "I suspect she'll check in at the hotel first. She's reserved a suite of rooms at the St. Regis."

Was I the only one who didn't know Liam's family was rich? A suite at the St. Regis could fund a small country for a least a year.

"Well, I'm sure she'll need time to settle in." My father tried to slither out of the room like the snake he was, but my glare froze him in place. I wasn't about to let him get away with sneaking off after putting me in this position.

"I still don't understand why she's coming now," I said. "She has to know I wasn't prepared for all this. Hasn't anyone told her I haven't made up my mind yet?"

"She'll expect us to go to her." Liam ignored my questions and spoke directly to my father. The two of them carried on a conversation as if I wasn't even in the room. "She likes to surround herself with the comforts of home."

"Yes, I imagine so. Though..." Dad threw an arm over Liam's shoulder with a faraway look in his eyes. "Spending time at the St. Regis is hardly a sacrifice. You know, perhaps we should all get rooms. Do you think the clan would mind footing the bill? Things would run much more smoothly if we stayed close by. Then again, your mother may prefer to head directly to Scotland. I haven't been back in years..."

"You two can go wherever you like, but *I'm* not going anywhere. Do you hear me?" I crossed my arms and glared at them in turn. I didn't bother to disguise the mocking tone in my voice. "Except maybe China. Or Singapore. Maybe Bali. I hear the weather is lovely this time of year."

Liam inched closer to me and winked, making my heart jump. He bent down and whispered in my ear. "I'd find you even if you left the country."

I tried to ignore my body's involuntary reaction to him. "What if I left the planet? I've always wanted to join the space program."

He chuckled, brushing up against me. "There's no place you can go that I can't find you. You're part of me now." He pressed his hand flat against his chest, and even that simple action made him somehow hotter.

"Stop teasing me."

"I'm dead serious." He gave me a pointed glare, and my knees went weak again.

Gah! I needed to get away from Liam before he turned me into an Ivie-shaped puddle on my mother's dusty old carpet. Could he really track me to the ends of the earth? Or the solar system? The man penetrated my defenses with every little word or glance... like kryptonite. "Dad, can I speak with you in the kitchen?"

My mother burst through the door with her purse dangling by one strap from her shoulder. "Angus, what's wrong? You said to come home right away? Is Ivie... oh, there you are, dear. I didn't see you. Is everything all right?"

Tears welled up behind my eyes, threatening to spill over in torrents. "Liam's mother is coming to town."

My mother's face twisted into the most evil expression I'd ever seen on her. "Marion? *Why?* Why is she coming *here?*"

My father winced. "Rose, I'll explain everything to you in private."

"Oh, no!" My arms flailed through the air like I was a juggler who'd lost her balls. "I'm sick of everyone discussing *my life* in private. Why is everyone still keeping things from me? I'm the one who's supposed to accept my fate and marry a man I barely know. I at least deserve to know what's going on."

Liam's face fell, and I knew I'd hurt his feelings, but I didn't have the time or the inclination to worry about it.

Dad scratched his head the way he did when he had trouble solving his scientific crossword puzzles. That was me: an impossible puzzle he couldn't figure out. "Ivie, I explained this to you already. It's tradition for—"

My foot came down on the floor with a *thwack,* sending up a mini dust cloud. "I don't give a flying—"

"Ivie!" My mother shrieked, and my dad caught me by the arm and dragged me into the kitchen like a spoiled toddler.

"But, Daddy," I whined. "I don't want to bind to Liam. I love Jack."

"I didn't want to have to tell you this, but marrying Liam may be the only way you can ensure Jack's safety." He kept his voice down, biting off each word and spitting them carefully out.

I stopped in my tracks, letting him stretch my arm until it hurt. "What are you talking about?"

"Marion McDougall isn't the forgiving sort." He checked over his shoulder. "Walking away from your commitment to Liam would be a slap in the face to her. And you need to be nicer to the boy. None of this is his fault."

"Not his fault?" I wrangled my arm out of his grip and did my best to get my point across without raising my voice, though I had no idea why I cared if Liam or my mom heard me. "What about me? None of this is *my* fault either! I never made a commitment to Liam. I didn't even know I was a sorceress a year ago."

Dad seemed to ignore me as he went to the cupboard and grabbed a coffee cup and a half-empty bottle of Macallan. He poured two fingers of whiskey into the cup then downed it before turning back to me. "Nevertheless, you were betrothed to him."

"Is that even legal? I was a baby!"

He poured himself another drink and sat down, this time savoring the scotch with a groan. "That's how they've done it for centuries. If I could undo the promise, I would."

A new thought hit me, and I had no idea how it'd managed to escape me before. "How did you marry Mom?"

I could tell by the shock on his face he was taken aback. "What?"

My spine straightened, and I wiped my eyes as the first potential contingency plan for escaping my so-called fate sparked in me. "If all the marriages are arranged, how did you marry Mom?"

Dad cleared his throat. "I was given a special dispensation to marry your mother."

"How?" My senses lit up with possibilities. "Can't we do that? Get a special dispensation for me to marry Jack?"

If he even still wants to marry me. After what'd happened that morning, I wasn't sure anymore.

My father clucked his tongue against the roof of his mouth then rinsed the sound down with another swig of scotch. "I'm afraid that won't be possible."

I wasn't above pleading. "But if they did it for you, maybe—"

Dad jumped up from his chair, tipping it over. "It just isn't! And that's the last I'm going to say about it. You need to accept your fate. If you *don't* marry Liam, Marion will assume—quite correctly, I'm afraid—that you've spurned Liam for Jack, and she won't hesitate to retaliate. Trust me, retaliation is one of her special talents, and you *don't* want to see her in action."

The more I heard about Liam's mom, the less I wanted to meet her. "How well do you know her?"

Dad emptied the rest of the bottle into his cup and brought it to his lips. "Too well for my taste."

I couldn't wait to escape my parents' watchful eyes. It was as if they saw me as a ticking time bomb. For more than an hour, they took turns engaging me in mundane conversations about the weather—sunny and warm with a slight chance of the apocalypse—and the newest neighborhood gossip. Apparently, *we* were the neighborhood gossip since someone had recognized the unmarked government car in the driveway. It was all I could do not to explode while they went on pretending nothing was out of the ordinary and waiting for the phone to ring and announce Marion's arrival.

And Liam was no help. He'd refused to speak a word to me after the mini-meltdown in which I'd all but proclaimed I'd rather engage in illicit acts with a goat than be bound to him for the rest of my life. He'd planted himself in my father's chair, piercing my heart with his damned baby blues and sending texts to persons unknown.

The whole situation had me wound up tighter than a Herve Leger bandage dress. I couldn't breathe. So despite Liam's pledge to find me no matter where I went, I snuck out the back and caught a cab to Chloe's house, leaving her rental car in the driveway. At least there, I could stuff myself with Thin Mints while I waited for my turn at the gallows.

My phone vibrated, dancing across the face of the glass-topped coffee table on a path to the edge. I reached over and hit 'decline.' I'd turned off the ringer after the twelfth time Mom called, but that hadn't stopped her. All nine of the Scottish clans could have been descending on Atlanta for all I cared. I wasn't picking up the phone for anyone but Jack.

I'd left him several messages of my own, but I couldn't blame him for ignoring me. He'd done nothing to deserve the hand he'd been dealt—other than falling in love with me. And *that* seemed to be on par with crossing paths with black cats or walking under ladders these days. After having his ass handed to him by Liam, I couldn't blame him for licking his wounds in a quiet corner somewhere. But at the same time, I wished he'd given me at least some indication as to whether or not he even wanted my attention anymore.

"Would you please get off your ass and do something?"

My head shot up at the bite in Chloe's voice. She stood in the entryway with her phone pressed to her ear, dressed to kill, as usual. I certainly hoped I wasn't on the endangered species list.

I pointed to my chest. "Are you talking to me?"

She scrunched up her face and waved me off. "I'm serious, Jon. Your brother isn't picking up his phone. Ivie's dealing with a crisis of epic proportions. You would think so, but I'm telling you, this makes the whole Matt situation look like a minor hiccup. Well, on a scale of Mary Poppins to Cruella DeVille, I'd suggest you keep a close eye on your hide. Maybe if you weren't gallivanting all over Nevada, waving your wand where it doesn't belong... Oh, don't give me that pathetic excuse again. I saw the pictures on TMZ. And just FYI, my father's a plastic surgeon, so I can spot a pair of fake tits a mile away. She *totally* got hers on clearance." She wandered out of the room, leaving me with my buzzing phone and the last box of Girl Scout cookies.

I nestled back into the plush sofa. The air around me pulsed, and I got a distinct whiff of butterscotch candies. I sat up, bumping my knees on the coffee table as Liam shimmered into focus on the opposite side.

I brushed the crumbs from my front and stood to face him, wielding half a sleeve of cookies like a light saber.

He didn't even crack a smile. "Drop the weapon, Little Debbie."

"What are *you* doing here?" I lowered the cookies and straightened my spine. "You do know you can't just pop in and out of people's houses whenever you like? Don't you have to be invited first?"

Liam clamped down on the inside of his cheek with his teeth to keep his grin at bay and maintained an icy distance. "You're mixing mythologies. Vampires have to be invited. Sorcerers can pop to their hearts' content." He reached out and snatched a Thin Mint from the top of the sleeve and popped it into his mouth. His sudden aloofness threw me off balance. I couldn't remember a time when he hadn't flirted with me—not since that first day in the lab. "Mum's arrived. She'd very much like to meet you."

He spoke to me as if I was an employee, and I didn't like it. Guilt bubbled up from the pit of my stomach. *I'd* done this to him. *I'd* hurt his feelings. For the first time since I'd discovered I'd been put under a spell, I felt sorry for someone other than myself. "That's nice, but I'm not sure I'm ready to meet *her*."

"Too bad. I've been sent to collect you." His stony facade cracked along the edges, and a bit of annoyance spilled out. He scowled as he eyed me from head to toe, lingering just a little too long on the neckline of my silk tank. "You might want to change. Mum isn't fond of the way you Americans dress. Either way, we're expected in ten minutes."

"Fine." I tossed the cookies onto the table and grabbed my phone before storming out of the room with a huff. "You do realize we'll never make it across town in ten minutes at this hour, right?"

I didn't expect him to follow me, so when I spun around to find him directly behind me I gasped, drawing in another lungful of his delicious scent.

My visceral reaction seemed to thaw him, and his signature smirk made a brief appearance. "Traffic won't be a problem."

I waited for him to elaborate, but he didn't say another word. He just stood in the doorway of my room, staring me down like I was a double-chocolate lava cake topped with mint chip ice cream and a heavy dose of whipped cream. His intense gaze made me squirmy. "Stop looking at me like that."

His brows came together in a tight furrow, and he tilted his head to the side. "Like what?"

I caught my lower lip between my teeth and held it while I studied his lost expression and cleared my throat. "Like you can't breathe without me."

He brought his mouth within a whisper of mine but didn't kiss me. Instead, he feathered his lips against my ear. "I can't."

The resulting shudder ran from the top of my head down to the chipped pink polish on my toes.

He brushed against me as he stepped back and gave me a wink. "Now, go on and get dressed. My mother hates to be kept waiting."

Chapter 17

THE INSIDE OF MY MAKESHIFT closet looked as disjointed and out of sync as I felt. After moving out of Jack's townhouse, I hadn't bothered to sort or organize my clothes. I'd just shoved them into the first open slot I could find alongside Chloe's overflow. Her Dolce and Michael Kors mingled with my various off-the-rack brands and thrift store finds. *Gucci meets Goodwill.*

Finding something to wear would be an almost impossible task. I had no idea what Liam's mother expected of me or if I wanted to live up to her expectations. Dad made it seem as if she held my future in the palm of her magical hand. I had my doubts, but until I met the woman face to face, I had no choice but to believe him.

With a quick game of eeny meeny miny moe, I grabbed something of Chloe's—an Alexander McQueen white crepe maxi dress with three-quarter sleeves, a modest slit up the side, and a jewel neckline that wouldn't show even a glimpse of cleavage. I did a quick change then pulled my red hair into a tight bun, securing it with a few pins. I finished the outfit off with a pair of sensible white flats, shoes that would have brought Betsey Johnson to tears but wouldn't slow me down if I had to make a run for it.

I dumped my purse on the bed, plucking out my favorite lip gloss, a pack of cinnamon Tic Tacs, and my debit card, and stuffing them, along with my phone, into a white quilted Marc Jacobs clutch. With one last peek in the mirror, I headed out to face the music.

Liam looked up when I opened the door. "Ivie, you..." His mouth dropped open, and his eyes followed every contour of my body from head to toe.

I shifted from one foot to the other, uncomfortable with his meticulous inspection. "Come on. Let's get this over with."

"You look..." He tried again then shook his head and took my hand, gripping it a little too tightly in his. "Hold on, and whatever you do, don't let go."

The first thing I noticed was a prickle of static running over my skin. The fine hairs on my arms stood on end, and a steady current of air rushed around me, giving me goose bumps. The hallway shimmered in and out of focus, and I felt as though I floated in a pool of lukewarm water. Just as I was getting used to the weightlessness, I was jerked off my feet and pulled into the dark.

My stomach lurched as the sensation of being rolled into a tight ball and turned completely inside out hit me. Somehow, I resisted the urge to regurgitate half a box of Thin Mints, swallowing down lump after lump that crawled up my throat. I snapped my eyes shut and tried to scream, but the vacuum swallowed up the sound. Then as quickly as the out-of-body experience started, it stopped.

"We're here." Liam squeezed my hand then released it.

I opened my eyes on the elegant lobby of the St. Regis hotel. Giant crystal chandeliers hung from the ceiling, sending dancing light over the shiny hardwood floors. We stood beneath one of two sweeping staircases, out of direct view but still in the open. But the breathtaking view had nothing on the excitement threatening to burst out of me.

"Will you teach me how to do that?" I beamed at Liam, my pulse still thrumming in my veins.

He bit back a grin of his own. "Do what?"

I dragged him behind an enormous planter and lowered my voice to a whisper. "Disapparate."

Liam laughed. "You're adorable when you're excited, but I think you've been reading too much Harry Potter. *Disapparate* isn't even a real word."

"So?" *All the more reason to use it, as far as I'm concerned.* Most of what I knew about witchcraft and sorcery came from a youth spent reading and rereading the Harry Potter series, followed by more than one weekend of binge-watching all eight movies with Jack. And the more I found myself submerged in the reality of it, the more I realized reality was far stranger than fiction.

"We call it *siubhal-ama.*" The words rolled off his tongue in what I assumed was Gaelic.

I opened my mouth to repeat what he'd said but changed my mind. "You can call it whatever you like. I'll call it disapparating. And you really need to teach me. Soon." I thought of all the places I could go once I'd mastered that little trick: Paris, Rome, this little burger joint in the worst part of town. I could be in and out before anyone had a chance to harass me. My mouth watered at the thought of a juicy double bacon cheeseburger.

He leaned in close enough to kiss me but pulled back before our lips touched. "I promise I will, but right now, we need to get upstairs. If I know my mother, she's already sent out a search party."

"Why didn't you dis—transport us straight to her room?"

"The clan put a block within the hotel. Other than a few sputters here and there, the only places magic works are the lobby and the ballroom. That's where—" He didn't finish the thought, but the way his eyes tightened as they swept over me made me afraid to ask.

As soon as we stepped off the elevator, we were greeted by a welcoming committee: three hulking Scotsmen in authentic regalia. I couldn't help gawking. I'd seen men in kilts before—my father was known to don one on special occasions—but I'd never seen men of *this* stature wearing red-and-green tartan kilts with white knee-high socks and black buckle shoes. None of them wore shirts, just matching sashes emblazoned with the McDougall family crest that barely covered their impressive chests.

My face flamed as I continued to stare. I wanted to ask Liam why they dressed that way, but I didn't dare.

"Afternoon, Liam." The tallest of the three men shook Liam's hand. His fingers had to be as thick as fence posts.

"Good to see you, Callum. I didn't think you and Finn would make the trip."

"Aye, we were supposed to stay home, but your mum insisted."

Liam nodded but didn't interject.

"So who's the lovely lass with you? Is this *her*?" A man with dark hair and a thick red beard stepped forward.

"Aye, Duffy. This is Ivie."

"Good to see ya, Ivie." Duffy gripped my hand in his but didn't squeeze. Instead, he brought my fingers to his lips and kissed my knuckles. He stared into my eyes and gave me a look that made my blood run cold. "Glad you could make it."

"Okay, boys. Time to step aside. I'm sure Mum is tired of waiting."

"Oh, you can say that again." Callum barked out a laugh, and the other two joined in. "Go on in. The door's unlocked. She's waiting for ye."

I followed Liam into the empty parlor. A fire blazed in the stone fireplace, and an old black-and-white Cary Grant movie played on the flat-screen TV with the sound muted. The pillows from one of the two overstuffed sofas had been rearranged. Half of them spilled onto the floor. A glass of red wine sat untouched on the cocktail table. But there was no sign of Liam's mother.

"Is this the right room?" I whispered, and even that seemed too loud.

"Mum?"

"Is that mah darling boy?" Marion McDougall's breathy voice called out from the bedroom in an accent so thick I could barely understand her.

Liam reached out and took my hand—to steady himself or me, I wasn't sure. "Aye, 'tis."

The woman who stepped out of the bedroom both shocked and intimidated me. She would've been about the same age as my parents, but unlike my parents, who looked every bit of their ages, the years had been kind to her.

Like her son, she had thick raven-black hair—though hers hung in loose curls just above her shoulders—without a wisp of gray. She had delicate features and a fine bone structure with curves in all the right places. But it was her mesmerizing crystal-blue eyes—the exact color of her dress—that trapped me in their depths from the moment they locked on to mine.

"Well, as I live and breathe." Marion seemed to glide across the floor as she closed the distance between us, her feet barely touching the floor. She reached for Liam's free hand but never broke eye contact with me. I was like a fly caught in her web. "If you aren't the spitting image of your father."

I opened my mouth, but my voice failed me. I had to clear my throat twice before I could make a sound. "We have the same eyes."

"That you do." She cupped my cheek in her cool hand, and I felt the power humming below her skin. "And the same stubborn streak, so I hear."

Heat shot up from my chest to my hairline, and the overwhelming need to flee pulsed in me.

Liam cleared his throat. "I saw Callum, Duffy, and Finn when we came in, but I'm assuming the others are here too. Where are you hiding them?"

Marion removed her hand from my face and turned toward Liam with a chuckle. "They're playing tourists."

With the connection between us broken, I sucked in a quick breath, my first real breath since she'd come into the room.

"Though I have no idea what the draw is." Marion shot another icy glance my way. "I'd sooner finish our business here and be gone. But despite what some may say, I'm not a monster."

A chill cut through me. I had the distinct feeling Marion McDougall was every bit the monster people claimed her to be.

My phone buzzed in my bag. I did my best to ignore it, but no sooner had it stopped than it started up again.

Her lips curved up in a polite smile, a gesture far too chilly to be genuine. "Are we keeping you from something, dear?"

She made me squirm, and I debated lying and pretending the situation didn't make me all kinds of uncomfortable. But in the end, I coughed up the truth. "Actually, if you wouldn't mind, could I have just a moment?"

"Of course." She motioned for me to carry on, and I took advantage of the reprieve to dig my phone from my borrowed clutch.

I had two missed calls and a text from Jack. I brought up the messages and held in the sigh as I read what he'd said.

Jack: I miss you, sweetheart. Can't we just leave all this craziness behind and run away together? Please? I'll go to the ends of the earth if it means I can keep you with me. I love you so much.

Tears welled up in my eyes. Jack still loved me. He still wanted me. And I was stuck in the presidential suite at the St. Regis with Lady Macbeth and her spawn. With my back to Liam and his mother, I tapped out a quick reply.

Me: I love you too! I want that so bad. You have no idea.

Marion cleared her throat. "Ivie, I think we need to get a few things straight."

I spun around with my thumbs still hovering over the keyboard.

"You seem to be laboring under the misconception that you have any say in what happens to you." She plucked the phone from my fingers and exited the screen without reading it then slid the device back into my bag and zipped it shut. She took my left hand in hers and fingered my engagement ring. I'd gotten so used to wearing it that I'd almost forgotten I had it on most of the time. "It's time for you to sever your ties and accept your fate."

I knew it couldn't be a coincidence that she used the same words my dad had. I wished my father were there to explain. "I-I'm sorry, but I don't know if I can do that."

Her eyes flashed with a white heat, and a barely perceptible tremble shook her delicate hands. "This is not a debate. You *will* complete the binding ceremony. Instinct tells me to demand it be done immediately, but I promised my son I would give you time to settle your affairs first."

"Settle my affairs?"

She waved a hand. "Say your goodbyes. Tie up loose ends. Whatever you feel the need to do. I'll give you one day. Twenty-four hours. But come this time tomorrow, you *will* be bound to my son and honor the promise made to me over three decades ago."

Three decades ago? I didn't understand what she meant by that, but there was no mistaking the demands she was making of me now.

"What if I don't? I was engaged to another man when I met Liam. I made a promise to him first."

"I don't care about your petty promises!" She moved with the grace of a cat, capturing my face in one hand as her voice rang in my ears. "Your family owes me a life, and I will collect it. Make no mistake about that, little girl. I. Will. Collect."

Her slight form blurred in and out of focus, then she quickly pulled herself together and backed away with a smile, leaving me shaken.

My legs wobbled beneath me. If Liam hadn't grabbed hold of my arm, I might have collapsed to the floor.

"Liam, be a dear and tell Finn to have my dinner sent up. I'm positively famished." She kissed Liam's cheek then turned to leave the room as if she hadn't just shattered my entire world into a million tiny pieces. "I'll see you tomorrow afternoon, Ivie. Don't be late."

After disapparating us back to Chloe's, Liam followed me wordlessly into my room and sat on the edge of the bed while I paced in front of the window. "I'm sorry. I know this is difficult for—"

"No!" I jabbed my finger into the air as if I could stab him from across the room. The tears that had threatened to fall all day finally broke free, rolling down my cheeks in a steady stream. "Don't you say that. You don't get to say that to me. You have no idea how I feel. You're not in my head. Or my heart. You can't possibly understand."

He stood and took a step toward me then stopped as if he'd changed his mind. He was treating me like a fragile doll, and I hated it. "You're wrong. Since the first moment your soul touched mine in that spell, I've felt what you felt. I'm sorry the incantation was interrupted. I'm sorry your heart was left torn between two loves, but believe me. I do know how you feel."

"Then how can you force me to walk away from him?" I didn't bother to wipe the tears. I just let them fall. What was the point if my heart was breaking? "If you know how I feel, you must know how much he means to me."

"I do." He dropped his eyes to the floor. "But I also know *you* mean that much to *me*."

"Then let me go."

He raised his head, his eyes brimming with unshed tears. "I can't do that."

I turned my back on him. I couldn't bear to look at his face anymore. The blue eyes I'd grown so fond of reminded me of his mother. "Get out."

"Ivie, wait." He closed the distance between us and reached out to me.

"No!" I shrugged away from him and hurled my borrowed clutch at his chest. It bounced off with a *thwack*. "Get out! I want to spend my last twenty-four hours with the people who *aren't* trying to destroy my life."

"You mean Jack." When I nodded, he gritted his teeth and ran a hand through his dark hair. His patience seemed to have run out. "Fine. Go see Jack. Say your goodbyes. But don't do anything stupid. My mother doesn't make idle threats."

A bitter laugh bubbled out of me. I wanted to hurt him. I wanted him to feel every bit of my gut-wrenching pain down to the bottom of his soul. "Let her retaliate. I don't care what she does to me anymore."

"It's not you she'll hurt." He spoke so softly I almost didn't hear him.

"What are you talking about?"

Liam dropped onto the bed again, resting his elbows on his knees and burying his face in his hands. He stayed like that for a long time. Then he picked up his head and locked his eyes with mine. "Ivie, if you cross her, my mother won't punish you. She'll punish the people you love."

Chapter 18

Y HAND SHOOK AS I reached up to ring the bell. Standing on the outside of Jack's door felt strange. I didn't think I'd ever had to knock before. I just walked in. Everything in me told me to unlock the door and go inside, but I didn't even have my key anymore.

I dropped my hand and stood there in a daze for several minutes, listening to Jack moving around inside, going about his day, oblivious to my presence or what I'd come to say. He had no idea I was about to destroy us both, all because of a promise someone made for me before I was born. I hated my father. I hated Liam. But mostly, I hated Marion for being the catalyst in all of this.

My fingers twitched as I reached out again, but instead of ringing the bell, I rested my hand on the knob and let the magic flow out of me. It had gotten easier to control in small doses. Almost immediately, blue light sparked from my fingertips, and I used it to turn the lock and let myself in.

"Jack?" I stood in the foyer and called out to him. It would have been easy to simply walk across the room and find him, but it wouldn't have been right. Not this time.

"Ivie?" Jack walked out of the kitchen, one of those red-and-white-striped towels in his hands and surprise written on his handsome face.

My heart skipped a beat at the sight of him, and I sucked in a quick breath. I'd almost forgotten the rush I felt in his presence: like standing at the top of a mountain, like magic.

He dropped the towel and jogged toward me, scooping me into a crushing hug. "You're here."

I let him hold me for a moment before wriggling free. As much as I loved being in his arms, I wanted to see his face so I could memorize every freckle, every crease that formed around his eyes when he smiled. I never wanted to forget a single thing. "I had to get a ride. My car's still in the shop, and I left Chloe's rental at my parents' house."

Everything felt off, like we were out of sync, almost as if we were two people who'd run out of things to say and were being overly polite to one another, but that was the furthest thing from the truth. There were so many words that needed to be said, and I wasn't sure if I'd have enough time for all of them.

Jack squeezed my hand. "You should have called me. I would have come and gotten you."

I shrugged. I didn't know what to say. I didn't want him obligated to take me back after I ripped out his heart. "It's okay. I'm here now."

He exhaled, and his Adam's apple bobbed as he swallowed. "Did your dad—"

"No." I didn't need to hear the rest. I knew he wanted to know if the spell had been removed. I wanted to tell him yes with everything in me, but I wouldn't lie.

"Oh." He nodded. Disappointment etched across his features. "What are we gonna—"

"Not now." I pressed a finger to his lips. "Let's pretend it's a month ago, and I never went to the lab that day. There's no Liam, no spell, nothing but you and me and a wedding to plan." The idea sounded so good, I actually grinned.

Jack's smile had an edge of sadness to it, but it still warmed me all the way to my toes. He wrapped his arms around me like he never wanted to let go, and it really was as if the past month hadn't happened. "I really like that idea."

I knew I had to tell him. The words were on the tip of my tongue—bitter and cold like freezer-burned ice cream. But I selfishly wanted these last few hours with him. And I knew I wouldn't get that if he knew. He might never forgive me for keeping it from him, but years from now, when my time with Jack was nothing but a distant memory, I'd still have this moment.

Jack buried his face in my hair, breathing me in as if he was savoring me the same way I was savoring him. I felt rather than heard his words. "What's wrong, sweetheart?"

I swallowed down a sob. I told myself I wouldn't cry, wouldn't spoil our time together. I forced a smile into my voice. "Nothing."

"Don't lie." He let out a shaky laugh. He was nervous, and I couldn't blame him at all. Everything about that moment screamed "Shakespearean tragedy." "You're a horrible liar."

I held onto him for dear life, my heart stuttering behind my ribs. "Am not."

"Are too." He scooped me up and carried me to our room. He laid me down on the bed then crawled over me until he had me spread out under him. "Is it that bad?"

My hold on my emotions faltered, and a sob broke free. I couldn't do anything but nod.

"Oh, baby." Jack rested his forehead on mine then reverently kissed each of my eyelids, then my nose, then finally pressed his lips to mine, kissing me like he'd never see me again, as if he knew the truth even though I hadn't said the words—maybe never would say the words.

I tasted my own tears in our kiss, and I didn't want to cry my way through our last moments. "Make love to me?"

"You don't even have to ask."

We didn't speak as Jack took his time removing my clothes then his own. For a long time, the only sounds in the room were the whispers of fabric falling to the floor. Jack only asked one question as he slowly entered me. "Are you okay?"

"Mmhmm." I hummed out my response, concentrating on the feel of him so I could replay the moment later.

He didn't move for at least a minute. He stared into my eyes and held himself still inside me as if our connection could save us from everything.

When neither of us could wait any longer, he started to move. He took long, deep, unhurried strokes, taking his time luxuriating in my body, skating his hands over my skin, touching me everywhere he could reach.

Much too quickly, he had me climbing toward climax. I tried to slow it down, but we were so in tune with each other, his body knew exactly how to bring mine to the edge and push me over. And he did, shattering right along with me.

I had no idea how long we lay there breathing in the dark—our hearts beating in tandem—before he asked me the question of the hour. "Are you going to tell me what's wrong?"

I shook my head, burrowing my face into his shoulder until it muffled my voice. "I don't want to."

He tipped my chin up, bringing his eyes to mine even though we could barely see each other. "Why?"

"Because it'll change everything." I whispered the words as if that would take the sting out of what I had to say.

He hugged me, tucking me into his side and resting his chin on the top of my head. "It doesn't have to."

"Yes, it does."

"Okay." He gave one resolute nod. "Then don't tell me. Don't say it out loud. Then nothing will change."

"Okay." Had we just said it without saying it? Did he know what I had to do? I might never know for sure. But either way, we'd agreed to leave it unsaid. That would have to carry me through the dark times. I believed Jack understood, at least on some level.

It had to be close to dawn, though I didn't bother to check the time. Instead, I stayed awake and listened as

Jack's breathing changed, and he drifted off to sleep. It killed me to slip out of his arms, gutted me to get dressed without saying a word, and left me empty and cold as I kissed him goodbye, whispering "I love you" one last time. I slipped my engagement ring from my finger, leaving it on the bedside table with no note. No goodbye.

Then I left. And I prayed I'd be able to forgive myself someday.

"You have to eat something." Chloe pushed a plate of scrambled eggs and toast across the table toward me.

"Why?" I took a sip of sour grape juice and made a face. "Everything tastes like disappointment."

Chloe chuckled and shook her head. She didn't have a clue. "Why are you being so melodramatic this morning? I thought you talked to your dad yesterday."

"I did. It didn't go the way I'd expected." I took the fork she all but shoved into my hand and picked at the eggs without taking a single bite. Like a picky toddler, I'd mastered the art of rearranging the food on my plate.

Chloe spread a thin layer of jam on her toast and took a big bite, chewing and swallowing before going on. "I thought you said your father agreed to remove the binding spell."

I couldn't look her in the eye.

"Ivie?" Chloe waved her bread like a white flag. "That *is* what you said, isn't it?"

I shoveled a forkful of eggs into my mouth so I wouldn't be able to answer.

Chloe dropped the toast and leveled a glare at me that rivaled even Marion's. "Come on. Out with it."

The eggs turned to dust in my mouth, but I forced myself to choke them down. "Actually, what I said was my father apologized for putting the spell on me, and we had a nice long talk about it."

"Then he removed it." She raised her eyebrows and waited for me to respond.

"I never said he removed it. I said I was getting married. I never said to whom."

"Oh, my God. Ivie, no!" She bumped her juice, spilling what was left onto her plate. "What were you thinking?"

Her outburst caught me by surprise, making me so angry I had to tamp down the crackle of electricity inside me. "I was thinking I didn't have a choice. I was thinking I'd like for Jack to grow old, even if it means he does it without me. I was *thinking* I'd rather not be responsible for anyone I love dying." I pushed away from the table and stood up, throwing my napkin onto my plate. Fresh tears blurred my vision. "You really have *no* idea what I was thinking."

"Oh, Ivie. I'm so sorry. I didn't know." Chloe ran around the table and pulled me into a fierce hug. She squeezed me almost hard enough to put my pieces back together. "So what's the plan?"

I rested my head on her shoulder. "What do you mean? There is no plan."

"What do you mean, there's no plan?" She scoffed. "There's *always* a plan."

I shook my head. "Not this time."

Chloe pulled away and grabbed my shoulders, holding me at arm's length. "Hold on just one damn minute. I don't know about the *new* you, but my best friend Ivie Marie McKie *always* has a plan."

I chuckled as I wiped a tear from my cheek with the back of my hand. "I think you have me confused with you. You're the one who always has a plan. And they always manage to get me into more trouble than I was already in."

"Hey, now!" She feigned outrage. "My plans are brilliant. In fact, if memory serves, one of my brilliant plans landed you a certain magician-slash-veterinarian."

Raised eyebrows were my only reply.

"Oh, you know it's the truth. You were ready to write him off when I talked to him."

Sadness washed over me as the realization that I'd never see Jack again hit me. "Yeah. I was an idiot."

Chloe pulled me in for another hug. "We'll figure something out. We always do."

I would've given anything to believe her, but I'd given up on last-minute miracles.

"I'm gonna go pack. I'm supposed to be at the St. Regis by six o'clock. *And not a minute late.*" I mimicked Marion's icy tone.

"Okay. You pack. I have an errand to run." She stared me down with a familiar sparkle in her eyes. She was plotting something. "Promise me you'll be here when I get back."

I crossed my fingers behind my back. "I promise."

She nodded, clearly pleased with herself, then grabbed her purse and her keys and ran out the door as if she'd been shot out of a cannon.

Chloe hadn't been gone more than a few minutes when I thought I heard a knock at the door. "Did you forget something?"

No one answered me, but I heard the knock again, this time more insistent.

After everything I'd been through, I didn't have the energy to get up. "It's unlocked!"

The knocking turned into pounding, and I dragged myself over and peered through the peephole. *Liam?* I opened the door with a huff and planted my hands on my hips, blocking the entrance. "What are you doing here? I still have six hours left before I have to be at the St. Regis."

He pressed out a smile, his dimples making a brief appearance. "You always look so happy to see me."

I glanced down at my ripped T-shirt and sweatpants and covered the chipped toenail polish on my left foot with my right. "Well, you do bring out the best in me."

Without letting his smile slip once, Liam stepped around me, inviting himself into the house.

"Come in, why don't you?"

I didn't catch a hint of sarcasm in his reply. "Thanks."

I couldn't help being amused by his boyish charm, but I wasn't in the mood for company. I rubbed soothing circles on my throbbing temples. "Seriously, Liam, why are you here?"

He whipped his head around as if looking for something... or someone. "Where's Chloe?"

"I don't know. She said something about running errands. She should be back soon. But you didn't come here to see Chloe, did you?"

"No." He laughed, a nervous sound that sparked my curiosity.

I let out a sigh. "I wish you'd—"

"Give me a moment, please." He held up a finger then spun around and muttered a few words under his breath in Gaelic before turning back to me and clearing his throat. "I feel as though we've gone about this the wrong way. Our courtship hasn't been conventional, by any means."

Courtship? I almost laughed but somehow managed to rein it in.

"But despite the fact that we've only known each other for a short time..." Liam continued with his obviously rehearsed speech. "I feel as though I've known you my entire life. From the time I was old enough to understand what the binding ceremony was, I knew I would one day take those vows with you."

It started with a prickling at the back of my neck as I realized where he was going with this. My stomach sank into my toes. "Liam, no."

"Please, let me finish." He begged with his eyes, and I was powerless to deny him. "We'd never met. I'd never even seen you. But nevertheless, you rested in my heart as a promise for the future."

"No, no, no... Liam, please don't." I'd never been a fainter, but when he took my hand and went down on one knee, my legs gave out beneath me, and I sank to the floor beside him. This couldn't be happening: the sequel to my worst nightmare.

He grabbed my free hand to steady me. "We're not both supposed to be down here, you know."

"Well, you're not supposed to be proposing to me." I dragged in a ragged breath. "I just gave Jack's ring back last night!"

"I know." He fished in his pocket and pulled out a silver circle with a huge emerald set in the center of a double ring of diamonds.

"Liam..." Words failed me, and shock froze me in place.

"You needed a new one." His hands shook as he positioned the ring and slid it over my knuckle. "This ring has been in my family for centuries, though I added a few new stones especially for you."

The diamonds? My heart stuttered then went off like firecrackers in my chest. "I..."

"Don't say anything." He took me by surprise, silencing me with a kiss.

I should have pushed him away, but despite having my heart shattered in tiny pieces over a several-mile radius, I liked it. I threw myself into the kiss. Guilt rolled over me like a tidal wave, drowning me.

Liam pulled away first, whispering words I didn't understand. "*Tha gaol agam ort.*"

I pressed my fingers to my tingling lips. "I really need to learn Gaelic if I'm going to be around you."

Liam laughed and kissed my nose. "It means, I love you."

Tears welled up in my eyes as my heart broke all over again. I wished with all I had in me that I felt the same way.

"No... don't cry, Ivie." He put his forehead to mine. "Everything will work out as it should. You'll see."

Chapter 19

REAKING MY PROMISE TO CHLOE was the easiest thing I'd done in days. And that wasn't saying much. I didn't think there were enough pieces of my heart left to break, but I was wrong. I couldn't be there to see the disappointment in her eyes when she realized I'd given up. I'd already had my goodbye with Jack, and it nearly broke me. I couldn't go through another one with her.

Liam helped me pack the rest of my essentials—my toothbrush, a few changes of clothes, and assorted other odds and ends. I'd left everything else behind with a note telling Chloe to donate it all to Goodwill. Most of it had come from there anyway. Then we'd disapparated to the St. Regis lobby. Since we still had a few hours to kill before the sand ran out on Marion's edict, we bypassed her room, and Liam took me to a more modest suite instead—modest by Marion's lavish standards, that is. The furnishings weren't quite as over-the-top luxurious, and the sitting room—though tastefully decorated—didn't come with a fireplace. The mini-apartment still came with two spacious bedrooms and a fully appointed marble bathroom with a tub larger than some backyard pools.

"Where are we?" I sat on the edge of the sofa, careful not to touch anything. I had no idea whose room we were in.

Liam froze in the threshold to the bedroom. "This would be my room. Well, *our* room after tonight. I've been staying here since I arrived in Atlanta."

"Oh." I imagined my face had turned several shades of red, and I tried to remind myself there were two bedrooms. "What exactly happens during the binding ceremony?"

Liam blushed to his hairline. "Your father didn't explain it to you?"

I barked out a laugh. "No. I think my father was hoping I'd figure it out on my own."

Liam choked, and his already flushed face went up in flames.

"Oh, my God!" I jumped up to pat him on the back. "Are you okay?"

"Uh, yeah." He coughed a few more times, giving me strange looks before his breathing returned to normal. "I think I may have swallowed my tongue."

I laughed. "What happened?"

"I don't know. My saliva went down the wrong pipe?"

"Wow. That's..." *Weird?* "Unusual."

"You caught me by surprise."

"Me? What did I do?"

"I guess I expected you to be more prepared."

"Oh." I fell into the sofa. "Dad explained a few things to me about the traditions, but he didn't get into the actual ceremony, and I didn't ask. It's not painful, is it? They won't tie us down and brand us with red-hot pokers, with they?"

That made him laugh. "No, it won't be painful. No red-hot pokers or even tattoos. The ceremony is much like a traditional wedding where rings and vows are exchanged—but with a twist."

"A twist?"

"Like the spell in the lab but more intense."

"Ah." I couldn't imagine anything more intense than windows blowing inward and lights exploding.

"After that, the clan witnesses—are you sure you wouldn't rather talk with your mum? This is typically one of those mum conversations."

"You're referring to the wedding night?"

He chuckled. "I guess so."

"I'm not a virgin, Liam. I don't need my mother to explain how things—" A nervous giggle bubbled up my throat, and I swallowed it down. "You know, maybe you're right. This is definitely a mom conversation."

"Your parents are due here in a few hours. I'll make sure she stops in to see you."

"Thanks."

"I know this isn't what you wanted, Ivie, but—"

"You don't have to say anything. I understand."

At precisely six o'clock, after several clothing changes, I followed Liam in his dress kilt, paired with a crisp white shirt and jacket, into the Presidential Suite, wearing a black silk sheath that Chloe would've killed for. I personally thought it was a tad on the tight side, but Liam had been the one to select it, and he said it made me look very Audrey Hepburn-esque, even if my hair had gone back to a vibrant shade of fire-engine red.

Marion greeted us at the door with a painted-on smile and a bottle of pale-pink champagne.

"Right on time," she cooed then turned and handed the bottle to someone standing to her right. I did a double take, averting my eyes from the rippling chest muscles of the half-naked man in a kilt. I had no idea how I'd missed him when we'd come in. "Now, Duncan."

Duncan opened the champagne with a loud pop and a splash then scurried off to the banquet-sized table where several glasses were already lined up.

Marion took the first glass and held it up in a toast. "Today is cause for celebration. Finally, after far too many years of waiting, the wrongs of the past will be righted with the hopes and dreams of the future." She waited until Liam and I had our glasses to bring hers to her lips.

"Cheers!" She downed her glass and held it out to Duncan for a refill.

"Not so fast, mum. You aren't as young as you used to be," Liam cautioned her, but she waved him off.

"Youth is wasted on the young." This time, she sipped more slowly.

"Oh, look." Marion grabbed my hand and hauled it up to her face to inspect the ring. Her eyes filled with tears. "You're wearing it! This ring belonged to my mother and her mother before her. It looks lovely on you, Ivie. And the diamonds were a nice touch, Liam. You have magnificent taste." She beamed at him over her shoulder. "You get that from me."

Liam's cheeks pinked. "Thank you, Mum."

"Now, back to business." Marion's tears evaporated instantly, and she dropped my hand to bring hers together in a loud clap. "I've already seen to the arrangements. The ceremony will begin at the stroke of midnight. The grand ballroom has been reserved, and our guests are scheduled to arrive at eleven. As I'm sure you know, the head of the McKie family would traditionally perform the ceremony, but under the circumstances..." She slid her eyes in my direction. "I'll be performing the spell myself."

I didn't understand the break with tradition, but I was afraid to ask questions. I stole a peek at the half-naked clansman standing guard in the corner and wondered where my parents were. Liam had said they were supposed to be there.

"Are your rooms satisfactory? I would have preferred you stay in the room adjoining my suite, but Liam felt you might be self-conscious."

I swallowed the knot in my throat and reminded myself to thank Liam later. "It's fine. Beyond fine, actually. I would have been perfectly happy with less."

She made a sound in the back of her throat. "You need to get used to the finer things. A McDougall is never satisfied with less."

In a stroke of brilliant timing, someone knocked at the door, and Duncan let my father in. I stopped myself before I asked him where my mother was.

"Marion." Dad greeted Marion with caution, approaching her as if he half expected her to whip out a dagger and plunge it into his chest. I didn't know what it was, but I knew there was more to their history than I'd been told.

"Angus." Marion's lips curved into a stiff smile. She eyed his wrinkled shirt and worn blue-and-green kilt before focusing her attention on the manila folder in his hands. "Is this the paperwork we discussed?"

My father's eyes traveled from her face to mine then back again. "Yes. I've brought everything you requested." Dad held out the packet, and Marion nodded to Duncan, who took it.

"For a man who's dedicated much of his life to flying beneath my radar, I find it almost comical that you weren't able to elude mere mortals."

"Well, the FBI—"

"Are not sorcerers. But not to worry. As per our agreement, once the binding is complete, I'll take care of your little predicament. It shouldn't be too difficult." She snickered, and I felt the sting of Dad's embarrassment.

Dad gave a little bow. "I would be in your debt."

Marion wheeled on my father, all traces of amusement stripped from her face. As the tension in the room climbed, the temperature dipped. I felt the chill all the way across the room. "Make no mistake about it, Angus. You've been in my debt for the better part of four decades." My father flinched back, and Marion cackled. "What's wrong, Angus? Afraid I might follow through on my father's threat?"

My father coughed up a nervous laugh. "It may have crossed my mind."

"Not to worry." She patted his shoulder as if he were the family pet. *Ironic.* "In a few hours, my father's dream will finally be realized, and you will finally be able to rest easily."

I had no idea what they were talking about, but my suspicion that my father knew Marion better than he'd let on was confirmed.

"Duncan, I believe I've worked up quite the appetite—and just in time for dinner." She glanced at her bodyguard, and he gave a subtle nod. "I've arranged for a feast in the ballroom. If you'll excuse me, I'd like to change first. Callum will see to it you don't get lost on your way there."

At the mention of his name, Callum entered the suite from the adjoining room. "If you'll come with me..."

We followed Callum through the sitting room and exited the way we'd come in. He led us to the elevators and pressed the down button. I don't know why that made me giggle, but it did.

"Private joke?" Liam whispered in my ear, giving me tingles.

"It just seems so ridiculously normal to take the elevator once you've disapparated."

Liam smirked as the doors slid open, and we joined an older couple on their way down. "Yes, well, aside from the block, most of us do try to blend in whenever possible."

I stole a glance at Callum's exposed physique and had to suppress another giggle. "I don't think he's blending in all that well."

Liam joined me in snickering.

I'd almost forgotten my father until he cleared his throat. "Your mother is waiting for me in the lobby. I'll collect her and meet you there."

I nodded. "I'll see you in a few minutes."

We both eyed Callum, who stared straight ahead as if he hadn't heard a word. I wrapped my arms around my dad's waist and pulled him in for a quick hug. A feeling of dread hung over me as if I'd never see him again, and it was all I could do to keep from begging him not to disappear.

Too soon, the elevator stopped on the mezzanine, and Liam took my hand, leading me through the open doors. I watched Dad's guilty expression over my shoulder until the doors closed again.

As we entered the ballroom, a cacophony of voices and boisterous laughter greeted us. At least a hundred people sat around a long banquet table in what reminded me of a scene straight out of a Harry Potter movie. Baskets of bread floated through the air as greedy hands reached up to grab the rolls before they were gone. Glasses of dark-red wine refilled themselves as fast as they were emptied. Giant platters of roasted meat appeared and disappeared as the hungry crowd descended on them like ants at a picnic.

A bear of a man leaped out of his seat near the head of the table with a mug of what looked like dark beer in his hand. Foam spilled over the side as he staggered into a new seat at the opposite end and sandwiched himself between two curvaceous brunettes.

My eyes widened as the man grasped a breast in each hand—one from each woman. "Did he just...?"

Liam groaned. "One of the drawbacks of having magic in the ballroom: it takes some getting used to."

Getting used to? I hadn't been to as rowdy a gathering since my college days, and instinct had me melting into Liam's side.

"You're shivering." Liam rubbed warmth into my bare arms.

I continued to watch the mayhem from a safe distance. "Are they always so..."

"Spirited? I'm afraid so. But not to worry. They won't get out of hand." He nodded to the burly men in kilts lining the room like soldiers. "Mother never travels without the full guard."

"Are all these people here for the ceremony?" I tore my eyes from the festivities long enough to watch Liam's expression.

He sighed and squeezed my hand. "I suppose I should've warned you. Talk of our binding reached legendary status before I was old enough to understand the ramifications."

"But why?" I tried to think back to anything my father had said that would explain the fascination with our wedding. "Dad said arranged marriages are standard practice. What's so special about ours?"

Liam's mouth fell open, but he closed it just as fast.

"What aren't you telling me?" My suspicions grew with every moment he stayed quiet. I searched the room for my parents, but neither they nor Marion had arrived. I reached for my cell phone to text my mother before remembering I'd left it with the rest of my things in our suite. "I'll find out eventually, you know. You may as well tell me."

He reached up and scratched the back of his neck. "It's a long story."

I crossed my arms and leveled a death glare in his direction. "I guess you'd better start talking."

Liam licked his lips, but before he could spill his guts, one of the revelers, a red-bearded giant, noticed us standing there and rose to his feet with gusto.

"Ah! The happy couple has arrived!" He raised his pint over his head, sloshing dark ale down his bare arm. "This occasion demands a toast!"

"Toasts!" A chorus of voices thundered their approval as the clan went berserk. Buttered rolls flew into the air like confetti, and the sound of popping corks reminded me of fireworks on the Fourth of July. All around the room, the clinking of glasses sounded, and mugs rose in the air.

Redbeard turned to face Liam. "May your mattress be soft and your knob—"

"Hey now, there's a lady present!" The man who'd been groping the two brunettes shoved Redbeard out of the way and raised his glass to me. "To your continued fertility and Liam's ability to knock you up on the first try!" He barely got the words out before roaring with laughter.

The entire clan focused on me as my face went up in flames. Liam—the coward—kept his eyes trained forward, probably studying some imaginary spot on the opposite wall.

"Now you've gone and embarrassed the girl." An older woman in a sparkly red gown, probably Liam's grandmother, shoved her way through the throng and patted my arm. "Don't mind them, lassie. They're all jaked on ale."

A groan came from somewhere in the back. "Aww, come on, Agnes. We don' get to attend a binding every day! Let us have our fun."

"Ha! Fun my arse." Agnes shook her head. "You louts are gonna give the poor girl performance anxiety."

Redbeard barked out another laugh and nudged Liam's shoulder. "She's not the one who needs to worry about performance."

"That's right!" The big bear guffawed. "And don't forget we'll be awarding points for style."

Another hairy-chested sorcerer pushed his way from behind and circled his kilt-clad hips twice before jutting them forward with a grunt. "And extra points for deep penetration."

I whirled on Liam and my words tumbled out in a frantic jumble. "You're supposed to give them a play by play after...?"

The crowd got conspicuously quiet, and Liam's mouth fell open, but Marion walked into the room before he had a chance to answer.

After what seemed like a century of silence, a loud bellow came from the crowd, and a beast of a man with legs the size of tree trunks and braids in his beard hurled himself toward Marion with a battle cry worthy of Mel Gibson in *Braveheart.* Before he'd even covered half the distance, two members of the guard tackled him to the floor, where the three of them wrestled until they were in hysterics. Marion seemed to eat up the attention, cheering them on from the sidelines.

I hadn't seen anything that insane since Chloe dragged me to the Black Friday sale at Neiman's, and they only had one pair of the studded black velvet Louboutins in her size, and two other women wanted them. Chloe took down the underwear model pretty easily, but I thought for sure the circuit court judge would press charges after Chloe threatened to shove the business end of her stiletto up her—

"Where did you go?" Liam put his lips up to my ear, and I jumped.

I kept my eyes on Marion as she made her way through the crowd. "What are you talking about? I'm right here."

"In body maybe." The longing in his voice got my attention, and I glanced his way long enough to catch his gaze lingering over my curves. "But in spirit..."

I turned back to where Marion danced a jig with the bearded giant while people threw rose petals at them. I had no idea where the rose petals had come from. "I was just watching the show."

"Yes, well... My mother never disappoints," Liam grumbled as he dragged me away from the entertainment and toward the now-vacant table. "Come on. Let's eat while they're distracted."

Chapter 20

$\mathcal{A}$LMOST TWO HOURS WITH THE clan exhausted me. Unlike the treatment they gave Marion, the guard had no problem allowing burly drunken men in kilts to manhandle me, jostling me around the room like a basket of hot bread. Even Liam seemed to get a kick out of the attention I'd gotten, though he never let it go too far before stepping in.

As I feared, my parents never showed up. Both Liam and Marion swore they had no idea where they'd gone or why they would have left without seeing me. I didn't know whether to believe them or not. I didn't think Marion would ever gain my trust, and despite the unnatural draw I felt toward Liam, he was still a virtual stranger.

As soon as we'd finished eating but before I had more than a few superficial bruises, I fled the banquet hall with Liam and Callum close on my heels.

When we reached the suite, I whirled on Liam, my index finger pointed at him like a loaded wand. "You're either going to tell me *exactly* what's going on, or you're going to make yourself scarce for a while. We have three hours before the ceremony, and I have a lot of questions."

Liam blanched and backed away from the open door. "Those are really questions best directed at your—"

"Parents. I know." I finished his thought and gave him the best approximation of a smile I could manage. "So if you see them while you're wandering around the hotel, how about you send them on up?"

His head bobbed up and down in a frantic nod. Then Liam turned on his heel and power-walked down the hall toward the elevators.

"How about you, Callum?" I crossed my arms and arched a brow in challenge. "Feel like answering some questions for me?"

Callum threw his head back and barked out a hearty laugh. "I'm afraid that's above my pay grade, lass."

"Well then, it's been nice, but I think I'll head in and take a nap or something." I waited for him to follow Liam, but instead he stood toe to toe with me, mirroring my position with his massive arms crossed in front of his sash-covered chest. "That's your cue to leave."

"I'm afraid I won't be leaving."

"What?" My arms dropped to my sides, and I took an involuntary step into the room. "You're coming in to watch me sleep?"

He laughed again. "No. I'll be standing out here, guarding your door to make sure no one gets in. For your protection, of course." He didn't mention the fact that no one—namely me—could get out either, but the unspoken promise was written in his stony expression.

"Yes, I'm sure the St. Regis is a hotbed for attempted sorceress kidnappings, especially this time of year."

He pressed his back against the opposite wall without acknowledging me. His eyes seemed to gloss over as he locked his attention on me. I watched him until the door clicked shut, and I was on the opposite side.

As soon as I was sure Callum wouldn't let himself in, I set off in search of my phone.

I was sure Liam had put my bags down in the sitting room, but I couldn't find them in there or in the second bedroom. After swallowing a panic attack, I ran to the main bedroom and found my clothes hanging in the closet and my bags lined up on the floor beneath them.

"Who..." I stopped dead in my tracks as I discovered a stunning emerald-green satin ball gown spread out on the bed with a delicate red-and-green tartan sash beside it.

I ran my fingers over the smooth satin, almost swallowing my tongue when a woman cleared her throat behind me. I whirled around, nearly giving myself whiplash. I didn't recognize the slender redhead in front of me, but I knew from her tartan sash that she must have been part of the clan.

"Hello, Miss Ivie." She held out her hand to me with a smile, and I blinked at it. "I'm Nora, your dresser."

"My dresser?" I scrutinized the woman from top to bottom. She couldn't have been much older than me. She was about my height and weight, though she didn't have my ample chest. We could have been sisters.

"Your..." She shifted her turquoise eyes toward the ceiling, as if trying to pull the words out of the air. "Attendant. Yes, that's what you might call me."

"Attendant." I'd officially become a parrot. But Nora beamed as understanding dawned on me. "You mean, you're here to help me get dressed?"

"Yes, miss."

"You're a..." I almost said "witch" but bit back the word for fear of her reaction. I let the question hang there, hoping she'd finish it for me.

"A sorceress?"

"Yes!" I let out the breath I'd been holding. "A sorceress. Are you?" I managed a few more words this time, but still, she must have thought I'd lost my ability to speak.

Nora chuckled as she smoothed the wrinkles from the dress where I'd touched it. "No, miss. My father is a sorcerer, but my mother..."

"So your mom's a muggle, like mine?"

Nora tilted her head and looked at me sideways. "A muggle, miss? I'm not sure I understand."

Maybe Liam was right when he said I read too much Harry Potter. "So even though your father's a sorcerer, you don't...?"

"Have the gift? No. It's extremely rare, actually. Mortals muddy the gene pool, I'm afraid. You're a rare jewel indeed."

"So you're a-a servant then?"

Nora whipped her head toward me with fire in her unusual eyes. "I am not! I volunteered for the job. My mother's Marion's hairdresser, and, well... it's quite an honor to be part of a binding ceremony, especially this one. Not everyone was given the privilege. I had to request special permission to miss my classes to come here."

"You're in school?"

Her anger dissipated, and she smiled. "University. I'm studying to be a teacher."

"I'm a teacher... well, I *was* a teacher. I really miss it." I slumped down on the bed, careful not to mess up the dress.

"You look exhausted, miss. Would you care to take a short nap? I can hang the dress—"

"No. Thank you, but I need to find out where my parents are. They didn't show up for dinner. And to be perfectly honest, I'm much too nervous to sleep. Until a few days ago, I had no idea about any of this." I waved my arm around the room.

"I understand. It *is* a lot to take in." Nora stepped over to the bedside table and opened the drawer. As if she could read my mind, she handed me my phone. "Believe me, I'd be nervous in your place, but you should at least grab a quick catnap. You'll be needing your strength for later. "

A bubble of nervous laughter climbed up my throat. "Will I be expected to do a lot of heavy lifting?" Images of me carrying Liam over the threshold ran through my brain like a slide show.

"I suppose that depends on your point of view." She blushed crimson.

"Huh?"

"Well..." Nora tugged her lower lip between her teeth. "I wouldn't imagine you'd engage in any acrobatics for your first time."

"My first time?" I was back to repeating her every word.

She let out a frustrated groan. "You Americans don't say much, do ya? I'm talking about consummating the union. After the binding ceremony?" When I didn't comment, she went on. "The clan has to witness your consummation."

"What?" I shot up from the bed, clipping the lamp with my elbow and knocking it to the floor.

Nora winced and clutched her hands together in front of her as if praying. "I'm sorry. I assumed you knew."

"The whole clan?" My entire body went up in flames, but Nora seemed oblivious to my horror. All I could think of was Liam alluding to that very thing when we'd spoken earlier. No wonder he'd turned several shades of red when I didn't understand what he was trying to say. Redbeard's comments suddenly made perfect—yet horrific—sense.

"Well, the leaders..." Nora glanced at me, shrinking back as if I might attack her. "And of course, the parents."

"Oh, no!" I paced in front of the bed, exchanging glances between the dress and Nora. "I'm not having sex in front of my father!"

"It's traditional!" Nora pleaded with me as if I'd stripped her of her belief in Santa, the Easter Bunny, and the Tooth Fairy in one sweeping proclamation. "The clan leaders have to be certain the deed has been done, so to speak. It's quite the production. Afterward, they take the bloodied sheets and burn them over a ceremonial fire."

Burning bloody sheets? I had to find a way out of this. I would absolutely *not* be part of a pornographic display for a bunch of strangers, Marion, and my parents.

"I'd rather get on my knees for a goat than have sex in front of my family and Liam's mother."

Nora coughed to keep from choking. "I-I don't think we brought any goats. I could go ask if ya like."

"No! Please don't ask. I need to be alone."

"Would ya like me to draw a bath for you?"

"Just please go. I-I just need some time to think." Or plot. There had to be another way out of that hotel without going past Callum.

"All righty, then." Nora shrugged as if this was all commonplace. And maybe it was in her world. It sure as hell wasn't in mine. "I'll be back in an hour to dress you."

The instant I heard the suite door close with a quiet snick, I hit the autodial for my mother.

"Hello?"

"Mom! Where are you?" My voice got progressively more frantic and high pitched. "You and Dad were supposed to be here for dinner, but you never showed up, and now I'm freaking the hell out because these crazy people expect me to not only marry a man I barely know, but to have sex with him in front of the clan leaders!" I left off the part of about my parents being present. The situation was bad enough.

"Is that you, Ivie?" I immediately recognized her bored tone.

"Don't you dare pretend you don't know it's me. My patience is hanging by a red-and-green tartan thread at this moment." I plopped down on the bed, this time not giving a single thought to the stupid dress or whether it got wrinkled.

"I'm sorry, dear. Your father wasn't feeling well, so we decided to sit dinner out." She didn't sound sorry. Not at all.

"He wasn't feeling well? Are you kidding me?" If I could have pulled her through the phone, I would have. Better yet, if Liam had taken the time to teach me to disapparate— and the hotel wasn't on magic lockdown—I would've been standing in my parents' living room, throttling her within an inch of her life. "Do you have *any* idea what's going on here? I feel like I've been sold to a white slavery ring in order to get Dad out of trouble with the government."

"Oh, no. It isn't like that at all. This is all a big misunderstanding that goes back long before I even met your father."

"Big surprise!" I'd already heard enough to know this was all on Dad. "What I'd like to know is, why isn't he here fixing things instead of leaving me to fend for myself?"

Mom dropped her voice to a whisper. "He is. He's working on something right now. That's why we weren't there. Ivie, I can't talk right now, but I promise, we'll be there before the ceremony."

"You'd better be. Because—"

The line went dead.

Before my phone had had a chance to cool off, I tapped out a text to Chloe, bringing her up to speed. My phone rang almost immediately.

"They can't make you have sex in front of your parents!" She sounded as scandalized as I felt. "That's just sick. And I know for a fact they can't make you marry Liam. I looked it up. Forced marriages are illegal, even in Scotland. You have to find a way to escape."

I climbed into the glass shower to make sure Callum wouldn't overhear our conversation. "I can't escape. Jack's life is at stake here."

"I also know for a fact Jack would rather die than let you go through with this."

"Did you tell him?" The question came out in a shrill squeal.

"Of course I didn't tell him." She cleared her throat. "I told Jon, and Jon told him."

"Chloe!" As much as I couldn't tell him myself, part of me was relieved Jack finally knew the truth.

"You can get mad at me later. Right now, we need to figure out how to get you out of there."

"Well, good luck with that. There's a guy outside my door who looks like an extra from *Braveheart*, and I have an attendant in the other room waiting to dress me." Even if I could get past Nora, I'd never get by Callum.

"Listen, if we could outsmart that scary guy with the gun in Vegas, we can slip past some dude in a kilt."

"No. It's hopeless. In a few hours, I'll be married to Liam and trying to explain to the elders why they won't have any bloody sheets to burn."

Chloe laughed. "That's so gross."

"I know, right? What's wrong with these people?"

"After seeing the things your dad's been up to lately, I'm beginning to think it's something in the sorcerer gene."

"Don't remind me." I heard pounding from the next room. "I've gotta go. Someone's at the door."

"Okay, go get the door, but don't lose faith. We'll figure out a way to get you out of this, Sabrina."

I only wished she could.

The pounding got louder the closer I got to the door. "Hang on. I'm coming." No sooner had I grabbed the handle than it flew open, nearly knocking me off my feet.

"Ah, there you are, lass. I thought maybe you'd somehow managed to sneak by me." Callum stood like a linebacker in the doorway, blocking my view of the hall.

I coughed over a laugh. "Right, because you'd ever let that happen."

"No." He smiled without showing his teeth. "I wouldn't."

"Are you going to let me in?" My mom's voice came from directly behind Callum.

"Mom?" I gave my bodyguard the "what-the-hell" face, and he stepped aside with a chuckle.

My mother squeezed past him, nudging me back from the door, then closed it in his face. "Finally. I thought he'd never let me in."

"What are you doing here?"

"Make up your mind, Ivie." Mom rolled her eyes and put her hands on her hips. "You either want me here, or you don't want me here."

With a whimper, I pulled her into a hug. "I do. I want you here."

"I'm not sure you will after I say what I came here to tell you."

"What do you mean?"

"I have a confession to make, and I'm afraid you'll hate your father when I'm done. And believe me, that's the last thing I want to happen."

"Mom?" My stomach did a full rotation. The lamb chops I'd eaten for dinner threatened to make a reappearance.

She dropped her purse and walked over to the sofa and sat then got back up, wringing her hands together until they were red and splotchy.

My pulse kicked up a notch. "You're really scaring me."

"I swear to you I had no idea about any of this, not until after you changed your father back."

"Just tell me what's going on. Please." I sat on the sofa and patted the spot beside me until she nodded and joined me.

"I never told you any of this because I didn't want to worry you, but when he first changed back, he had nightmares. He went on and on, ranting about some promise he'd made. I had no idea what he meant by it. I mean, honestly, it could have been anything. I never expected it to be..." She got up and paced. "Things only got worse when Liam arrived. It took me a while, but I put two and two together and realized whatever promise your father had been talking about involved Liam.

"About a week ago, after we'd gotten another letter from Scotland, he finally admitted what he'd done. I wanted to tell you then. Guilt had all but eaten me up—to think some of this is actually my fault in an indirect way—but he'd already set everything in motion. There was nothing I could do to stop it.

"Ivie, I'm so sorry. I wish I could fix this for you. I wish I'd known when you were younger, or at the very least, before your magic presented itself. I would have warned you. Your betrothal to Liam should have never been allowed to happen."

"Rose." My father stood in the doorway with his mouth agape. "You've said quite enough!"

"Daddy?" I stared, openmouthed, at my father as he panted to catch his breath. He looked as though he'd run the whole way there.

"Rose, you shouldn't have—" Dad eyed Callum, who stood off to the side, still very much in the room.

"Shouldn't have what?" Mom jumped up from the sofa. "Told our daughter the truth? Don't you think she deserves to know?"

My father turned to Callum. "Would you excuse us?"

Callum shot me a glance, and when I nodded, he let himself out of the room, closing the door behind him.

Once my bodyguard had gone, Dad turned to Mom with a sigh. "No, I mean, you should have waited for me. It should be me telling her the truth, not you." He waved us toward the sitting area again and waited while Mom and I took our places on the sofa before sitting in the chair opposite us. "I was a lad of thirteen when I first met Marion Kincaid."

Chapter 21

"THERE WAS A TIME WHEN you could've searched for miles around without finding anyone as lovely as Marion Kincaid. She had fire—so full of life—you couldn't help wanting to be around her. And I was no different from anyone else in that regard. She played as hard as the boys, but not a single girl could hold a candle to her. Marion flirted with everyone. It didn't matter who they were. But no matter how much she flirted, she'd been promised to me." Dad wore a huge grin as old memories seemed to overtake him. I had the urge to stick my fingers in my ears and chant "la, la, la" until he finished talking, but if my mother could sit ramrod straight beside me without a single wince or groan at anything he said, I could stick it out too. Still, listening to my dad talk about another woman with such obvious affection threw me off balance. It would break my heart to hear Jack talk about a past love that way. I could only imagine how my mother felt.

"Our clans weren't close," he continued. "But a match between them had been brokered over many generations. Ours was the first to produce viable heirs. Luckily for us, Marion and I developed a quick bond. I would have done anything for her, and she felt the same. For five years, nothing came between us.

"After my father's unexpected death, we were forced to delay our binding ceremony. Naturally, as his only son, all of his responsibilities fell on me. I spent more time out of the country than in it, but Marion's dedication never wavered. She helped my mum run the family holdings without once complaining. She would have waited for me forever; I have no doubt.

"I'd just completed university and started a new position when I met your mother. I'd gone to London on business, and there she was at the local pub with a group of friends."

"What was Mom doing in London?"

Dad threw a wink at Mom. "Studying at Oxford for her semester abroad."

I whipped my head around and gaped at my mother. I'd had no idea she'd studied at Oxford.

"Close your mouth, dear." Mom smirked. "You'll catch flies."

Dad laughed, but the besotted look he gave Mom soothed some of the anger I'd felt toward him and filled me with hope. "I had to believe fate had brought us together. I knew instantly Rose was the woman I was meant to spend my life with. Don't get me wrong. It wasn't easy by any stretch, but despite the obstacles in our path, we wasted no time working toward that goal. I made arrangements to leave the country in secret, and we eloped without telling a soul."

"Wait..." I slid toward him until I sat on the edge of my seat. "You didn't tell Marion?" Why I felt sorry for her, I had no idea. But maybe I understood her just a little better.

"No, I told no one. I should have been man enough to tell her in person, and believe me, the guilt still keeps me up at night. As you can imagine, she didn't take it well." He winced.

Understatement of the century.

I couldn't imagine Marion taking much in stride. "She was humiliated? Angry?"

"Humiliated and angry didn't even begin to describe her emotional state." Dad steepled his hands and rested his chin on the point. "The McKies have a rather long and distinguished pedigree in the sorcery world, and as I said, the match between our families had been planned for generations. So when I, uh—"

"Jilted her?" The fact that he'd left her for my mother hadn't escaped my notice, but for some reason, a twinge of sympathy for Marion festered in me.

"I suppose so, yes." Dad lowered his head and exhaled with an uncomfortable chuckle. "My hasty departure had shamed her in front of the whole clan. And a lack of other available matches forced her to marry an aging clan leader, a widower, and not a warm man at that. Rumors went around for years that he'd killed his first wife for failing to give him a son."

I gasped. "How Henry the Eighth of him."

Dad let out another tense laugh. "My rash decisions had trapped her in a loveless marriage with a cruel man who'd lost most of his faculties. But over time, Marion managed to align herself with McDougall's power center. When her husband died while Liam was still a boy, Marion rose up as the clan leader."

My brain ached with information overload. Dad's confession explained why Marion would hold a grudge against him for all these years, but not how Liam—or I— fit into the equation. "Dad, I still don't get what any of this has to do with me. You broke her heart. That's awful. But why am I here?"

My parents shared a strained look, and my stomach dipped. "What?"

Mom cleared her throat. "I'm sure you'd noticed your father and I waited a while before having you, but what you probably didn't realize is we tried to have children for years with no luck. The doctors chalked it up to bad timing, but I always felt as if something more sinister was in play. And then your father—"

Dad took over. "I'd heard through an old acquaintance that Marion struggled with fertility for years. I felt guilty, of course, especially given her husband. But then when she did finally conceive—"

"We found out we were expecting just a few months later." Mom jumped back into the conversation with a vengeance. "I swear to you, it was as if Marion had cast a spell to keep us from bearing children until she was able to."

"I didn't believe it at first. She would've had to be..." Dad lowered his voice to a faint whisper. "Well, not just a little bit *insane*. And accepting that would mean we were in far more danger than I'd ever dreamed. Soon after giving birth to Liam, Marion petitioned the clan council to sanction me for having broken our agreement. My sins had come back to haunt me. "

"They couldn't have just fined you? A 'here's a few grand and a slap on the wrist' sort of thing?"

"Unfortunately, no. Not only had my parents agreed to the arrangement, but I'd signed a contract, something similar to a prenuptial agreement, if you will. But stronger. It involved dark magic."

"You ditched out on a magical contract, so Marion wanted you punished. And what? You offered me up in trade?" The conversation was heading in a direction that made me uncomfortable and not just a little pissed off.

"Oh, no, Ivie!" Mom grabbed my hands and squeezed them between hers. "Your father would *never* offer you up in trade."

"No, mah wee bonnie lass, *you* were always what, or rather who, Marion wanted. She demanded a betrothal for a betrothal. She wouldn't rest until *my* daughter was promised to *her* son."

"If I wasn't even born yet, how did she know you'd even have a girl?" I darted my eyes back and forth between them.

My parents shared another uneasy glance, and this time my stomach plummeted.

Dad leaned forward and rested his elbows on his knees. "The infertility, the sudden pregnancy, all of it was her doing. Her hatred had made her stronger than I could've possibly imagined. She wielded dark magic the way your mother wields a credit card."

Mom scoffed, but her blush told me he'd been dead on.

I blew out a breath and sank back into the cushions. "So I'm guessing the council agreed?"

Dad nodded. "I always figured I'd have years before I had to face up to it. And there was always the possibility you'd be born *sine magicae*."

Sine Magicae?

Mom must have read the confusion in my face. "A mere mortal, dear."

I nodded and waited for Dad to continue.

"As you grew up, I regretted not fighting the council. Signs of your impending magic were everywhere. To say I had second thoughts would be a gross understatement."

"And you never told Mom any of this?"

"Oh, God, no, not until it was clear Marion would be making the trip. I'd hoped you and Liam would..." He shook his head as if to clear the thought. "On the day you were born, the council mandated that you be bound to Liam on your thirteenth birthday. Dread filled me until I couldn't sleep at night. The only way I knew to prevent it was to block your magic. I put a spell on you when you were young, but with every growth spurt, I would have to refresh it. I hoped the clan would scry for you, and when they didn't sense your abilities, the mandate would be null and void."

"But...?"

"I had this brilliant idea to cloak myself as well. If I took myself off the radar, they'd have an even harder time searching for you with a locator spell. You can't scry for a sorcerer when no sorcerer exists."

"What happened?"

Dad leaned back in his chair and laughed. "My simple little cloaking spell had a few side effects I didn't expect."

I widened my eyes and waited.

"Fleas." As if the mere mention of them made him itchy, Dad scratched his head.

I laughed. I remembered the dog well, and then Dad had somehow managed to swap the dog for a cat and ended up as my trusty familiar during the ordeal with my cheating ex. *Oh, my God, Matt!* "So when I turned Matt into a skunk—"

"You set off a signal that lit up Scotland."

"That's how they found me?"

Dad's lips pressed into a hard line, and he nodded. "I did try to mitigate the damages as much as possible, but as I was a cat, my paws were tied. Jack did the right thing, keeping you moving. That threw the clan off for a while. And of course, they couldn't find me anywhere on the map, so the possibility of an anomaly must have tripped them up. But once you'd changed me back, there we were, like two glowing lanterns in a church window for all the world to see.

"The first letter came just weeks before Liam arrived. And when he got here, well, I had to fib just a little when he learned you were already engaged to another man. That wouldn't have gone over well with Marion. Between that and the trouble with the FBI, I've had my hands full."

"What little fibs did you tell Liam?"

He waved me off. "That's not important anymore. The boy has been unbelievably helpful over the past few weeks. He's been well trained. I only wish I had his control. And the transporting from place to place, that's a rare gift, indeed."

"So basically, you're saying you let things go on the way they were because Liam's been helping you dig yourself out of trouble?"

"Well... there is that, but if I could have sent him on his merry way, I would have. Discovering his talents was just an added bonus. You must know, I feel horrific guilt for all of this and what it's meant for you. I should have told you right away. Doing the spell without your knowledge was a bad decision on my part, and I only hope you can forgive me someday, but I'm afraid nothing would have changed. If you don't agree to the binding with Liam, Marion will retaliate. None of us will be safe. She'll hold your mother and me responsible. And I'm afraid Jack will be her first target."

My pulse thundered so hard that I felt it in my fingertips, my throat, my hair. My father had jilted Marion and brought all of this down on me in the process. Not that he would have known that would happen when he walked away. But none of that would help me now. I was totally screwed.

"I don't know what to think." I stood and paced over the plush carpet. I sank into the deep pile, but my feet must have been as numb as the rest of me because I felt nothing. "Liam's... *nice.* And I do feel something for him, but I also know what I feel isn't real. It's the product of that little spell you put on me."

Dad, at least, had the decency to blush. "A necessary evil, I'm afraid. I couldn't have you rejecting him offhand. He would have gone straight to his mother and told her we'd failed to honor another betrothal."

My heart skipped as a sudden thought hit me. "Liam's feelings aren't just a result of that spell, are they?"

"You have to understand," Dad explained. "He was groomed from a young age to accept your betrothal. It would've never occurred to him to reject it."

"This is crazy." I dropped into my seat again. "Straight-up insane. You know that, right?"

Dad shrugged. "Old traditions die hard."

Old traditions needed to die. *Hard.*

"So I have no say in this? I marry Liam, or everyone I love suffers?"

My mother used the sleeve of her blouse to dab at her eyes.

"It's incredibly unfair." Dad gripped my shoulders and looked me dead in the eyes. "And for that, I am immeasurably sorry."

Nora arrived at nine, giving my parents the perfect excuse to escape before the shock wore off and I went all ninja witch on them. *Not a bad idea.* In fact, it sounded better and better with every passing minute, especially after Nora scolded me for wrinkling my dress. *My ugly emerald-green wedding dress.*

She shot me a look that would've had big strong Callum's balls climbing back inside his body. I didn't even *have* balls, and I shuddered. "This wasn't wrinkled when I left ya here with it."

"You told me to take a nap." *Which, of course, I didn't.* But she didn't need to know that.

"Not on your dress!" She huffed, grumbling as she scooped up the dress as if it were her child. "This'll have to be sent down to the laundry to be steamed, unless you'd care to use a little magic to fix it. Oh, wait. The block. I forgot."

I laughed. "Trust me. You wouldn't want my help anyway, unless you'd like to see that dress turn into a potted plant or something. In case you hadn't heard, I'm not exactly known for my control." So I lied. I'd gotten much better at the simple spells, but even if I was able, I'd refuse to lift a glowing blue finger to help the McDougalls drag me to the altar. I held on to the hope that something would make us late, and the entire hotel would turn into a shoe box at the stroke of midnight. A girl could wish, anyway.

"No. That would never do." Nora muttered to herself as she stomped to the door. "You'd better get in the shower.

And unless you want to be embarrassed later, I suggest you shave."

My lips fell open, but not a sound came out. Would my humiliation never end? I'd become the poster child for living with the sins of the father.

The girl who'd been so sweet to me not two hours earlier slammed the door behind her as she went out.

I cranked on the hot water and stepped under the scalding spray, wondering how my life had spun so completely out of control. If only I'd let Matt kick me out all those months ago instead of turning him into a woodland creature... or if I'd left Dad in his kitty-cat form. Maybe the clan wouldn't have found me. I knew my thoughts were bordering on selfish, but didn't I deserve a little happiness in my life?

I'd only finished shaving one leg when Nora pranced back in with a perfectly pressed gown. "That was fast." *Too fast.*

A scarlet stain spread over her cheeks. "I ran into Duffy in the lobby. He was kind enough to wave his wand over it."

The images her comment brought to mind made me blush. "I hope you were being metaphorical."

"Of course." She giggled, and I had to squash the image of any *member* of Marion's guard whipping out his wand and rubbing it all over my dress. "Did you need any help in there? You're gonna use every drop of hot water in the hotel if you don't hurry."

I made a few more passes over my shins before rinsing off and wrapping myself in one of the hotel's luxurious bath towels. "What time is it?"

Nora's impish face lit up. "Time for hair and makeup."

Over an hour later, my hair was curled within an inch of its life, making me wish I still had the pixie cut from my pre-sorceress days. And Nora must have learned how to apply makeup from the cast of *La Cage aux Folle* because I looked a little like my dad in drag.

"You don't think I'm wearing a little too much..." I waved my hand around my entire face.

"Mascara?" Nora studied my false eyelashes like an entomologist with a new species.

"No. Well, yes. But what I really mean is, I don't normally wear this much makeup. I'm pretty sure Liam won't even recognize me."

"You look beautiful." The vacant look in her eyes told me she had no idea what I meant. Then the clouds cleared, and she whipped her head toward the sitting room.

"*Who... was that cleared... no one informed me.*" Bits and pieces of a conversation between Callum and another man filtered through the door. I could tell Callum was agitated. "*No one sees Miss McKie without permission from Chief McDougall!*"

Someone wanted to get into my room in a big way, and I could only think of one person who'd stand up to a half-naked sorcerer to see me.

I bolted across the room, dragging Nora behind me as she tried to keep me from tripping on the train of my skirt. We almost wiped out twice on the way to the door. I would've never expected Nora to be so athletic.

I practically ripped the door from the hinges. "Callum, what's going—" My eyes practically popped out of my head, and I choked on my tongue, unable to make more than a few guttural sounds as I stood face to face with Jack and his older, more broody brother, Jon, wearing Clan McKie traditional kilts with matching blue-and-green plaid sashes... and nothing else.

Chapter 22

WILLING MY LEGS TO HOLD on just a little bit longer before giving out, I eyed Jack, drinking him in from head to toe and paying special attention to his exposed chest. Even with his hair sticking up in all directions and bags under his blue eyes, he looked amazing—tired, but amazing. I resisted the urge to tackle him to the floor and bit back a groan. The ever-present tingle that materialized whenever we were near each other prickled over my skin as an entire colony of butterflies set off from their hiding places to flutter around my stomach.

This is so not the time to fall apart, Ivie!

While Jon argued—in a far better Scottish accent than mine—that my dad had sent them to escort me on his behalf, Jack returned my perusal with a barely contained snicker. The urge to glare at Nora and scream, "I told you so!" took a backseat to Callum's icy glare. The gears in my brain spun like a hamster on a wheel. If I didn't come up with something fast, we'd all be toast. Finally, an idea came to me. "Oh, good. You're here!"

Callum whipped around as Nora tripped over her shoes to get a better look at Jon. I couldn't blame her. If I hadn't already fallen for Jack, Jon's devil-may-care attitude and swagger might have sucked me in like a tractor beam. And I had to admit, he looked good, even if he did need a haircut. His dark hair curled up where it grazed his neck. As if he'd heard my thoughts, Jon shot me a wink, and I sent up a quick prayer that Nora didn't recognize the Amazing Jonathon Blake from his TMZ appearances.

"Dad said he'd be sending a few of his favorite clansmen to escort me to the ballroom. I hope that's not a problem, Callum." I flashed him a toothy grin and batted my twenty-pound eyelashes in his direction. With the smile frozen on my face and my eyes twitching, he probably thought I was having a seizure.

"Why didn't I know about this?" Nora narrowed her eyes, giving both Jon and Jack another once-over before turning her attention back to me.

"Come on, Nora. You're so big on tradition, I figured you'd already know that, in America, it's customary for the bride's family to walk her down the aisle. Since we aren't having a traditional American ceremony, my dad wanted to at least give me that much." It wasn't hard to bring out the tears under the circumstances. Just seeing Jack's face fall when I said "bride" was enough to bring them back to the surface.

Nora lowered her eyes to the floor, but I caught her peeking under her lashes at Jon more than once. "Yes, of course. That makes perfect sense."

Callum crossed his massive arms and huffed. The vein in his forehead pulsed as if sending out Morse code, and I wondered if sorcerers could stroke out. "Nobody cleared this with me."

"There she is!"

We all turned in unison as if we'd synchronized the motion.

In what had to be the most constricting Herve Leger dress she owned, Chloe alternated between power-walking and jogging down the hall toward us. The lilac strapless bandage dress wrapped her body like a tourniquet from chest to mid-thigh. I had no idea how she took a breath in that thing, let alone walked.

Chloe stopped directly in front of Callum, her Lucite platform heels bringing her almost to his shoulder. "Well, hello, handsome." She bit her lip and reached out to grab his arm, giving it a squeeze.

Callum turned so red he was almost purple, and a violent cough ripped out of me as I tried to keep from laughing.

"Oh, my heavens. Are you okay, Miss Ivie? Can I get you a drink?" Nora slapped my spine hard enough to dislodge my back teeth.

"No," I sputtered, catching my breath. I glanced at Chloe, and she winked. "I'm fine."

Callum darted his eyes down the hall in both directions before settling them on Chloe's face. "And who might you be?"

Without missing a beat, Chloe spread her lips in a smile worthy of an orthodontia ad and shoved her hand toward him. "Chloe Jamison, the wedding planner. Ivie's mother hired me to make sure her daughter's wedding went off without a hitch. So here I am." Her expression turned serious, and she leaned in as if she had a secret to share with him. "I'm assuming you have the itinerary? I'll need to be brought up to speed immediately."

Callum didn't take her proffered hand, but he did steal another peek at her cleavage before exhaling. "Miss Ivie, did you know your mother would be sending a—what did you call yourself?"

Chloe rolled her eyes then said the words slowly, enunciating each syllable. "A wed-*ding* plan-*ner.*"

He rotated his head from side to side as if he still didn't comprehend her meaning. "That would be Miss Nora's field of expertise. My job is to stand guard."

"Well, then." Chloe turned to Nora and cranked up her smile to full volume again. "I guess it's you and me!"

Nora's eyes widened until I almost worried they'd fall out of her delicate face as Chloe linked their arms together and dragged Nora into my suite. Jack slid past Callum's radar, keeping pace with Chloe as she had Nora show her around the sitting room.

Jon cleared his throat and signaled with his head for me to go in before mimicking Callum's posture. "I suppose it can't hurt to have two of us stand guard, aye?"

He didn't have to tell me twice. I hurried into the room, sending up another prayer for Jon to say as little as possible. His accent might have been better than mine, but that wasn't saying much.

The instant the door had closed behind me, Jack wrapped his arms around my waist. He yanked me off my feet, dragging me to the side.

I swallowed a squeal, turning in his arms and planting a breathless kiss on him before realizing what I'd done. "Oh, my God. What are you doing here?"

Jack did a quick sweep of the room, but since we could hear Chloe oohing and ahhing over the marble fixtures in the bathroom, we knew we were safe for the moment. "I've come to rescue you."

"Rescue me? In a kilt?" I zeroed in on Jack's exposed stomach muscles then back up in time to see him smirk. "And yes, you look amazing, but that's not the point."

His eyebrows pulled together in a deep furrow as the severity of the situation hit him. "Right. The point is, I can't let you marry... or bind yourself... to Liam. I love you. You're worth fighting for."

As much as I wanted to, I didn't have time to melt at his words. I had to get him out of there. If Marion found him, all my sacrifices would've been for nothing. "Jack, under any other circumstances, I'd not only be flattered, I'd agree with you. But you don't understand."

"Ivie—" Jack whipped his head to the side as Chloe's voice got closer. "Damn it, come on. You need to listen to what I have to say." He grabbed my hand and pulled me into the adjoining room.

As soon as the door closed behind us, I wheeled on him with my pulse pounding in my ears. "No, *you* need to listen to *me*. There is no other way this can end. I'm a sorceress, and you've never been comfortable with that fact." He opened his mouth to argue, but I silenced him with a finger over his lips. "Think about it. I've dragged you across the country on a wild goose chase after using magic I didn't even know I had. I almost got you killed by my crazy neighbor. You got your ass kicked in a magical showdown with a sorcerer." I ticked off each one on my fingers. "You were arrested. I was arrested. I lost a job I absolutely loved. All because of magic."

"None of that was—"

"It doesn't matter whose fault it was. It happened because of *me*."

"I don't care." Jack pressed his lips into a tight line, and I recognized the stubborn set of his shoulders.

He could lie to himself but not to me. "Yes, you—"

"No." His voice dipped, and he rested his forehead against mine. He panted, hot against my face. "I don't."

I let out a shuddering breath as Jack skated his hands up my arms and over my shoulders.

He locked his eyes on mine and sank his fingers into my hair. "You listen to me, Ivie McKie. I love you for who you are—sorceress or not."

With his fingers rubbing soothing patterns on my scalp, I'd lost the will to fight. I barely had the will to speak. "It'll never work out. I can't have a normal job or a normal life." His hands stilled for a second, and I jerked out of his grasp. "For once, I'm going to do the right thing."

He flinched as if I'd slapped him, and my already broken heart shattered into a million pieces. "Ivie, no."

I sucked in a deep breath and kept going as if I wasn't dying inside—as if saying goodbye to him again didn't destroy me. "I'm sorry, Jack, but I'm going to marry Liam and move to Scotland where I can be with other people like me, where I can blow up labs until I learn to control the magic, and where I'll have someone to help me the next time I turn random strangers into domestic pets."

"Stop." Jack grabbed a hold of his hair with both hands and paced. "I know why you're doing this, and I won't let you. Chloe said you're afraid Liam's mother will retaliate against me if you walk away, but sweetheart, I'll tell you what I told her. I'd rather die than let you bind yourself to someone you don't even love." Jack stopped pacing and grabbed both sides of my face to lock his gaze with mine. A sad smile crossed his lips, and his voice dropped to a whisper. "And if you think for even half a second I'm going to walk out that door and let you consummate *anything* with *him* in front of a bunch of strangers and your parents, well, you don't know me very well."

My broken heart hammered against my ribs as I blinked back tears and pressed my lacquered lips to his. *A goodbye kiss—because nothing has changed.* I still couldn't allow him to sacrifice his life for me.

"Ivie, it's almost time!" Nora shouted from the other room, making us jump apart. "You'd better not have wrinkled that dress!"

I wrenched myself farther away from Jack before I changed my mind. "I have to go."

Jack grabbed for my hand, but I pulled it away before he could get a good grip. "Damn it, Ivie. No, you don't. Come with me. We'll just disappear. Name the place, and we'll go there."

I shook my head as tears spilled over my lower lashes and down my cheeks. My lips moved, but barely a whisper came out. "They'll find me."

"Then we'll keep moving. I'll do whatever it takes to be with you." He stalked toward me until he'd backed me against the wall.

No matter how hard I tried to hold it in, a sob slipped out. "Jack, you don't understand!"

"Then explain it to me." His eyes glistened with unshed tears as he slammed his fist into the wall beside my head. "I know you love me. Why won't you run away with me?"

"Because in less than an hour, Ivie will be bound to me." Liam stood in the open doorway, flames sparking from his eyes. He slammed the door and crossed the room. Instead of confronting Jack, he cupped my face in his hand. "Are you okay?" I nodded, and he whipped around to face Jack. "Don't look so surprised. I've told you before, we're connected. I can feel her stress. I can tell when she's upset, and as usual, you're the reason."

Jack took a step toward Liam, danger flashing in his own eyes. "Have you ever stopped to think maybe *you're* the reason she's upset?"

"Me?" Liam pressed a finger into his own chest. "You think I'm the reason she's upset?"

Jack nodded once, his jaw clenched, and the vein in his neck bulged more with every breath he took. "Everything was fine before you got here. We were happy."

"You call that happy?" Liam turned his eyes to the ceiling and barked out a humorless laugh.

"I'm right here!" I shouted, but they ignored me.

One long stride brought Liam within striking distance of Jack, and I waited for him to throw the first punch. But he had a more damaging attack in mind. "Ivie's never been anything but a plaything to you. You kept her in a box, only taking her out when it served your purpose."

Jack froze in place with his head tilted to one side. He'd gone so still, I thought for half a second Liam might've actually hit him. "What the hell are you talking about?"

"You used her for her magic." With his hands fisted at his sides, Liam circled Jack like a boxer in the ring. "Tricked her into doing your bidding."

Jack's mouth dropped open, and he rocked back on his heels, looking defeated.

"Don't look so shocked. Did you think I wouldn't find out? Her father told me what you've done."

"My father?" I took a hesitant step toward Liam as, one by one, the pieces fell into place. "What did my father tell you?"

"He told me how your precious magician had used you, forced you to perform magic, then took advantage of your heightened physical state afterward, forcing you to do unspeakable acts." Liam spoke to me, but he stared at Jack with hatred in his eyes. "He told me how you'd been completely mesmerized by him, unable to see through his façade." Liam turned to me, and the affection in his expression chipped away at my defenses. "I took a vow to protect you from people like him, Ivie. I won't back down now, not when we're so close to being one."

"Liam, you don't understand." I cautiously laid my hand on his forearm, and the corded muscles jumped beneath my fingers. "My father lied to you."

Pain flashed in Liam's eyes. "You're still defending him? After everything I've just told you? You still want him?" He turned on Jack like a rabid dog, a spark of blue light dancing along his fingertips as he pointed at him before it fizzled out like a match in the rain. I saw the moment he realized what had happened. His fists clenched at his sides, and he launched himself at Jack.

"Liam, NO!" I jumped on his back like a spider monkey, knocking his hand away before he could punch Jack. We crashed into the bedside table, smashing my second lamp in a day and sending shards of glass everywhere. I kept my arms coiled around his neck, holding on for dear life. "Please, don't hit him. Just give me a minute to say goodbye."

Liam huffed out a heavy breath as his muscles relaxed. He nodded.

I unwrapped my arms and slid off his back, glancing down at my wrinkled dress. "Nora's gonna kill me."

"She'll have to go through me first." His lips curved into a sad smile as he crossed to the sitting room door. He pointed at Jack. "One minute."

As soon as Liam closed the door behind him, I dropped to the floor with my dress puddling around me like an emerald pool.

"Don't even say it." Jack stood over me, his face set in a determined scowl. "I won't let you say goodbye to me."

"I know." I smiled through my tears as I thought back to our last goodbye. He wouldn't let me say the words then either.

"You don't love him." He stared at the closed door.

"No," I whispered, but I knew he'd heard me when he brought his eyes back to mine. "I don't. But I love you enough to let you go. To keep you safe."

Jack crouched down beside me, running his long fingers through my tangled hair. "We've been through worse than this, sweetheart."

"Uh, actually, no." I laughed through a sob. "We haven't."

Jack grunted out his agreement. "So maybe this is the worst thing we've had to deal with, but that doesn't mean we should give up!"

I gazed up at his stubbled jaw, clenched so tight I was sure it would shatter, and wondered how I'd survive without seeing his face every morning. "You're only saying that because you don't know what I've done. You'll hate me when you find out."

Jack sat down, smoothing the wrinkles in my dress with his finger. "What could you have possibly done to make me hate you?"

"Do you remember that first night in the woods?"

He raised his eyebrows and smirked. "Are you kidding me?"

"Right." The corners of my lips tipped up only to fall again. "Of course you do. Well, apparently, your idea of a magical convergence was dead on the money, and I did it, and now you only love me because I accidentally put a binding spell on us."

His eyebrows came together as he frowned. "What are you talking about?"

"Don't you see? You love me because of a stupid spell I didn't even know I was capable of. It's like the spell my father put on me. I love you. I know I do. I feel it with every fiber in my being, but my feelings aren't real. And whatever you feel for me, that's not real either. It's the spell. Just like with Liam."

Chapter 23

Jack's face went ashen. "That's not possible. I'm not a... I don't have the power to... Ivie, you know I made that up. Nothing that happened to us in the woods that night was magic. Well, it was, but not *that* kind of magic."

"Then I must have done it myself. I've been to see a witch doctor, and he said it's true." I couldn't control the wail that ripped out of me.

Liam cleared his throat from the doorway. "That isn't possible."

My head snapped up, and I stared at Liam through a steady flow of tears. "Have you been listening this whole time?"

He ignored my question and continued. "In order to perform a binding spell like the one your father performed, you would've needed a potion made up of parts of yourself and parts of Jack—blood, fingernail clippings, hair—I'm assuming you didn't have any of those things."

I shook my head, mesmerized by the soothing tone in his voice.

"And since Jack isn't a sorcerer, even if he'd had those things, he couldn't have done it. Then there's the whole issue of intent. I'm going to assume you didn't intend to bind yourself to him that night?"

I shook my head again.

"Without a potion and without proper intent, it's highly unlikely a novice sorceress would have successfully performed such a complex spell by accident."

"Oh." I blinked at Liam to bring him into focus.

He shifted his weight, and the sadness in his eyes made me want to cry. "So you really don't have any feelings for me?"

I started to shake my head and stopped myself. "No! I do. But..."

"But those feelings came from the spell."

"Yeah." I nodded.

"And what your father said about Jack..." He glanced at Jack, who sat as still as a statue beside me. "None of that was true?"

Jack and I both shook our heads.

Liam sank to the floor beside us and scratched his head. "I don't know what to say. An apology doesn't seem to be enough after everything—"

"My dad told me about his relationship with your mother and how he jilted her for my mom. That's what really caused all this. So it's me who owes you an apology."

Jack grabbed my hand and slid his fingers between mine. "I should have neutered him while he was still a cat."

"He did some horrible things. And he told some impressive lies to cover up for them. But my dad's still right, you know. Nothing has changed." I squeezed Jack's hand. "If I don't bond with Liam, you'll pay the price. Or my parents will. Or someone else I love. And I can't let that happen."

"That's a horrible reason to want to be with me." Liam let out a strained laugh.

"Do I really have a choice?"

"Maybe." Liam's eyes lit up, but before he could finish his thought, Nora pushed her way into the room with Chloe hot on her heels.

"We're gonna be late!" Nora skidded to a stop a few feet from where Liam, Jack, and I sat cross-legged on the floor. "What on earth are ya doing? Marion's already sent someone to make sure you were on your way. It's past eleven!"

Chloe shoved past Nora to stand over us. "Clearly, you're not familiar with American traditions. They're *praying*." She stretched the word into two long syllables.

Nora pressed a hand to her chest and jumped back as if she'd stepped on someone's fingers. "Oh. I-I'm sorry I interrupted your prayers. I hate to rush you, but how long will you be?"

"Not much longer at all." Chloe widened her eyes at me and mouthed "hurry up" as she grabbed Nora by the shoulders and steered her out the door, pulling it shut behind her.

"If you've got a plan, you'd better talk fast." Jack hopped up, nodding toward the door. "I don't think even Chloe can keep that one at bay for long."

Turning from Jack, I caught Liam's blue eyes and held them. I was close enough to feel his warm breath on my face. "You hinted at a choice. What did you mean?"

Liam's eyes darted to my lips then back again. He took a deep breath before speaking. "Did you ever wonder why Mum never retaliated against your parents directly? She would've had a number of opportunities over the years."

His powder-blue eyes pulled me in again, and I had to look away to concentrate on his question. "Mom and Dad said Marion put a spell on them to make it harder to conceive."

Liam groaned. "That's an old rumor, one I'm not entirely convinced is true. But even if she did interfere with their fertility, I'd hardly call that revenge, considering they did ultimately have a child."

"Okay, but..." My mind went blank. I'd taken everything my father had said at face value. Marion would retaliate. It never occurred to me that she'd had years to take her revenge but never had. It didn't take long for the thought to sink in and fester.

"Think about it for a moment. Once your dad committed to someone else—once he was *married*—my mother faded into obscurity."

I cocked an eyebrow in his direction.

One side of his mouth tipped up. "I didn't say she forgot. And she certainly never got over being scorned. But she didn't retaliate because she couldn't."

"Why?" Jack asked the burning question.

"I'm getting to that." Liam glared at Jack.

Jack held up his hands with his palms facing Liam. "Sorry. Go on. You've got the floor."

Liam exhaled through his nose before continuing. "It's all about the rules."

He was talking in circles, and I didn't understand what he was getting at. I wanted to shake him until he spit it out. "Rules?"

"There are certain rules even sorcerers have to follow. Your father broke one of those rules when he walked away from the promise he'd made to my mother. But a betrothal doesn't carry the same weight as an actual marriage vow. Once your father had made that vow with another, Mum had no choice but to back down."

Jack's face split in a wide smile as understanding dawned on him. "So—"

"Exactly." Liam nodded at Jack. "If Ivie marries you, Mum will have no choice but to let you go as well." He turned to me with a sad smile. "I'll no longer have a claim on you, so neither will she."

"Why are you telling me this now? Why not before? You knew how I felt." A flicker of anger sparked in me. Liam'd had the solution to my problems all along and withheld it.

He lowered his eyes and fidgeted with a loose thread on his kilt. "Because I thought you were being manipulated by Jack and needed my help. And now..." He lifted his head. "Ivie, I care about what happens to you. Believe it or not, your happiness is the most important thing to me.

I wish it could've been with me, but if that's not possible, at least I'll know you're happy."

I'd lost count of how many times I'd cried over the course of the past several days, but Liam had brought me to tears again. "Thank you."

"Don't thank me yet. We still have to figure out how to get you out of here without using magic."

I swallowed my fear and winked at Jack before looking Liam dead in the eye. "I've been in worse jams than this one."

"I can't learn to disapparate in five minutes!" Panic paralyzed me as I stood in the middle of the sitting room with Liam, Jack, and Chloe. They were counting on me not to fail. But this whole idea had failure written all over it.

"Yes. You can." Liam took my trembling hands in his and squeezed. "Relax and concentrate."

"Disapparate?" Chloe nudged Jack. "Isn't that a Harry—"

Jack bit back a grin. "Not now, Chloe."

I let out a frustrated groan. "It doesn't matter what it's called. I absolutely cannot learn to transport myself magically from one place to another in five minutes. It took me almost six months to learn how to drive. That little brat Jenny Byrd called me MARTA all the way through junior year because of that. She said I might as well learn the name since I'd be taking the bus for the rest of my life. Even when I *did* finally get my license, it was after lots and lots of *practice*. I can't practice disapparating until I'm in the ballroom. And I'll only get one shot at it—one shot that I have to pull off in a room filled with angry sorcerers!"

Jack gave my shoulders a squeeze. "Relax. Don't think about that now."

"Right." All the breath whooshed out of my lungs as he massaged my tense muscles. That room full of sorcerers was all I'd thought about since the moment Liam sent Nora on a mission to the ballroom to get my parents. Our plan wouldn't work at all unless we could get the people I cared about out of the building before Marion discovered I'd disappeared.

"Ivie. Look at me." Liam grabbed my chin and tilted my face toward him. "It's not as hard as it looks. Just listen to the sound of my voice and relax."

I nodded as much as I could with Liam holding onto my chin and Jack's hands on my neck.

"Good. In order to *siubhal-ama*, you have to visualize your destination. Pick a spot, and concentrate on nothing else. Don't think about anyone in the room with you. Don't think about your parents or my mother. You have to clear everything from your mind so you can *see* where you're going and believe you'll arrive." He let out a breath and stepped back.

"So I have to have been to the place I'm going?"

"Not necessarily, but it definitely helps."

"What else?" I waited for the next steps so I could catalog them in my brain.

He shrugged. "That's it."

"That can't be it." I flailed my hands in front of me. "Where's the catchy rhyme for me to recite while I'm concentrating?"

"Sorry," he said as he tucked his white button-down into his kilt. "That's really all there is: no rhymes, no spells, just good old-fashioned sorcery."

I watched him in my peripheral vision. "Why do I think you've given me the Spark Notes version?"

"Spark Notes?" Liam scrunched up his face and scratched his head.

"Never mind," I said with an exaggerated huff. *Stupid sorcerer.* He'd probably skipped over half the steps for the sake of brevity. With my luck, I'd end up splitting my atoms and scattering them over the entire state. "That can't be all. Imagine yourself traveling there, and you'll arrive? If it was that easy, everyone would do it."

"I never said it was easy." He grinned and tapped my nose with his index finger.

I reached out to grab it, but he snatched it away at the last second. "Yes. You. Did."

"No. I said that's all you have to do. Executing the *siubhal-ama is* amazingly difficult. Most people have a problem wiping their mind of anything else long enough to make the trip." Liam stepped around me, escaping to the bedroom, but when he turned around, I was right behind him.

"So you're telling me when you brought me to the hotel, you thought of nothing but the destination?" I glanced at the bed and leaned in so I could whisper. "You didn't imagine what would happen in this room after the binding ceremony?"

"No." Liam's face flamed. "Not while I was transporting you."

"Are we done with magic lessons?" Jack stood in the doorway with his arms folded and his jaw tense.

Liam cleared his throat, hesitating before taking a step back from me. "Yes. We're done. As long as Ivie can keep her head clear, she can do it."

"Good." Jack nodded. "Chloe, as soon as Angus shows up to distract the bodyguard out there, you need to get Jon and get out of here." He didn't leave room for argument.

"You too." When he moved out of the doorway without agreeing, a flicker of panic had my stomach doing somersaults. I chased him into the sitting room. "Jack, you need to leave with them. I can't do this unless I'm sure you're safe."

"No. I'm not leaving you." Jack shook his head, adamant. I knew that look. He wasn't going to back down without a fight. And we didn't have time for that.

The flicker of panic grew into a full-blown attack. My stomach plummeted, and I had to swallow down the urge to scream. "You can't stay! In order to disapparate out of here, I have to walk into a room filled with sorcerers. And this time, they won't be unarmed. And oh, God... Marion. Jack, if she finds you here, she'll—"

Jack cupped my face and leaned in until his breath filled my lungs. "Listen to me very carefully. I. Don't. Care. I'm not leaving without you."

My eyes burned, but I didn't have any more tears to shed. I turned to Liam for help. "Make him leave. Please. I can't do this with him here. I'll be too distracted."

"I'm sorry, Ivie." Liam walked over to the chair and grabbed his jacket from the back. "Jack's right. I actually think you'll be far more distracted if he isn't here. You won't be able to get him out of your head long enough to disapparate."

"Did you just say—"

He winked. "It's growing on me."

Not a minute later, we heard my dad shouting in the hall. "What do you mean, I wasn't supposed to send people to escort my daughter? She's *my* daughter!"

"Okay, that's my cue." Chloe pulled me in for a quick hug. "I'm out of here. It'll take me a few minutes to get Jon and clear the building—not that Marion has a clue who we are. So do me a favor, Sabrina. Don't worry about us. I'll see you back at my house." She jogged to the door and mouthed, "Good luck!" then slipped out into the melee.

"I've come to escort her myself." Dad strutted into the room, his kilt swinging with every step, then slammed the door in Callum's face. "We'll be out in a few minutes!"

"Daddy! You came." I ran straight into his arms, hitting him like a sack of potatoes and making him stagger back.

Dad sat me on my feet and dusted himself off. "Well, of course I did."

"Where's Mom?" I'd been so excited, I hadn't noticed she wasn't with him.

"Home." He shot a scowl at Liam. "Seems she came down with a terrible headache right about the time Liam here texted her with the plan."

"Oh, thank God." I grabbed him in another bear hug and buried my face in his chest like old times. "I was afraid you wouldn't help."

"Oh, I'm not here to help." He patted my back the way he had when I was small. "I'm here to talk some sense into you!"

I wrenched myself out of his embrace. "What?"

"I still believe marrying Liam is the right thing to do. He'll make you happy. Look at him." Dad wagged a finger at Liam. "He adores you. Why would you walk away from that?"

"Daddy—"

"Did he tell you he has a castle?" Dad ran over and put his arm around Liam's shoulder. "In Scotland?"

I whipped around to gape at Liam. "You have a castle? As in a *real* castle? With a moat and a drawbridge? That kind of castle?"

"Uh, sweetheart?" Jack waved a hand to get my attention.

Liam blushed. "It's not a big castle."

"But still..." Visions of lavish balls and glass slippers clouded my thoughts.

Jack blew out a breath. "Still standing right here."

I shook off my fairytale fantasy and turned to Jack with a sheepish grin. "Sorry. I was having a Cinderella moment."

Dad cleared his throat. "In all seriousness, you need to remember your heritage. It's in your blood, Ivie. Sorceresses belong with sorcerers. You need to embrace that side of you. That's what nature intended."

My dad's words threw me further off balance. He was right. I was a sorceress. And giving up everything to be with Jack didn't make any sense. But love didn't always make sense.

"Do you remember telling me how you felt when you first saw Mom? How everything inside you lit up, and you knew at that instant she would be the one you'd spend forever with?"

"Of course, but your situation is different."

"No, Daddy, it's not." I turned so I could see Jack's face. "When I look at Jack, I see my future. I see a couple of kids running around in the yard, and I see burned casseroles because I never learned to cook as well as Mom. And I see spells gone wrong—lots of them—and having to talk my way out of disasters every now and then. But it won't matter because without Jack, I see just darkness. And those confusing feelings I have for Liam, they're not real. You did that so I'd make the choice you wanted me to make. But I can't do that. I love Jack. Even after you tried to bind me to Liam. I still love Jack. I never stopped." Watching Jack's face light up at my words was all the proof I needed to know I'd made the right choice.

"Maybe this will simplify things." Liam let out a heavy sigh, and before I could stop him, he bent down and kissed me.

The instant our lips touched, I felt a dam break free inside me. It was as if fresh oxygen filled my lungs, and rejuvenated blood flowed through my veins. The piece of me that had been missing for weeks snapped back into place as if it had never been gone. And the piece of Liam that had rested in its place disappeared like it was never there.

He pulled away first, leaving me slightly dazed as he whispered against my lips. "I release you from the spell."

My father groaned. "Now why'd you have to go and do that?"

"Because it was the right thing to do." Liam backed away from me. "Now, I need to go before Mum comes looking for us. I'll wait for you to be clear of the ballroom before I tell her I released you from our betrothal. She'll be furious, but by the time she regroups, you and Jack will be married, and her hands will be tied."

Jack held out his hand to Liam. "Thank you."

Liam shook Jack's hand. "Take good care of her. And remember, I'm always just a spell away." He glanced my way one last time. "I wish you every happiness, Ivie Marie McKie. I'll never forget you."

"I'll never forget you either, Liam McDougall. Thank you for everything." I brushed a tear from my cheek, catching a glint of diamonds as I lowered my hand. "Liam, wait!" I made my way across the room, tugging on the ring as I ran. The stone sparkled as I held it out to him. "You almost forgot this."

He took the ring from me with a nod then turned and walked out the door.

Chapter 24

THE INSTANT LIAM CLOSED THE door behind him, the tension in the room shot up. I feared I'd have to hold Jack back to keep him from beating my dad senseless. Sadly, my dad probably deserved it.

For his part, Dad didn't look too worried. "I guess you'd like to know why I—"

"Nope." Jack directed a strained smile toward my father, but when he turned to me, his expression softened, and his voice dropped to a whisper. "We should get going. Are you ready?"

Right. I shuddered because I'd always wanted to attempt the impossible while facing down a firing squad. "I'm not sure if I'll ever be ready."

Jack cupped my face in his hand. "Just remember, I'll be with you the whole time. Succeed or fail, we do this together."

I leaned into his touch, greedy for his warmth. "That doesn't really give me any extra confidence."

"You can do this, sweetheart. I feel it all the way to my bones." He grazed his fingers down my cheek.

A rap at the door startled me, setting my already jangled nerves even more on edge.

"We're up," Jack said with a nervous smile. He reached up to push a few out-of-control curls from my face. "You've got this."

I nodded and pulled myself up to my full height. "Do I look okay?"

Jack brushed his soft lips against mine. "Beautiful."

"All right now, none of that." My dad crossed the room and stopped with his hand on the doorknob. He cocked an eyebrow my way. "Last chance to change your mind."

"Daddy." I groaned.

"Fine." His face scrunched up as he grumbled something under his breath. "Follow my lead."

Callum waited for us in the hall. He eyed my dress with a snicker but didn't say anything, though he had "it's about time" written all over his face.

Once again, Callum led the procession down the hall to the elevators and pressed the down button. He seemed particularly on edge.

The elevator arrived with a ding, and as soon as the doors opened in front of us, my dad snapped his fingers and tapped the face of his ancient watch in the worst bit of acting I'd ever seen. "Oh, now I've gone and done it. I had a gift. I've left it in the car. Don't move a muscle. I'll go fetch it and come right back."

Callum exhaled a long breath, and a deep scowl changed his features until I barely recognized him. "No. We've delayed long enough. We're going, with or without you."

"Fine, fine. You three go on ahead. I'll catch up." Dad bent down and pressed a firm kiss to my forehead, lingering just a little longer than normal. As he pulled away, I caught the emotions swirling in his emerald eyes. His voice was thick with tears as he said, "I'm proud of you, Ivie Marie."

"Come on. We're already late," Callum growled as he herded me into the elevator behind Jack. I kept my gaze locked on my dad's face until the doors closed with him on the opposite side. My eyes stung. That would be the closest thing to goodbye I'd get. I only hoped it wouldn't be forever.

Jack shifted his weight, turning so he stood between Callum's wrath and me.

"I don't know what you're plotting, Miss McKie, but I suggest you shut it down now." Callum eyed me like I was a shoplifter in a candy store.

The ride down seemed to take forever. The only thing keeping me from a full-on meltdown was Jack. His clean scent grounded me and kept me sane.

Even before we reached the ballroom, I felt the floor pulsing beneath my feet, almost like an earthquake. The vibrations rolled up my body, resting in the center of my chest and drowning out my heartbeat. The low rumble immediately preceded the trumpeting call of a flock of birds in the distance. *Birds? Inside?*

When Callum swung the double doors open, the wall of sound nearly knocked me off my feet. Instead of geese, at least fifty members of the McDougall clan stood on tables, playing bagpipes and drums. The droning sound gained volume until it detonated through the air. High above their heads, enormous crystal chandeliers jumped and shook with a tune of their own.

The crowd had grown by at least a hundred bodies since dinner, most of whom swung giant mugs of ale back and forth in front of them, sloshing the frothy liquid over the sides. The few people not holding mugs held each other and... *Are they really having sex in public?* I had to tear my eyes away from the carnage.

Across the expansive room, a few members of the clan surrounded Liam. I had no way of hearing their conversation, but the tense set of his jaw told me he wasn't happy with the direction it had taken. One thing I knew for certain: he wasn't keeping his mother occupied as we'd discussed.

My breath rushed past my lips in shallow puffs as the first wave of panic set in. I rose up on my tiptoes to search for Marion in the crowd but didn't see her. Our hastily thrown-together plan shook at its foundation.

I glanced behind me to where Jack stood like a statue, taking in the room with wide eyes. My fingers itched to grasp onto him, desperate to keep him close, but I knew better.

"I was afraid you weren't coming," Marion cooed from in front of me, making the hair on the back of my neck stand on end.

Had she seen Jack? Would she even recognize him if she did? As I turned back around, my heart hammered so loud I could almost taste it.

Marion's eyes narrowed, sending a chill skipping down my spine as she took in my disheveled appearance. "What happened to your dress?"

The gears in my brain whirred as I tried to come up with an answer that would satisfy her. My mouth fell open, and a single word tumbled out. "H-Hugs?"

"Hugs?" she snapped. "What on earth does that mean?"

"Too many hugs." Once verbal diarrhea started, I couldn't turn it off. "Liam hugged me, then Dad hugged me, then Mom had to hug me. I was just one big hugging machine. You may as well hug me too. I'm very huggable today." I opened my arms, but she didn't take the invitation.

"You're a mess. Your hair, your makeup. You look like you've been crying." Her delicate features twisted into an ugly scowl as she ran her eyes over me. Then she reached out like a cobra's strike, grabbing my left hand and yanking me off balance. She stared at my bare finger for a nanosecond before she let loose the mother of all shrieks. "Where's your ring?"

Everything in the room stopped: the music, the laughter, the swinging mugs of ale. Every head in the room turned toward me, waiting for my reply as Marion stared me down with blue flames dancing in her eyes.

Behind me, Jack gasped then went still. I didn't need to see him to know his muscles had coiled, ready to act. Like everyone else, he waited for my cue. But unlike everyone else, he knew exactly where my ring had gone.

"L-Liam?"

"What about Liam? Oh, for heaven's sake, child, spit it out!"

"Mother, wait." Liam pushed his way through the crowd, and I heaved in a much-needed breath. "Ivie gave me the ring to hold onto while she got ready, and I forgot to give it back to her."

Marion released my hand and held hers out to her son. "Give it to me."

"I don't have it." Liam's features smoothed into an impressive poker face.

Marion whipped her head around, mouth gaping. "What do you mean, you don't have it? Where is it?"

"Sorry, Mum." Liam shrugged as if his mother wasn't completely losing it right beside him. "With all the excitement, I left it in the room. I can go get it if you like."

The walls in the massive ballroom seemed to close in around me as I waited for Marion to respond. *Go get the ring, Go get the ring, Go get the ring,* repeated in my head like a chant.

Marion's eyes settled on something behind me. "Send Callum."

My hopes fell like a water balloon from the third-story balcony and went splat.

Liam directed a terse nod at his mother then turned and mouthed something as he passed by me, but I couldn't read his lips. I screamed in my head for him to turn around and tell me again but gave up when I remembered he'd lifted the spell that connected us. Callum shot a look in our direction, scowling at me before leaving the ballroom.

The moment the door closed behind Callum, the room erupted in activity again. The pipes started up where they'd left off, and the merriment resumed as if there hadn't been a break in the festivities at all. Near me, Jack cleared his throat, and I whipped around to see what he wanted and came face to face with Marion again.

"As soon as Callum returns with the ring, we'll get started," Marion said when Liam had returned to her side. Her gaze wandered toward Jack, but Liam cleared his throat to get her attention again.

"Mum, do you think I could speak with you for a moment?" He scratched his head and slid his eyes in my direction. Whatever he tried to convey to me wasn't getting through.

Marion checked the time on her diamond-studded watch. "Can't it wait?"

"No, it really can't."

With one last look at her watch, Marion huffed out an exaggerated breath. "Fine. But we'll need to hurry."

As soon as the two of them stepped out of earshot, Jack grabbed my elbow and led me away from the crowd. "Can you do it now?"

"Now?" I didn't recognize the squeak that came out of me.

"This may be our last chance." He spoke through clenched teeth, his eyes darting around the room as he walked us backward toward the rear wall.

Following the path of his gaze, I counted twelve guards around the perimeter of the room, all of them with their eyes locked on me. I stumbled over the stupid train on my dress, and Jack caught me before I hit the floor. "They're watching me."

"I know." Jack angled his body in front of me, protecting me, but the action seemed to attract more attention from the guards.

Two of the men from the back of the room inched forward, and I noticed blue sparks emanating from their fingertips. The larger of the two, a ginger-haired giant, who looked like a slightly larger, less friendly version of Redbeard, smirked at me as he approached.

"Jack?"

"I see it." He reached his hand back and took mine. The muscles in his back strained as he edged me farther away from the approaching guards. "Can you get us out of here?"

Liam's instructions ran through my head like pages blowing in the wind. *Concentrate on a destination, and know you'll arrive. Block all other thoughts from your mind, and just go...*

"Ivie?"

Jack's voice broke my concentration, and my eyes snapped open to see two more guards approaching from either end of the room. They were slowly flanking us as what sounded like the battle music from *Braveheart* played in the background.

"Okay, sweetheart." He squeezed my hand. "Now would be good."

A bubble of panic rose up and spilled over, sending tremors down my arms and legs. "I can't do it. I can't clear my mind!"

"Yes you can," Jack said in a calm voice. "Don't think about anything but Chloe's living room."

With a nod, I squeezed my eyes shut. *Chloe's living room. Chloe's living room. Chloe's—*

"Hey!"

My eyes flew open just as the ginger guard poked Jack in the chest with his blue-light special.

"What're you doing here?" His accent was as thick as molasses on a cold day.

I peeked around Jack to give the giant a timid glare. "He's taking my father's place at the ceremony?"

"Well, that's not how it works, lassie." Beneath his bushy red beard, he grinned. "This here's the McDougall clan, and we don't take kindly to outsiders in our midst."

"I'm an outsider."

"You won't be for long." He reached around Jack, wrapping his giant paw around my arm and giving it a yank.

"Let. Her. Go." Jack laid both hands on the guard's chest and shoved.

Other than the ripple of muscles down his chest where Jack had pushed, the guy didn't budge. He blinked at us in turn as if we were a pair of ants at a picnic. Then he tossed his head back and let loose with a roar of laughter.

This time, not only did every head turn in our direction, but they made a hasty path toward us until a glowing circle of blue surrounded us.

My fingers clung to Jack's as I made another attempt to wipe everything from my brain but Chloe's living room. But when the red-haired guard grabbed onto Jack with both hands, lifting him high above his head, ready to toss him like a caber in the Highland Games, I lost my temper.

"Put. Him. Down." An unintelligible string of obscenities ripped through my thoughts, and prickles of intense heat danced over my skin. I didn't waste a single second contemplating my options as I lifted my blue-sparking finger and pointed it at the man.

He dropped Jack to the floor with a sickening thud, and a thick red haze clouded my vision. With one last flick of my finger, his kilt exploded into a million red and green tartan pieces.

"I did it." My lips curved up at the corners as I stared down at his beady black eyes and white-striped tail.

Another of the guards surged forward, and I zapped him too. And the one after that. The space around us filled with tartan confetti, until I stood surrounded by a small army of pissed-off skunks, and the rest of the crowd had sufficiently backed away.

At my feet, Jack groaned, and I bent down, grabbing his hand and pulling him to his unsteady feet. "Are you okay?"

Before Jack could answer, Callum reentered the ballroom. He did a double take at the scene in front of us before locking his furious stare on us.

"I'd be a lot better if we were somewhere else. Anywhere else." Jack pulled me behind him again, slipping his fingers between mine and squeezing. "I don't even care where you take us, but please, get us out of here. Now."

This time when I closed my eyes, I saw a blackened circle in the middle of the woods. I concentrated on that spot until I smelled the charred remnants of a fire long since burned out. As the sensation of being rolled into a tight ball and turned completely inside out hit me, I heard Marion's shrill scream in the back of my head, but it was too late. We'd already landed in the middle of the woods in the exact spot where Jack first kissed me all those months ago. We didn't make it to Chloe's living room, but we were safe.

Chapter 25

I STOOD IN FRONT OF THE full-length mirror in what used to be one of the old Maxwell farm stables. Six months after the renovation, I could still smell the hay and oats lingering in the air—and a trace of something a little *less* appealing.

Until yesterday, I'd had no idea this part of the farm existed. I didn't even know the Maxwell farm did weddings, not that I'd spent much time on the farm if I could avoid it.

If anyone had told me back in October that I'd be getting married just yards from where a goat had tried to accost me, I would have said they were crazy. And yet, there I stood, adjusting the bodice of my Goodwill wedding gown—a purchase that'd brought Chloe to tears, and not happy ones—waiting to marry the love of my life.

"Hold still," Chloe said through gritted teeth as she pinned a line of loose fabric at my waist. She secured the last one and let out a long sigh. "I can't *believe* after everything we've been through, you still ended up wearing off the rack. And from *Goodwill*!"

I caught her eyes in the mirror. "After everything we've been through, what I'm wearing doesn't really seem to matter much, does it? I'm marrying Jack."

"Of course. You're right." She shook her head and flashed me a watery smile then stared out the window as she dabbed at her eyes with a wadded-up tissue.

I placed my hands on her shoulders and peered around her. Caterers hustled back and forth, rolling carts across the gravel parking lot toward the big white tent behind the barn.

How Chloe'd managed to pull together an actual wedding in a day, I had no idea. Maybe she had a bit of sorceress in her too.

I rested my chin on top of my hand. "Have you seen my dad?"

She slid her eyes toward me and shook her head before looking out the window again. "Jon drove by the house again to see if he'd gone home."

"And...?" Hope colored my voice. Just once, I wished my dad would come through the way he'd promised.

Chloe's face fell. "Nothing."

I dragged myself away from the window and went back to the mirror to fiddle with my hair.

She watched my reflection with a wistful sigh. "You're going to ruin all my hard work if you don't leave it alone."

I let a loose curl slip through my fingers. "Where is he?"

Chloe faced me. "Sweetie, this is your dad we're talking about. Who the hell knows where he might be?"

With a halfhearted nod, I perched on the edge of a black velvet wingback chair, careful not to pull out the pins after Chloe'd painstakingly secured the back of my dress. "He'll be here." *I hope.* "He promised."

Someone knocked on the door then pushed it open without waiting.

"Jon!" Chloe rushed over and covered his eyes.

He swatted her hands away, laughing. "What? It's not like she's naked."

She growled and stamped her foot like a pissed-off toddler. "No one's supposed to see the bride before the wedding!"

Jon wrapped his arms around his wife, lifting her off the floor. He gave her a big smacking kiss on the lips before setting her on her feet again. "I'm pretty sure that rule only applies to my brother."

"Did you find my dad?" My pulse thrummed with a dangling thread of hope.

"Yep." Jon beamed, and I jumped up to hug him.

"Thank you." I rested my cheek against his chest, listening to the steady beat of his heart until he pulled away with a crooked grin.

"No thanks needed." He fell into the wingback chair I'd vacated. "I gave up looking and found him right here in the parking lot. Funny, right?"

"Sounds like my dad." I laughed as a huge block of weight lifted off my shoulders. With everyone accounted for, the wedding could finally go off without a hitch. "Okay, Chloe, what's our status?"

She checked the screen on her iPhone. "T-minus thirty-four and a half minutes. We're waiting for everyone to settle in."

"Knock, knock." My dad poked his head into the tiny room, doing a quick search until his eyes landed on me. "Oh, good. Everyone's decent."

Jon coughed up a laugh. "Guess that's my cue to leave."

I pulled Jon into another hug, jumping up to wrap my arms around his neck. "Thank you so much for coming."

"What?" He grinned down at me. "Did you really think you could've kept me away? I thrive on danger!"

"You thrive on cheeseburgers and imported beer." Chloe swatted him away with a big smile on her face. "Now get out of here, and make sure your brother makes it to the altar, would you?"

He shot her a salute on his way out.

"He didn't have to leave on my account." Dad squeezed into the room, dragging a huge black garment bag behind him.

Chloe and I looked at each other. "What's in the bag?" we asked at the same time.

Dad hung the bag on a hook then turned and took both of my hands in his. I'd never seen him look quite so serious. "I owe you an apology, twelve years' worth of apologies, if I'm being honest, but at the very least, I owe you the most spectacular wedding a girl could imagine." He scrunched up his face as he surveyed the room. "One that doesn't take place in a dusty old barn."

"Daddy..." I squeezed his hands.

"No, hear me out. I should have been honest with you the moment Liam arrived, but I wasn't. And because I wasn't, I almost cost you the man you love. And since we didn't have time to plan the elaborate wedding you deserve, your mother and I bought you a gift, a little token of our affection." He dropped my hands and turned to tug down the zipper. "I hope your mum got your size right."

The instant he'd peeled back the top corner of the bag, I recognized the buttery silk of my dream gown.

"Oh, my God, Ivie. It's the dress. It's really your dress!" Chloe flew to his side and helped my dad ease the gown out of the bag as if it were made of spun gold.

"Dad..." At a loss for words, I ran my fingers over the bodice then whipped my head around to gape at him. "Where did you get this? Because if this is another one of your spells, I don't—"

He stilled my hands. "It's not a spell. Your mother insisted on paying for it the day you tried it on. But with everything going on, she'd completely forgotten about it hanging in the back of the closet."

"But where'd you get the money? Do you have any idea how much this gown cost?" Despite my reservations, I couldn't take my eyes off it.

His eyes sparkled with amusement. "As I understand it, the store heavily discounted it because of a bit of water damage. But I suspect a thorough cleaning was all it needed." He winked, and I took that as my cue to drop the subject.

After all, I could forgive one little magical cleaning, couldn't I?

Chloe hung the Colette Original on the hook beside the mirror and wasted no time unpinning the back of my dress. "Let's get you out of *this* so you can wear *that*."

Dad averted his eyes and headed for the exit. "I'll just wait outside then."

Before the door had closed behind him, a pile of Goodwill satin lay in a heap beside me, and Chloe had me stepping into the Colette gown.

The ruched silk bodice hugged me from my chest to my hips, exactly the way I remembered it. I fingered the row of clustered pearls at the dropped waist, where the floor-length tulle skirt flared out around me. My eyes met Chloe's in the mirror. "I'm afraid to blink and have this all be a dream."

"It's not a dream."

Jack.

I spun around to see him standing in the open doorway in a fitted black tuxedo. His usually chaotic hair had been slicked back and to the side in a rather tame style that made him even more handsome, setting off a deep ache within me.

Chloe squealed and ran to shield Jack's eyes. "What is it with you Blake brothers? You know you can't be in here!"

I tried not to smile at his obvious disregard for the rules and failed. "Don't you know it's bad luck to see the bride before the wedding?"

Jack's grin got wider. "Sweetheart, we've already had a lifetime's worth of bad luck. I think the odds are finally in our favor."

"Where's Jon?" Chloe glared at Jack, and I imagined a plume of smoke curling from her ears. "He's supposed to be keeping an eye on you."

"He's got his hands full with our mother. She isn't thrilled with the venue or the short notice." Jack stuffed his hands into his pockets and propped his shoulder against the doorframe, his feet crossed at the ankles—the poster boy for serenity. "But I'm sure you can tell I don't care."

I shot a glance at Chloe, and she looked as horrified as I felt.

"She's not coming back here, is she?" The color drained from Chloe's face.

Jack laughed. "I don't think so."

"Good," Chloe and I said with matching shudders.

Jack pulled himself away from the door and eased his way farther into the room. "Chloe, could I borrow Ivie for just a minute? I promise I'll give her back as soon as I say what I came to say."

"Fine." She huffed, but I caught her fighting back a grin as she shook a finger at him. "But just *one* minute. We're on a tight timetable here."

As soon as Chloe closed the door behind her, Jack scooped me into his arms, careful not to wrinkle my dress. His lips feathered over the shell of my ear. "You look amazing."

One touch and he had me purring like a satisfied kitten. "You shouldn't be looking."

"I'm sorry." He kissed my temple and took half a step back to admire my dress. "No, I'm not. I just couldn't wait."

Wiping the grin from my lips proved impossible. I glowed under his careful inspection. "We're getting married in less than thirty minutes."

"I know. But I needed to do something first." A serious expression washed over his face as he watched me for a moment.

I tilted my head and analyzed him sideways.

He shook his head as if to clear it then reached into his pocket and pulled out my engagement ring. The sun hit the stone at an angle, sending light dancing across the walls. "You left this at the house, and I thought you might want it before you walked down the aisle."

"Oh, Jack." Tears sprang to my eyes, and I blinked them back.

I held out my left hand, but he took my right, sliding it onto my finger. "For safekeeping. You can put it back where it belongs after I put the *other* ring here." He picked up my left hand and kissed my bare ring finger.

I choked back a sob. "I will."

He let go of my hand to brush a strand of hair from my eyes, his fingers lingering on my cheek. "You know, I thought I'd freeze to death the night we met. I knew you were just as cold as me, stomping through the woods behind a man you'd never met like this furious kitten. So determined but not a bit scared."

I leaned into his touch. "I was terrified."

"Well, you didn't show it. You impressed me, but more than that, you took my breath away." He drew in a ragged breath then blew it out, and I felt a shudder run through him.

My heart kicked up a notch, my stomach dipping and swirling as I waited for him to go on.

"I think I fell in love with you that night. And I've loved you every day since." He rested his forehead against mine, his fingers slipping to my neck, where he slid them over my racing pulse point.

My heart hammered so hard I could hear it. Or maybe that was Jack's heart.

He brought his lips within an inch of mine, and I could taste the mint on his breath. "I can't wait to marry you. Thirty minutes seems too long to wait."

"I love you. So much." My throat threatened to close up.

Jack bent down to brush his lips to mine then checked the time on his watch. "Happily ever after in T-minus twenty-five minutes?"

I nodded, and he kissed me again.

"Nothing but good luck from here on out." With a wink, Jack slipped out the door and headed back to the tent where we would be getting married in T-minus twenty-five... make that *twenty-four* minutes.

Time seemed to stand still. Every passing tick of the clock felt like an eternity—an eternity where I stood in a former stable, afraid to sit in my beautiful gown, waiting for someone to come get me so the ceremony could start. I checked the time on my phone again. Jack had left me twenty-*six* minutes ago.

Where is everyone?

I tapped out a quick text to Chloe. *Where are you?* And waited for her reply.

Twenty-eight minutes.

My satin peep-toe Jimmy Choos—a wedding gift from Chloe—pinched my feet. I couldn't wait to kick them off, but I wouldn't, not until we'd walked down the aisle, making me *officially* Mrs. Jackson Blake.

A ceremony that should've started four minutes ago. I chastised myself for wondering what my father'd done to cause another delay. After waiting another ten minutes and sending several unanswered messages to Chloe, I set out on foot.

The sound of violins floated through the air like delicate flower petals, the music getting louder as I approached the giant white tent. I peeked inside to see a small crowd had gathered, waiting... like me... for the ceremony to start, but no sign of my parents... or Chloe and Jon... or my groom.

I marched toward the farm office where Jack should have long since finished getting ready, my shoes scraping the skin off my heels as I went.

I'd almost reached the door when it swung open, and Liam stepped out. My heart thudded to a stop. The insane attraction I'd felt toward him just over twenty-four hours ago had evaporated, leaving nothing but a warm familiarity behind. "Liam?"

"Ivie." He breathed out my name like an apology and scrubbed his hand over his unshaved face. He looked a wreck, like he hadn't slept since I last saw him. And the faint odor of skunk clung to his clothes like cheap cologne.

Seeing him on my wedding day felt all kinds of wrong. "W-what are you doing here?"

He took a tentative step toward me with both hands out in surrender, and his silky voice cracked. "I tried to stop her, Ivie. I swear I did."

"Where's Jack?" An icy finger slid down my spine as I pushed past him to enter the office. "Jack?"

"Baaaaaahhhh."

I whipped around toward the source of the bleating and... laughed. A solid-brown billy goat the size of a large dog sat on the floor facing me. He had a large bouquet of lilies in his mouth and a crooked black bow tie around his neck.

Despite the inappropriateness of the situation, I gave Liam a slow round of applause. He'd gone to a lot of trouble to prank me on my wedding day. And I knew he couldn't have done it alone. "Okay, you can all come out now. Ha ha. Very funny. Chloe? Jon? Jack?"

The goat jumped to its feet, its little hooves clicking like two pairs of expensive heels against the floor, and I held up my hands, palms facing the animal as I backed away. "You stay right where you are, Mr. Goat. I've spent entirely enough time with *your* kind."

"Ivie." Liam's voice came closer, and when I turned around, I found him standing directly behind me.

Ignoring the tortured look in his periwinkle eyes, I balled up my fist the way my dad had shown me all those years ago and gave him a halfhearted punch to the arm.

The goat bleated again, this time more insistently, and somewhere in the back of my mind, reality threw darts at my fragile bubble. "So was this your idea? Or Jack's?"

"I don't think you understand." Liam reached for me, but I pulled my hands away and took a quick step back, shaking my head the whole time. I couldn't let him touch me, not when I was so close to losing it.

"It's a good prank." I gulped in a lungful of sweet air. Jack's clean, outdoorsy scent clung to everything around me. "I almost fell for it too. I mean, a blue-eyed goat? Genius."

The goat rubbed its head against my leg, and my heart skittered to a stop before taking off again. Just as I decided to flee to safety, something plinked against the floor at my feet.

It only took a quick glance down for the entire room to shift, tilting to the side like a carnival funhouse. Black spots swam across my vision.

I must have swayed on my feet because Liam reached for me and called my name. "Ivie..."

Without even looking at him, I waved him off and bent down to pluck the diamond wedding band from the dusty old floorboards.

As I crouched in front of him, the goat inched closer until he'd almost rested his forehead against mine. My head snapped up, but before I could bolt, I caught his familiar blue gaze. I took a deeper look, and he almost seemed to smile at me. *It can't be. Can it?*

"Baaaaaaaahhhhhhh!"

"J-Jack?"

Other Books by Erica Lucke Dean

Red Adept Publishing Books
To Katie With Love
Suddenly Sorceress (An Ivie McKie Novel)
Ashes of Life (with Laura M. Kolar)
Splintered Souls (Flames of Time: Book 1)

Cinnabar Silk Books
Craving Caine (with Elise Delacroix)
Diamond Duplicity (with Elise Delacroix)
Ruby Ransom (with Elise Delacroix)

About the Author

After walking away from her career as a business banker to pursue writing full-time, Erica Lucke Dean moved from the hustle and bustle of the big city to a small tourist town in the North Georgia Mountains, where she lives in a 90-year-old haunted farmhouse with her workaholic husband, her 180 lb lap dog, and at least one ghost.

When she's not writing or tending to her collection of crazy chickens and diabolical ducks, she's either reading bad fan fiction or singing karaoke in the local pub. Much like the main character in her first book, To Katie With Love, Erica is a magnet for disaster and has been known to trip on air while walking across flat surfaces.

How she's managed to survive this long is one of life's great mysteries.

* 9 7 8 1 9 4 0 2 1 5 6 6 2 *